The Tale of
Snow White and Rose Red

Cover design: Luisa Galstyan

Typeset: Arcturus (main text)
                Mala tempora currunt (titles)

Author website: www.tim-maddox-books.square.site

Social media: @TimMaddoxAuthor on X/Twitter
                Tim Maddox, Author on Facebook
                TimMaddoxAuthor on Instagram

ISBNs: 979-8-9921954-2-2 (hardcover)
                979-8-9921954-3-9 (paperback)
                979-8-9921954-4-6 (e-book)
                979-8-9921954-5-3 (classic cover paperback)

The Tale of
Snow White
and
Rose Red

By Tim Maddox
First Published March 25, 2025

Thank you for picking up this adaptation of Snow White and Rose Red. I hope you find the story to your liking.

The genesis of this tale was in finding fairy tales that have slipped out of the public consciousness. Many of our modern mainstream adaptations seem to use the same tales over and over again. It is my hope that we can dig through the vast collection of our ancestors and bring some old favorites back to light.

This is my personal favorite from that initial search into fairy tales. My adaptation is based on the text from Andrew Lang's "Blue Fairy Book" from 1889.

I encourage you to read the original, as well as the rest of those tales. I find the Blue Book has a number of tales that are well-represented, though a few are quite different in their late 19th century vintage, making it a good starting point for those seeking the old stories but still want some familiarity.

Thank you again.

Prologue

Rose Red watched as the wren hopped closer and closer to where she sat. The greater part of her concentration lay with the small flock at her feet, but she hoped to sway one more to the flock this time. To prove that there was no question of her magical skill.

"Do you think you can reach it?" her father asked softly.

Rose nodded, and the wren fluttered back a few feet. She scowled at her mistake. "Quiet words, no motion." She said before her father could remind her.

He chuckled. "Try again."

She exhaled and focused on forming the bond. The magic that the North Hunters used to sway an animal was simple in execution. One reached out with their mind and effectively bound the creature to their will. Upon forging a successful bond, the animal would act tamed until the bond was severed.

One rite to receive the mark of a hunter among her father's people required a demonstration of holding multiple creatures under sway. Birds were traditionally used to assess a new hunter, as her father was assessing her now. Larger animals in the north were difficult to find in suitable groups and required more effort to form the bond.

Rose focused on the wren. It turned to look at her. Rose let out a slow breath as she could feel the bond forming. *I've almost got you.*

A stick snapped right beside Rose, and she jumped in fright. The wren and the rest of the birds fluttered away the moment her concentration broke.

"Father!" she exclaimed. "I almost had a dozen that time."

The words met with hearty laughter. "You did, but you should be able to maintain the bond even with a sudden sound."

Rose couldn't help but laugh with her father. He had given her a good startle, and if she'd seen the same thing done to her sister, Rose knew she would have laughed at the sight.

Once the laughter subsided, Rose cast her gaze towards the trees. "Do you want me to try calling them over again?"

He shook his head and stood. "I think you've proven enough for today. How about we practice your archery?"

She smiled and reached for her bow as she got to her feet. Triumph flowed through her. Her father knew she would pass the test of swaying. That meant the greater hurdle before she could begin her hunts was proof of her prowess with a bow.

Her training this summer had mostly revolved around archery. She had improved much, and the training bow now felt light when she drew it back. It was only a matter of time before she carved her own bow.

Once she did, Rose would begin her rites. Her hunts. Until then, she had to wait and make do with what she had.

Rose took a moment to take in the view from the knoll. From where she stood, the woods stretched all the way across the valley floor until it stopped against the mountains to the south. Wild rivers and streams glistened in the early afternoon light, the mightiest being the one that flowed from the reedy lake to her left. The many waterways cut through the trees from the reedy lake and protected meadows before they finally reached the settled world.

The first signs of civilization appeared at the edges of her vision. The settlements to the west were the nearest to their cottage, with the town of Fernglen serving as the home of the local lord. Rose visited there roughly every moon during the summer; her mother and sister made the trip to that side of the woods every couple of weeks to sell dyes.

The eastern settlements, hidden beyond where the reedy lake rested, were unfamiliar to Rose. She'd been to Middleton only twice in her life. While the widening river inspired awe as few people could ever hope to swim across it, there was little else of interest to draw her there.

Rose exhaled with a wide smile. From here, she overlooked her father's informal kingdom, which one day would be hers to share with him.

She breathed a laugh at the thought. The woods were not her father's by title, for he had none in the lowlands. These woods were his insomuch as he helped the king's rangers maintain the woods as a royal hunting ground.

That said, the rangers maintained only a small portion as a true royal forest for the king and his court to hunt in, and those pockets were far from where she stood. One lay to the southwest of Fernglen; the other was east of the hills beyond the reedy lake. The lands south of the large waterways had occasional problems with bandits, but the northern woods rested peacefully under her father's watch.

This was where she belonged, with nature as far as the eye could see. Much like how her father described the north, only with much less snow and even fewer people.

Rose heard the clicking sound her father would make with his tongue. Smiling at him, she joined him by the line of stones on the ground. They stood behind the line and looked at the target tree. Rose or her father would say which knot the other would aim for, then they'd send all but two arrows towards it. Her father insisted on keeping those in case of necessity. There was little need for that in the woods, but the north required strong habits.

"Aim for the third one on the left." He told her.

Rose nodded and drew back the arrow. A moment passed, then she let it fly. It arched through the air and struck the tree about a hand's width from the knot. It was decent for her first attempt of the day.

Before she could draw a second arrow, her father jested, "Your bow seems a bit small, doesn't it?"

"Well, I still -" Rose paused as the reason for the tone dawned on her.

Her father chuckled at her reaction, then nodded. "You're ready."

"How soon?"

"I will go north and bring the branch south before winter. Then we will carve your bow and start your hunts in the spring."

Rose barely kept hold of her bow as a joyous smile broke over her face. This was something she'd been dreaming of for years. The words that every new hunter heard when they passed their rites flew through her head. *Well done, huntress.*

Rose couldn't wait until her father spoke those words to her. "Can I go with you?"

He laughed at her eagerness. "You'll see the north soon enough."

She pictured the lands that her father had described during his stories beside the fire. Tribal settlements clinging along the sides of cliffs and along secret coves of the icy seas. Magnificent animals which had adapted to the frozen wilds and provided a greater challenge than anything Rose would find in the woods. Summers where the sun never set, and where the grand auroras guarded the day-less winter.

There were also the North Beasts, creatures that never bent their will to the bond. Rose felt her heart quiver at the thought of them, and that angered her. She shouldn't fear them, despite their strange resistance to magic. She would hunt them, not the other way around. "Will I see a North Beast?"

"In time," he said, pride welling up in his eyes at Rose's apparent eagerness to face the creatures. "You'll hear the words before you know it."

Rose smiled and looked down at her old bow. "Thank you for believing I'm ready."

"You've earned it, Rose," he replied before he lifted his bow to take aim, "but remember that our woods still holds its own adventures. Now then, let's..."

She saw her father's eyes shift, as though something unseen by her had caught his attention in the woods below. It lasted only an instant before a grin broke over his face. "Come on; let's go home early today."

"What is it?" she asked. Her father rarely ended a practice session early, especially to head home during the middle of the day.

"You'll see soon enough." He shouldered his bow and calmly turned to head back home. Rose retrieved her arrow and went with him. Rose wondered what her father had noticed. It could be something he saw, or something he smelled or heard. His senses were more attuned than hers, and the grin he'd made meant that it was likely a pleasant surprise waiting for her.

She kept her questions silent, knowing that she would learn soon enough. Instead, she enjoyed walking through the late summer scene. A few times she swayed a squirrel or a pair of rabbits that walked in front of them to practice some more, but other than that, there was nothing to disturb the majesty of the untouched woods.

The sun was halfway through the afternoon when they reached the meadow surrounding their cottage. Rarely did Rose see the cottage from the tree line while the sun was high, and whenever she did, she thought of how dull her mother and sister's lives seemed. Aside from going to town to sell dyes or buy other things, the cottage and its garden were their world, an unchanging pocket of civilization in the middle of the wilderness.

Such a life held little allure for Rose. In the woods, whether she was practicing with her father or gathering plants for her mother, something new was always waiting for her. Each day brought with it new encounters.

Still, the cottage would always be a special place. Their home rested on the spot where her parents had first met, him a young chieftain of the North Hunters and her a maiden of the lowlands whose family worked in dyes. After they married, they returned here in the early winter, where the place then provided the names for the yet-unborn girls.

Rose turned to look at the rose trees that marked two corners of the garden. Hers was the one standing alone with the deep red blooms that were the same color as her hair. At the other corner sat the pale white roses protected from the sun by the boughs of the old oak tree.

According to their mother, when she had seen the two trees, she prayed that her child would have skin as pale as the white roses and hair as deeply crimson as the red roses. When the twins were born the following spring, they each had one part of that prayer answered. And so, they were called Snow White and Rose Red in honor of that moment.

Rose and her father were a few steps from the door when she caught sight of her mother and Snow coming out of the woods from the direction of Fernglen. Snow was already running towards them, having set down her pack to run unhindered in her favorite dress. She rarely went to town without wearing it. Her mother had collected Snow's pack and followed at a more reasonable pace, but Rose saw she was watching their father with a look of confusion.

"You two are home early!" Snow exclaimed as she leapt into their father's arms.

"We are," he replied. "I had to speak with your mother."

"About what?" Snow asked in that pleading tone only she could manage.

Normally, their father would divulge some fragment of his reasoning when he heard that tone, but today, he merely smiled and stepped back. "You two go wait in the tree while I talk with your mother. I'll let you know after that."

Snow nodded. "Alright." Her shoulders dipped in disappointment, but that smile remained. There was little that truly disturbed Rose's sister. Instead, Snow took Rose's hand, and they left their parents alone.

"I should show you the new book I bought when they call us inside." Snow said once they were beside the old oak tree. Before Rose could reply, Snow climbed into its sturdy branches. Rose followed more slowly, only because the way into them wasn't as familiar to her.

"How are things in Fernglen?" Rose asked once they had reached their perch.

"Everyone's excited about the harvest festivals in a few weeks. I even saw a few of Lord Arrenton's knights practicing in the tournament field." Snow adjusted the white headscarf that directed her jet-black hair to cascade down her back. "Do you think you will go this year?"

"I probably won't," Rose replied, knowing that look from her sister. Snow always enjoyed the time in town, both for the gossip that spun new tales for her fantasies, and because young men rarely ventured into their part of the woods. The two suspected their father had something to do with that.

Snow smiled in jest. "Still afraid of feeling out of place?"

Rose gave her a feigned look of annoyance, then breathed a laugh. "I may have another reason." She then told Snow what their father had said about getting her bow.

"That's wonderful, Rose!" Her sister nearly knocked them both out of the tree as she hugged Rose. Once she let go, Rose was aware of that fairy tale look in her sister's bright green eyes. "That means we'll be going north soon. Do you think we'll get our cloaks before we go?"

Rose blushed. Receiving their cloaks meant that the young women of the North Hunters had reached adulthood. She wasn't ready to dwell on what that future held yet. She had to become a huntress first.

Then again, Snow would have no worries about that challenge in her future. Her sister cared not whether life kept her in the lowlands or carried her north; even the far desert lands had fantasies for her to chase if such a fate awaited her.

A butterfly lazily fluttered between them. Snow slowly put a fist out and tried not to frighten the insect. Then she extended her finger, and the butterfly landed on it. She smiled at Rose. "Remember when we would do this all summer?"

"You mean back when we were kids?" Rose replied jokingly. She'd moved past swaying butterflies with her father long ago, but still enjoyed the moments with Snow. The shift from the practical to the whimsical made the evenings with her sister memorable.

"We are still kids, at least until we receive our cloaks." Snow said, her eyes glazing over as she pictured what wonders might await them in their father's lands.

Rose glanced up into the tree, looking for a distraction from Snow's daydreaming. She could barely see a raven looking down at them and pointed. "Want to try swaying something bigger?"

She watched as Snow looked for the raven. Once her sister had found it, there was a moment of laughter. "I think I can sway it." She said and motioned for Rose to give her some space.

Once Rose had moved, Snow began using her bond. A few seconds later, the raven made a call and swooped down. Snow lifted her hand in front of it, and the raven settled on top of her hand.

"Well done!" Rose exclaimed.

"Thanks!" Snow replied as she stroked the bird's back.

"That's a big raven, isn't it?"

Snow shrugged. "I don't think it's much bigger than the ones in town. The rookery there has a few big ones among them."

"Really?" Rose couldn't quite hide her disappointment, though hearing about a new rookery of ravens interested her. Perhaps she would go with her mother the next time they had dyes to sell and check on this change.

Come to think of it, I haven't been in town for a while. I wonder if anything else has changed.

Rose reached out to touch the raven while trying to steal the bond from her sister. Snow shot her a mischievous glance, then simply kept stroking the bird. Replying with a smirk, Rose smacked Snow's hand.

"Stop!" Snow exclaimed jovially as she pushed Rose's hand away. The raven shifted to maintain its balance, but remained on Snow's hand. "You're not getting me to sever the bond."

"I wish I could," Rose said. "You control it so well."

"And I wish I could reach more than one at a time as easily as you can." She replied with a grin. "Guess that's the downside of being twins."

The two laughed for several moments, then Snow straightened up. Her eyes had fixated on the tree line to the meadow. The raven dashed away as Snow willingly severed the bond, a smile instantly on her face. "The Hunter's here!"

Rose turned to look. Indeed, the high chieftain of the North Hunters was walking across their meadow. Seeing him normally brought joy, but then Rose noticed he hadn't come alone.

Two others were with him, the older of whom had a hunting falcon on his shoulder. Rose had never seen a sun-browed falcon before, but those distinctive orange feathers were unmistakable. They were native to the desert lands and trained to track down magical creatures and items. They also had a vengeful quality, pursuing any magic which harmed their masters until they had taken it or died trying.

The Hunter coming alone was always joyous; him arriving with two others and such a bird could only mean one thing. "They must want Father for another hunt."

"What do you think it could be this time?" Snow asked, a hint of concern in her otherwise wonder-filled voice.

"I don't know." Rose turned to the cottage. Their father was already at the doorway wearing the hide-and-fur clothing that bore their tribe's red patterns. Yet his bow was missing from his hand, and Rose could see the concern on his face even from the tree.

He must have only noticed The Hunter earlier.

Their father walked towards the group with even steps. Without a word, the girls climbed down from the tree and hurried to their father's side. Snow adjusted her hair, and Rose soon knew the reason. The younger hunter looked to be around their age.

Rose inadvertently wondered what he thought of them. Both girls had the green eyes that were common among their people, but Snow's black hair was rare, and Rose's deep red was a strange blend of her parents' heritage.

More blatantly, neither wore the clothes of the North Hunters. Rose's short yellow and red dress was more of a tunic that was perfect for hunting in the summer weather, while Snow was in all appearance a lowlander with her long dress that was blue above the waist and undyed linen below. Even though their hems and sleeves bore designs reminiscent of those from their tribe, the stark difference had to raise questions in the strangers' minds.

She exhaled as she took her place at her father's side. *Snow's talk of our cloaks is getting to me.*

Their father held his hands before him and bowed his head. The girls mimicked the gesture. "Hunter," he said, "I wasn't expecting you to have company."

"I am afraid we are in a hurry." The ancient man said. "I need as many great bows as I can muster."

"What has come south?"

"A roc, though since it was young, the hunters who found it decided to follow it back north."

Rose looked at her father. The mighty white birds were the kings of the North Beasts. Her father had said that when full grown, their wings were more than a hundred feet across, and their beaks could swallow a man whole.

Yet their greatest danger was in the blizzards they could create. A hunter that didn't surprise the beast had to contend with the storm before he ever faced the physical threat the roc posed.

It was this reason that made their hunt prized above all others, and it was said that more hunters had died hunting rocs than any other North Beast. Their existence also made the North Hunters of immense value to the kingdoms south of it. They kept the unnatural storms from terrorizing the lowlands.

"What else have you found?" Her father's voice betrayed fear, and it made Rose uneasy.

"We found an eyrie."

Her father's eyes narrowed, and Rose's breath caught in her throat. Rocs were loners; her father had never told a story that contained more than two of them.

"How many did they find?" her father asked.

"Eight." The hunter with the falcon said. His red hair was becoming speckled with white. "I watched the eyrie for a week, and I saw no others join them in that time."

"Was there a nest?"

The speckled hunter shook his head. "Three of them are juveniles, but I saw no eggshells from where I could approach the eyrie. Either they destroyed them, or the nesting grounds are still further north."

Rose could hear the frustration in her father's sigh. She shared the feeling. The North Hunters had been searching for nests since the first rocs had appeared, when the great giant still roamed the north. Yet the birds seemed to breed beyond the reach of mankind. Only the frost dwarves dwelled far enough north to undertake such a journey, but they avoided contact with the North Hunters except to trade their wares for silver and sapphires.

That the hunters had found such a large group of rocs, yet couldn't see any signs of a nest, was disappointing.

A moment passed as her father considered the news, then he turned to his daughters. "I have to go."

"I'll get your bow," Snow said and hurried to the cottage before anyone could say otherwise.

"She's an eager one, isn't she?" the young hunter jested. Rose's earlier assessment had been right; he was older than her, but not by much.

"She is." Rose said.

"How goes your training for the hunting rites?" The speckled hunter asked her.

Rose glanced between her father and The Hunter before replying. "I can hold sway over ten now, and my skill with a bow is improving."

"I believe she will be ready to receive a hunter's bow once spring arrives." Her father added.

The speckled hunter turned to The Hunter. "No surprise, given whose tribe she belongs to."

"And your sister?" the young hunter asked.

"You are not worthy of her." The even tone of The Hunter spoke before either Rose or her father could create a favorable reply. "Not yet, anyway."

The young hunter dipped his head respectfully. Rose silently thanked The Hunter for answering. While a woman becoming a huntress was uncommon among her father's people, she knew that most North Hunter girls around her age still had more use of the magical bond than Snow did. Her sister could barely keep two birds under sway; Rose could arguably reach twelve birds, while ten was the requirement to begin your hunting rites. Her father could command a flock of hundreds when he wanted to show off to Rose, and who knew how many The Hunter could command if he so chose.

That said, Snow showed impressive control over her limited use of the bond. Even when laughing and fighting with Rose, the raven hadn't slipped from under her sway. *Maybe she's just a late bloomer.*

Her father went to speak, but The Hunter cut him off. "There is no need to defend Snow White. She takes after her mother just as Rose Red takes after you.

You accepted that possibility when you decided you would live in the south."

Her father bowed his head respectfully. "I know."

The sound of footsteps cut off any further discussion. Snow returned with the bow and quiver alongside their mother, who had a sack in her hand. Snow held the quiver out first, then handed over the bow once their father had fastened the quiver around his waist.

"Thank you, Snow." He said as he opened his arms.

Snow hugged him tightly. "I look forward to hearing how your hunt goes."

"I'll try to remember everything for when I get back," he replied with a smile. "I'll keep you up for a week filling those pages of yours." Snow chuckled, then let go of her father and went to wish the other three well on their hunt.

It was now Rose's turn to say goodbye to her father. "Good luck, hunter." She used the traditional saying as she wrapped her arms around him.

He laughed softly. "We'll start your hunts when I get back. I promise."

"Thank you, Father." she replied as she let go of him.

He then turned to their mother and took the sack. The two embraced for a long while. "Be safe." Their mother said finally.

"I will be," he said. Then the four North Hunters began their journey to the eyrie.

Chapter 1

A sound woke Snow White. She opened her eyes, yet did her best not to move as she listened carefully. The noise didn't return.

After a few seconds of silence, she began taking even, deep breaths as though she had slipped back into her dreams. It wasn't long before she heard movement again in the pale light.

Rose was awake, and she was trying to slip out quietly.

Snow continued her breathing pattern, knowing that it would fool Rose. She had once asked her sister what she sounded like when she was asleep, and Rose had imitated it for her. That knowledge helped Snow get away with sleeping in or resting during the day when Rose was around. It also helped her surprise her sister on the rare mornings Rose failed to be quiet enough.

She listened as Rose finished getting dressed and picked up her bow and quiver. The footsteps hesitated at the entrance to their bedroom, likely one last look to confirm that Snow was still asleep; then they left.

Exhaling, Snow gently lifted the blanket and moved to follow her sister. She treaded lightly across the bedroom as she listened for any noise Rose might make. The sounds of the fire being stoked reached her before she rounded the corner. Snow peeked into the room and saw that Rose was staring mournfully into the flames.

Despite the ember of mischief in her heart, Snow waited to be seen instead of startling her sister after she saw Rose's eyes. They had filled with tears, though none had fallen yet. Snow knew what they were for, and tears of her own formed.

It's already been a year, she thought.

Only the crackle of the flames kept the world from being completely silent. Snow watched while her sister would idly grab a new piece of wood and set it on the fire, yet otherwise remained still. She wondered what thoughts hid behind Rose's eyes; the only thing she was certain of was that they had to do with their father. Whether they were memories, regrets, or broken futures, Snow couldn't know.

Rose set another piece on the fire. A few moments later, it popped as the sap inside burned. Snow jumped and made a small sound, alerting Rose to her presence. Rose spun towards her. "Snow? I'm sorry, I thought I hadn't woken you."

"I heard the fire stir." Snow whispered with a smile to hide the lie. "You look like you're going out already."

"I was planning to, after I started some breakfast for when you and Mother woke up."

Snow chuckled softly, knowing that Rose's attempts at cooking left much to be desired. "I can take care of that, if you'll wait a little while."

A thought of protest crossed Rose's eyes, but she conceded without giving voice to the thought. "Thank you."

"Don't mention it." Snow then lit a candle using the fire and walked across to the kitchen. It didn't take long to prepare a small brass pot for barley porridge. First, she opened the grain ark to scoop out the barley, and noted how full it was. They wouldn't need to go into town for a long time for barley.

Snow then opened the door to the cellar. While having the door inside was uncommon in the lowlands, it was typical in the north to keep creatures from gaining easy access to it. Down there, she grabbed a handful of dried blackberries she and Rose had picked earlier that summer. She also eyed the clay jar of honey she'd bought a few weeks ago and brought that up to add to the mixture.

When she returned, Snow was pleased to see that Rose hadn't slipped away. Letting her sister remain in her thoughts, Snow quietly put the barley into the pot and ladled some water in from the water barrel. Once certain that the proportions were right, she carried the pot to the fire and set it on its hook. Rose built up the fire under it, and they waited.

Snow held out her hand to Rose, offering her some of her berries. Rose smiled and took a few. Otherwise, the only sound was the crackle of the flames.

The silence ate at Snow. Her sister had a lot on her mind, and so did she. Snow knew that talking with her mother helped take the edge off the pain for both of them, yet Rose had rarely opened up about her thoughts over the last year.

It was a rift that Snow wanted to bridge; she just wasn't sure how to do so. Snow still had their mother for the daily routines, and that structure had helped her support her mother since the burial. Rose had to wander the woods alone, doing the work of both her and her father to help keep life on the same course. Her sister's choice to leave early and arrive late further kept any long discussions from happening.

Though tempted to try again now, Snow knew today would be the hardest on Rose. If she were to ask about her thoughts, it would be better after they had visited the cairn. She looked at her sister. "Where do you plan to go today?"

"I haven't decided yet," Rose said.

"Will you be back before we leave?"

"... I don't know."

Snow nodded. "Then I'll make sure we bring lunch with us, so you won't have to worry."

The remark caused a soft laugh to escape from Rose. "I'd appreciate that."

Smiling, Snow checked the pot. The barley was just where she needed it to be, and she added the honey and what remained of the berries. "I assume you'll leave after you eat?"

Rose nodded. "I need time to think in peace."

Snow couldn't suppress a knowing grin. "Do you want me to pack something to take with you?"

"I'll be fine, but thank you." Silence returned until the porridge finished cooking and Snow ladled a helping out for Rose. Her sister bowed her head in prayer, then tasted the meal. "I'm glad you woke up."

Snow laughed softly so as not to wake their mother. "You're welcome." She then ladled out a half-portion for herself. "Rose, do you think you'll find peace in the north?"

The question slipped out before Snow could stop it, and Rose stared idly into the porridge. It was several moments before Rose looked back at Snow. "I don't know."

Silence followed the question while the pair finished their meal, and Rose stood to leave. Snow followed her to the door, and as her sister stepped over the threshold, Snow tapped her on the shoulder. When Rose turned, Snow hugged her sister. "Take care of yourself."

Rose was stiff for a moment, instinctively trying to maintain the stronger presence between the two, but quickly she returned the gesture. When they parted, Snow saw a tear had crossed Rose's left cheek. "Thank you. I will."

Snow watched her sister until she passed the oak. Knowing then that Rose wouldn't turn back, she retreated inside. *I should have waited to ask about the north tonight, or tomorrow.*

Sighing, she went back to their room and got dressed. Like her sister, she had three dresses to pick from. Normally she would wear one of the two woolen ones when working around the meadow, but today was a special if somber day and she slipped into the decorative blue linen dress.

She adored the dress. It was a birthday gift from three springs ago. Her mother had bought it undyed and had then used the menulia dye she made to give the torso and sleeves their rich blue hue. White petals and snowflakes then ran down the sleeves, intertwined with their tribe's patterns as though the patterns were the wind carrying them. The lower part of the dress fell to her shins and had remained undyed, with menulia-dyed petals and snowflakes dancing along the hem in a similar fashion as the sleeves. At the thought of them, Snow twirled a few times.

Rose's short golden dress she'd left in was also from that day, its hues gained from the aedelis plant. This pair of plants defined their mother's work. They grew in many parts of the lowlands, but none produced so rich a hue as in the region around Fernglen and Middleton. The hunt for this trove had led Snow's mother to the woods, and that enchanted first meeting with her father.

The sound of her mother stirring reached Snow's ears. She quickly tied her white headscarf and hurried to the fire to ladle out another helping of porridge. It wasn't long before her mother had dressed and made her appearance.

"Good morning, Mother!" Snow said cheerily as she held out the porridge.

"Good morning." Her mother nodded, though the smile didn't quite reach her eyes. She reached out and accepted the porridge from Snow's hand. "Has Rose already gone?"

"She has."

Her mother sighed. "I suppose I shouldn't be surprised. Did you see her before she left?"

"I did. I tried to get her to stay, but you know how she is."

After a nod, her mother tested the porridge. She chuckled. "I see you made sure she didn't do the cooking this morning."

"I know you both prefer when I cook." Snow then served herself again and took the pot out of the fireplace. "Do you want to be inside or outside this morning?"

The question caused her mother to smile. "I think I'll tend to the garden this morning, just so your dress looks presentable at the cairn."

Snow nodded, silently upset that she had put on the dress now instead of later. She knew the garden had more work to be done today. But the moment had passed, and after a quick prayer, she ate her food and took the pot outside to clean it. She ladled water from the rain barrel at the corner of the cottage and wiped the inside clean with a rag, then left the pot to dry.

With breakfast done, Snow took a deep breath of the warm autumn air. It had been a good growing season. The growth of their garden was evidence enough of that.

Though, with all the attention I've given it, is it any wonder how well it's grown?

She chuckled, knowing that many villagers spent as much time in their gardens as she did. Today, though, it would be under her mother's care.

Snow could sense why her mother wanted to be in the garden. The act of tending the garden reminded her of gathering aedelis and menulia in the woods, and Snow knew that the garden prospered only because of years under her mother's instruction.

Tending the garden would also let her mother see The Hunter when he appeared.

Turning back inside, Snow set about cleaning the cottage while her mother went outside. The morning passed quietly as Snow sought and removed every speck of dust, then washed the clothes that weren't being worn. Even after this meticulous journey, the sun was still a long way from when she would start preparing lunch.

Sighing, Snow turned to the shelf near the fireplace. A dozen books sat atop it. Four large ones held collections of tales that a merchant uncle had given their mother on her wedding day. Two thin ones, one red and one blue, were fairy tales that her mother had written with her own hand. The remaining six, all of varying sizes similar to the thin books, were Snow's journals that she had written of her father's hunts.

These were her primary memory of her father. While Rose spent the day learning the ways of being a hunter, Snow would spend evenings listening to his tales. Sometimes the stories would carry on until morning. She'd begun writing them down years ago, and she could tell when a story had been told by the growth of her handwriting.

In a way, it preserved her father's life better than the cairn ever could. The cairn would lose meaning as traditions changed; so long as others could read, the stories would remain.

She took one journal and sat at the table. Soon she lost herself in a hunt for a nathair that had appeared near one of the other tribes.

"Snow?"

She jumped at the voice and turned. Her mother looked at her kindly. "It's time."

Snow looked out the window and saw from the shadows that it was nearing lunch. "Sorry, I was lost in thought."

"I could tell. I already put the fish on the fire."

Snow's eyes darted towards the fire. Sure enough, everything for lunch was already among the coals. Snow then looked down at the journal. She was nearly two-thirds of the way through. A guilty smile crossed her face.

"Hello, the house!"

Snow leapt to her feet upon hearing the voice of The Hunter. She hurried out the door and sprinted past the oak, leaping into the ancient man's arms. "You're here!"

"I am," he said as he caught her. His visits had been more frequent this past year, and he had filled a portion of the hole that their father had left. "I told you I would arrive today."

Snow smiled as he put her down. Despite his immense age and the far distance to his homeland, The Hunter had never failed to appear when he promised to. "How have you been?"

"I have no complaints," The Hunter replied. His green eyes tracked upwards, letting Snow know that her mother was approaching. She stepped aside so that the two could greet each other.

"How are things in the north?" her mother asked as the two embraced.

"The beasts have been more active of late, but the young hunters are proving themselves up to the task."

"That's good to hear. Have any caught your eye?"

"There are a few who might be worthy of greater things, but they could use another winter to prepare."

Snow listened to the exchange with intrigue, questioning if The Hunter was perhaps thinking of stepping down as high chieftain. No one had held the title half as long as the ancient hunter, and since it was their custom for the chief to renounce their name when they took the title, it was possible that there was no one living who remembered The Hunter's birth name; besides him, of course.

Yet, Snow saw nothing physically weak about him. His stature was still tall and his shoulders broad, like a hero of old. Could he actually be considering stepping down?

Or was he considering replacements for those who had fallen at the eyrie? The loss had been great for all the North Hunters, and the numbers that were looking for eyries and nests were fewer than they had been in over a century.

"Snow White?" The Hunter asked.

She shook herself from her thoughts, not knowing when she had gotten lost in them. "Sorry. What were you saying?"

"I asked how you were doing, Snow White?"

"Life goes on." She replied without thinking. Her eyes darted to her mother, catching a moment of sorrow glaze over her eyes. Snow added, "I've been good though. No complaints."

"That is good to hear." He then touched the pack over his shoulder. "Where is Rose Red? I have a gift for the two of you. Has she gone already?"

"Rose left early this morning," Snow replied. "I believe she'll be near the fork until she meets us at the cairn."

He nodded. "She has always found more peace in that part of the woods."

"What are the gifts?" Snow asked, hoping that she wouldn't have to wait to receive her gift.

The Hunter chuckled, then reached into his pack and pulled out two fur-lined cloaks, one with a white hood and one with a red hood. Snow immediately knew which one was for her and reached for the one with the white hood. Her eyes noted the snowflake patterns sewn into the hood beside the tribal patterns of her father's tribe, and the pure white fox fur lining it.

"It's beautiful!" she said as she wrapped it around her. The Hunter and her mother looked pleased with the exclamation. "I love it."

"I am glad." He then looked at her mother. "I will go look for Rose Red to give her the other cloak, then I have to leave."

Snow tilted her head. "You're not going with us?" She had believed that he would stay to visit the cairn, and maybe even stay the night before he would continue on. Since he had brought their cloaks, maybe he would take them north as well.

The Hunter shook his head. "I visited the cairn before I came here, and unfortunately I cannot spare much time today."

"What's happened?" her mother said. Snow noticed that her voice was worried.

"The trouble is along the south range, beyond Fernglen." he replied reassuringly. "I found a group of bandits hiding by the pass this morning and informed Lord Arrenton. The princes are being hosted by the lord for Fernglen's harvest festival and I was asked for my help in guiding them to the bandits' camp."

"The princes!?" Snow exclaimed. Her sorrow, at first shifted by The Hunter's arrival and the sight of the cloak, now firmly slipped to the back of her mind. She stopped herself from falling into her thoughts, though, hoping that there was more to be learned about the two.

"Yes. Both will go with me, which is surprising."

"Why?" she asked. "What are they like?"

"Snow, -" her mother started, but The Hunter held up a hand to quiet her.

"The princes are much like you and Rose. The younger is a charming host who has a way with words and a love of festivals, while the older is a warrior who is more at home outside the castle walls than within them."

Try as she might, Snow couldn't help but picture being introduced to the two. Which would she prefer, the one like herself or the one like her father? "I wish I could go with you and meet them in person."

The Hunter breathed a laugh. "I know you would, but fighting is no place for you." He then got a look in his eye, one that Snow would see when he wanted to speak with her mother alone. "I would like something to eat before I head south. Can you fetch me something quick?"

Snow nodded and hurried inside. She found the fish slightly burnt on one side now thanks to the distraction The Hunter provided. Snow took them out of the fire and put one in a knapsack, along with a few small barley loaves and a chunk of cheese from the cellar.

Wrapping the knapsack up, she turned to leave. She stopped at the door, however. Outside, she could hear her mother talking in a low voice. "Are you sure?"

"I am," The Hunter said. "Spring will be the best time, and I have an uneasy feeling about leaving before then."

"Why?"

"Something is off in the air. I can't place it, but it's hung over me since I left Fernglen this morning. I would say that your visit to the cairn should be brief."

"Is it so dire?"

"It could be."

Snow wanted them to say more, but her mother fell silent. Thinking that she may arouse suspicion if she didn't return soon, Snow put on her cheery disposition as she hurried over. "Here you go, Hunter!"

"Thank you, Snow White." He then bowed his head and added, "I hope to see you all again soon." The ancient man then set his feet towards the woods and soon disappeared into it, running with an effortless stride that looked so much like her father's.

"He must be in a hurry to meet the princes." Snow said as she turned to her mother.

Her mother laughed. "I can imagine that they would want to get back to their feasting as soon as possible. Fighting bandits must be an inconvenience for them."

"I suppose so." Snow glanced again at the woods. Her father had kept the lands near their cottage safe, but bandits were a common rumor closer to the villages and towns. From what she heard, they were rarely men of skill.

Yet, skill doesn't mean you are safe in a battle.

Her mother walked back towards the cottage. "Let's eat. The Hunter thinks the weather might turn later today."

That probably is what he meant by something being off in the air, Snow thought. "What about Rose?"

"I'm sure he'll tell her the same thing when he finds her. She'll either be back shortly or we'll see her while we're with your father."

Snow nodded, knowing that it would be the latter case. They ate their meal in silence and then got their grave gifts together. Snow had taken a few blooms from her rose tree and a poem she had written. She didn't see what her mother had packed, nor did she know what Rose would bring. Snow also put Rose's food in another knapsack, as well as a few wooden cups, so they could drink from the spring near the knoll.

When they stepped out of the door, Rose still hadn't returned from her mourning in the woods. Not wanting to get caught by the weather that The Hunter had warned about, and unsure what Rose would bring, Snow took a few of the red blooms as well. Then she and her mother started towards the knoll where her father's cairn stood watch.

Chapter 2

Another arrow cut through the air and buried itself alongside its fellows. Rose forced a smile and went to retrieve them. She had spent the morning practicing just like most other mornings, yet despite having her best results, there was too much weight on her heart to be joyous.

After gathering her arrows, Rose sat down beneath the oak trees along the banks of the fork. The waters of the shallow brook rippled as they met the larger stream; the joined course flowing east towards the river that divided the forest in half.

The forks had served as the place where her father would come and think of nothing for a while. It held no splendid views, nor did the underbrush warrant much beyond a glance. Yet the gentle rippling of the waters and the rustle of the breeze in the oaks made the place perfect for thinking.

Her father had let Rose follow him there one day, and it became their own sacred place in the woods.

Rose wished she could return to those days, when she would think of nothing and listened to the sounds of peace. A time when everything appeared perfect. She'd hoped that today could be a reminder of such a day, but even a year later, the feeling of loss was still too great, her heart still too heavy in her chest to fully enjoy the sacred place.

Other thoughts, which had become prominent as the year progressed, hindered her efforts. Her family was surviving, but Rose and Snow were now adults. They would soon have to start down their own paths. Would those paths run together, or would they split? Who would tend to their mother, or would she have to leave the forest and live in the village without either Rose or Snow?

When I finally go north, will the weight still be such that I choose to not return?

Her sister's question from the morning echoed in her mind. Rose was struggling to find herself without her father, and she hoped that being around other hunters would help.

But what if going north doesn't help?

Rose shook her head and tried to push the thoughts away. She focused on the sounds of the fork, yet the thoughts refused to be contained. At last she gave up the hope for peace and stood. She would have to search again some other time; for now, she had to go to her father's grave.

Despite what she had said to Snow, Rose had planned to go home before walking to the knoll. Yet a glance at the sky told Rose that she had stayed here too long to go to the cottage and eat first. She would have to meet her family at the cairn.

Hopefully, The Hunter would be there as well when she arrived. His instruction had helped Rose's lack of further formal training in hunting and trapping, but as helpful as it was, it was also infrequent. Maybe he could stay longer this time and teach her. Perhaps he would bring a bow so that she could begin her hunts, or help her carve her own to replace the weak training bow.

Maybe he will take us north. Rose sighed at the thought, then shouldered her training bow and left the sacred place.

As she strolled through the woods towards the knoll, her senses noticed a strange chill in the air. It was faint, to where it may be a figment of her imagination. Rose couldn't be certain, but the time wasn't right for cold weather yet. Could it be that the thoughts of loss were turning an otherwise beautiful day cold?

She dwelt on the thought a while further, then her eyes caught a pair of rabbits hopping through the bushes, trailed by a dozen nestlings. Rose chuckled as two of the nestlings clumsily tried to keep up. The whole family heard her and stopped, looking directly at her.

Rose smiled and used her magic bond on the family. The rabbits responded and hopped over to her, with the nestlings following behind.

The sight brought a soft smile to her lips. At least she had grown stronger in this skill after her father's passing.

Rose sat down by an old oak tree and let the family play around her. She also used the bond on several songbirds in the nearby trees, and soon Rose found herself surrounded by song and play.

This continued for some time before the rabbits turned and sniffed the air. Rose held her sway over them as she looked up to see a pack of wolves come trotting out of the trees, four cubs bounding alongside their parents.

Grinning, Rose reached out to them with her magic. All six turned, then made their way over to her and the other animals. The father took a spot nearby while the mother and two of the cubs laid down beside Rose. As for the other two cubs, they began playfully fighting in front of her. The rabbits paid them no mind, just as her father had taught her the magic should work.

Rose allowed herself to laugh as she petted one of the wolf cubs, a tear forming in her eye. The weight in her heart became a little lighter. While he was a great hunter, her father had taught Rose how to use the magic in this way rather than only luring an animal in for the kill. She could do that as well and had needed to do so over the last year to provide for her family, but it was the creation of these moments that she remembered best.

Her father would say, "you look like you belong in one of your mother's stories," and she would grin and laugh without a care in the world. Then he would remind her of the role of a North Hunter in the lowlands. *Take only what is needed; nurture that which remains.*

Her heart sank again. She would never hear her father say the words she had always hoped to hear him say.

Well done, huntress.

Suddenly, all the animals tensed up, Rose's bond no longer influencing them. Every eye stared towards the bushes to the north.

Rose wondered what could have frightened them so much as to sever the bond without her also being surprised, but before she tried swaying them again, they all turned and fled into the woods. Even the birds took flight and disappeared into the uppermost branches of the trees, sounding warnings the likes of which Rose had never heard before.

A moment later, she found herself alone, left in the silence of the woods.

What was that all about?

She had never seen the animals act in such a way, even when a ranger happened upon them. Nothing had ever broken the magic so suddenly without her noticing. *What is causing them to act like this?*

A rustling from the bushes caught her attention. Rose turned to see a massive wolf emerging from the woods. Its fur was a dark grayish-blue, and its paws were bigger than her entire hand. But it was the blood-red eyes that held her attention the most. She'd only seen such eyes on albino animals, not one with such a dark coat. It was unsettling.

Rose tried to reach out to it through her magic, but she felt a new sensation through the bond. It was as if the magic was being absorbed into the creature. The wolf's red eyes gleamed at her with wicked intent.

Rose tried again to use the bond, and again the wolf didn't heed her. Her heartbeat rose rapidly as she reached for an arrow. *Why won't you listen?*

The wolf hesitated for a moment, and Rose took the chance to nock the arrow and loose it at the wolf's chest. The wolf made a small yip as the arrow hit, but then it twisted its head to bite the arrow. With little effort, the wolf plucked the arrow from beneath its fur, with barely a drop of blood on the arrowhead.

She felt her heart stop at the sight, and fear gripped her. *My bow isn't powerful enough to kill it!*

The wolf continued coming closer and was now less than a dozen yards from her. It bared its cruel yellow fangs in a silent growl, then it crouched down. Rose knew in an instant that it was going to pounce. Her mind tried to get her feet to run, but she remained frozen in terror.

Her ears caught the twang of a bow, and a second later, a long red shaft was protruding from the wolf's side. It made a loud cry as it fell, and only a few seconds later, it was dead.

Rose turned, knowing who the red arrows belonged to. The Hunter was hurrying towards her. "Rose Red, are you alright?"

"I- I'm fine," she replied as she tried to calm her nerves. "What was wrong with that wolf?"

For a moment, the ancient eyes regarded her with surprise, then they softened. "I suppose you've never seen one before."

"No, not like this. What's wrong with it?"

"There's not enough time for me to explain, for I am late as it is, but if you see another like this, run.

Run like all the other animals do. Now go find your mother and sister and tell them to stay home."

"Why?" Rose could see the flicker of something behind The Hunter's eyes. Something that, though she couldn't place it, scared her immensely.

He hesitated for a moment, trying to confirm his own thoughts before he spoke. "I feel a storm on the wind, and I fear this one is heralding a roc. You must be inside when it arrives, or you could freeze to death. Your mother and Snow White were still in the cottage when I left. If they waited for you, don't let them leave, and if they already left, track them down and hurry them back. And have your father's bow ready for me to return."

"Yes, Hunter!" Rose said as she turned towards the cottage, ready to rush to her family's rescue. If The Hunter feared the storm, she wouldn't dream of getting caught in it.

"Wait!"

Rose looked back and saw the man pull out a cloak from his pack. "Wear this. It will help if you should still be out when the storm strikes."

She recognized the pattern at once, but didn't bother to admire her cloak. She swiftly pulled it over her shoulders and secured it, then turned to say goodbye. The Hunter was already a dozen yards away, heading off to a place unknown to her. His haste only strengthened the warning, and Rose dashed back to the cottage as fast as her feet would carry her.

In time, she could see the cottage and she hurried to the door.

"Mother!" Rose called as she threw open the door. Only silence greeted her. She spent a few moments glancing around, a sinking feeling settling in her chest. *They're already at Father's cairn!*

Rose grabbed the lantern by the fireplace, then set it down and built up the fire. If a snowstorm did strike while they were out, having the cottage already warm when they returned would be a blessing. She also shuttered and latched all the windows to keep the warmth inside.

Having taken care of that, she hurried out the door, stopping only a moment to shut the door behind her to keep the coming cold out. Then she pulled the hood of the cloak over her head and took off running again.

Chapter 3

Standing around waiting at the rendezvous took far too much time for Prince Werner's liking. His dancing clothes were ill-suited for the forest, and though they had left before most of the others had arrived for the banquet, he was missing the courtly intrigues that took place before the dancing and feasting.

Why didn't I stop myself from joining this expedition?

Werner huffed as the memory of the morning returned. The Hunter had appeared at Lord Arrenton's manor saying that he had discovered a bandit camp after traversing the Cascade Pass in the southern range. Both princes were on hand to greet him, having arrived shortly after sunrise. His older brother, Roland, had insisted on the early arrival, and Werner didn't want to reach Fernglen and the festivities hours after his brother.

Upon hearing about the bandits, Roland had taken command of the company sent to capture the bandits. That had been no surprise. Roland would take any excuse to avoid the protected social aspects of princely life to chase the wild outdoors. The surprise came when Werner, in what he now thought to be a fit of madness, decided he would go along as well.

The prince had hoped that they could deal with the camp immediately, rushing out and claiming victory in the fight before returning to the feasting and courting he was so fond of. Instead, Roland had taken time to gather a larger force and agreed to rendezvous with The Hunter some distance from the bandits in such a way that they could avoid being seen.

Werner knew that facing an enemy with overwhelming force helped to ensure victory and that having The Hunter along would guarantee they approached unseen, but the prince was ready to be back indoors.

He stopped his pacing beside several of the young lords and said in a low voice, "This is taking entirely too long."

"I agree." Lord Finley replied in a low voice. "We probably could have already been back at the banquet already if your brother wasn't waiting for The Hunter."

"It's not like we don't know where the bandits are," Lord Mauvelin added. "This just seems like a needless waste of time."

Werner nodded in agreement, yet he couldn't deny that it was in keeping with his brother's ways. Roland had grown out of pursuing impetuous action when he was still young, moving carefully in everything he did. Roland wouldn't view this delay as anything other than a necessary part of some flawless plan that minimized harm to their company.

There was also The Hunter to consider. The high chieftain was renowned by all, and Roland's request for his participation in the attack meant it would be improper to proceed without him. The North Hunters may view it as a slight towards all of them if the princes' company attacked after such an invitation. That would have a significant effect on filling the winter banquet tables if the North Hunters decided not to send their young hunters south in response.

At least, if they viewed such procedural things as Werner's people in the lowlands did.

"Why did we come, anyway?" Finley asked. "It's not like they need our help. Not with this many men."

"Don't look at me. I'm only here because I followed the two of you," Mauvelin said.

"Well, then that's your mistake, my friend," Werner replied with a smirk. As much as he enjoyed the two, Hans Finley and Jean Mauvelin were classic hangers-on, getting a rise in their own status by being around the prince at courtly functions. That also meant they could shift some of the blame onto the prince whenever they found themselves out of place.

Finley gave him a glare and jested, "Then what was your mistake in coming, o golden prince?"

Werner grinned at the common wordplay for his hair and reputation, then glanced towards his brother. Roland was sitting with his back to them, gazing at the distant clouds. "My mistake is being Roland's brother," he said lightly.

"Maybe you should ask your brother if we could get moving?" Finley asked. "He may listen to you."

"He'll be here," a low voice said sternly, before Werner could reply.

Roland had heard them.

At once, the conversation died. For Finley and Mauvelin, the reason for their silence was simple. While Roland was amiable most of the time, few men his age wielded such a commanding tone of voice. The young lords knew from experience that this tone meant any meaningless conversation might get cut down by a sharp rebuke.

Add in the older lords and their men who would side with Roland in the face of battle, and the young lords' compliance was all but assured.

Werner, meanwhile, knew that he now stood alone in any potential rebellion to Roland's wishes. It was a role reversal that occurred often between the two. At least, out here in the forest.

Within the city walls or the great manors of the kingdom, the contrasts of the brothers made Werner more or less equal to his brother. Roland could hide his personal shortfalls in courtly procedure behind a cautious tongue and an air of mystique, while Werner played the courtly games with as much skill as expected of his upbringing and took pleasure in being the more beloved prince among their peers. In such events as the upcoming banquet in Fernglen, Werner would be ascendant between the brothers.

But out here, beyond the walls, there was no question who was the greater of the two. Werner had the martial skill expected of a second son and was no slouch in a tournament, but being in the wilderness was Roland's true nature. A deadly man, fully confident in his skill and comfortable with his own solitude, moving against the forces of the natural world.

Even The Hunter held personal respect for Roland. That red scarf around Roland's neck was all the evidence one needed of that fact, though Roland's preference to wearing his jerkin and chain mail even at a banquet enforced the image.

It was infuriating to be so insurmountably behind his brother in such things, and whether Werner admitted it aloud, that was why he had that sudden fit of madness and agreed to come on this expedition, to prove that he was perhaps still within striking distance of his brother. Even though that meant he was out here wearing his fine clothes under an ill-fitted jerkin, looking like some sort of jester.

He breathed a laugh upon thinking of his appearance and replied to Roland, "And how long will we wait? Night will fall before we get back if he isn't here soon."

For a moment, there was silence. Werner was aware of the eyes glancing between the brothers, but he held Roland's gaze.

Finally, a grin broke on Roland's face, and he chuckled. "True, but I believe you are thinking less of the coming dark and more of the dancing to follow."

Werner smiled, satisfied that his brother was humoring the situation. He tapped his jerkin. "Well, I am still dressed for the dance once I get this thing off, but that's because I thought I wouldn't have time to get properly ready."

"Ha!" Lord Handel's shrill voice rang out. "It'd be dawn before you were 'properly ready'."

The company broke into laughter, yet Werner kept his concentration on Roland's eyes. They remained starkly focused, the war games between himself and the bandits clear behind the smiling mask on his face, but Werner could see that his brother appreciated the momentary distraction.

Still, there was feasting to get back to, and Werner was ready to be back in his realm of mastery. "That is a fair point, Lord Handel, but at this rate, it would have been enough time. I say we start for the camp now before we risk having to travel back in the dark."

"What of The Hunter?" Lord Roxeter asked.

I'll have to hope he doesn't think my actions are a slight against him, Werner thought, then he said, "The Hunter already told us the location, and he can track such a large company as ours once he realizes that we have continued on without him. I'm sure he will understand when it is not us who are the ones that are delayed, and he will catch up with us quickly."

"Very well." Roland replied, much to everyone's surprise. "We have waited quite a while, haven't we?" Those words weren't in that commanding tone as before. There was a more unsettling mischief in the words that put Werner on edge.

The feeling intensified when Roland locked his eyes on his brother. "I will stay here and wait for The Hunter to explain our decision. There are things I wish to ask him, in any case. If you are so inclined, brother, you may take the men forward. Just try not to get killed before The Hunter and I arrive."

The silence that followed made Werner's skin crawl. All the experienced lords had their gaze on him, recognizing that Roland had given his brother a subtle challenge and opportunity. If they caught the bandits before Roland arrived, the honor would go to him.

That also means that the planning for the battle goes to me as well.

It was a chance he rarely had, and maybe only the third time that Roland was offering no help in the decision. His brother's face was stoic, with those piercing brown eyes seeming to read every thought in Werner's mind.

Werner felt less like a prince and more like a trapped animal faced with a powerful predator. It was a quality that served Roland well in the forest, but such intensity was also among his worst features in social circles. Werner had gained many conversations with ladies frightened by a mere glance of those eyes.

The thought decided the matter, selfish as it may be. *What better way to raise my status during the festivals than showing that I, too, am capable in the art of war?*

"I'll do it." Werner nodded to his brother, then turned to the older lords. "Lord Arrenton, you know the way better than the rest of us. We'll plan to encircle the bandits before they know we're there and take them with as few losses as possible."

The lords spoke among themselves, but it was Roland's reaction that Werner sought. A wry grin turned the stoic face, and the eyes mellowed in satisfaction. That was all he needed to know. His basic idea for the ambush was good. Maybe not the exact plan Roland had in mind, but one that he found acceptable.

Roland rose and motioned for him to follow. The brothers moved to a place where no one could overhear them. Roland spoke first. "Are you sure you're ready for this, Werner?"

"I knew it may get bloody when I decided to come with you," Werner replied with a grin. "Besides, who knows when the peace will be broken? I may as well get some taste of combat before I have to face death in a battle."

His brother breathed a laugh. "You're giving reasons again. There's no need to be nervous. You can rely on Arrenton and Roxeter to get everything set if you choose to attack before I arrive."

"I know, it's just... something about today feels off."

Roland's eyes narrowed. "In what way?"

Werner shrugged. "Well, I willingly chose to follow you into the forest instead of staying behind, and now you're having me lead this company into a skirmish. Not exactly what I expected when I woke up this morning." Roland laughed at the explanation, but Werner could see that there was something else on his brother's mind. "What were you thinking about?"

Roland waited a moment to collect his thoughts. "Today does feel strange, and I can't quite understand why. Something in the air. That's why I want to wait for The Hunter, to see what he knows."

"Should we head back, then?" Werner asked. His brother didn't immediately reply. It was rare to see Roland indecisive in the forest. That alone warranted concern. "What do you think it is?"

"I don't know." Roland turned to Werner with a dismissive smile. "It might be nothing but a coming storm."

Werner laughed loudly, interrupting even the conversations of the lords some distance away. "A storm? That's what has you worried?"

Roland laughed as well. "It does sound ridiculous coming from me, doesn't it?" His brother then straightened up. "You probably should get moving. I will catch up when I can."

Werner nodded his head. "Understood."

His brother then held out his hand. "Don't die on me."

Smiling, Werner shook his brother's hand and turned to the company. "Looks like a storm's coming. Let's move quickly so that we're not caught in it."

The entire company then got underway, though the prince took one glance back at Roland. His brother had returned to looking north, waiting for The Hunter.

Exhaling, Werner joined the others on the warpath, taking his place at the head of the company with Lords Arrenton and Roxeter to get their council on the eventual fight.

Chapter 4

The significance of the day seemed to affect even the animals, for as Snow and her mother looked upon the cairn, there wasn't a sound to be heard. The walk through the woods had the sounds of life, but they stopped at the knoll. Snow found it at once eerie and wondrous.

They had already been at the cairn for some time. The sun was clearly into the afternoon phase of its course, and Rose had still not arrived yet. Snow was starting to worry about what may have happened to her sister for her to be so late.

Hopefully, she will get here soon. Snow thought as she wrapped her cloak tighter. She was glad that The Hunter had given her the cloak, for the air had grown strangely cold, and as much as she tried to keep her father's life in mind, the chill was becoming a large distraction.

She willed her focus from the air towards the cairn that marked her father's grave. The cairn stood five feet tall and was visible all the way from Fernglen if the sun struck the capstone at the right angle. While mainly built of loose rocks from around the knoll, the capstone of polished black granite and two rings of cut white stone signified their father's status with their people.

The lower ring was for those who had killed a North Beast as proof of their prowess as a hunter; the second showed that he had been a tribal chieftain; and the black capstone was the sign that he had slayed one of the great rocs by his own hand.

Looking at it, one would know that it had been as well-lived a life as any North Hunter could ask for, even if it had ended far too soon. The only honor missing from the cairn was a third ring supporting the capstone, which would show that a hunter had become the high chieftain of all the northern tribes, The Hunter.

On the side facing away from the forested valley, there was a small shelf for offerings of remembrance to be laid. A bundle of frost lilies and arrows bound by a fur cord were already there when they arrived, a gift from their people that The Hunter must have placed before he'd come to their cottage. Next to them was one of his red arrows as a personal gift.

The flowers would remain until they withered, while removing the arrows was only done when fighting the North Beasts. It was an old belief that the spirit of the fallen hunter blessed the offered arrows and their spirit would be eager to add one more blow against the North Beasts to their legacy. Her father had told her of several stories where a lonely cairn appeared out of the snow and saved him against direwolves and farroclaws.

Snow and her mother had added their own flowers to the collection. Their mother placed the tulips she loved on the shelf with her own hands, while Snow had swayed a large squirrel to carry her poem and blooms to the shelf. Snow didn't know if spirits lingered near their graves, but if they did, she knew her father would smile seeing her use her bond.

She was still holding the red roses from her sister's tree. It was possible that Rose had gone out early in order to find something special to bring in remembrance. Her sister had her own ways and many memories in the woods, after all. Maybe a bloom from one of those special places would be her offering, and could explain why she hadn't arrived yet.

Snow and her mother stayed standing for a while longer, each lost in their own thoughts. Several times, Snow looked over to see a tear or two rolling down her mother's cheek. She offered the hem of her cloak to wipe her mother's eyes. While new tears had flowed at the gesture, Snow could tell her mother appreciated it.

In the back of her mind, Snow wanted to ask about the conversation between her mother and The Hunter. The part she had missed while inside seemed to have been about her and Rose. Yet she decided it would be best to wait until Rose arrived before asking. Snow thought it would be better for her mother to only tell it once instead of having to say the same thing again.

For her part, Snow thought of the long nights of recording her father's stories and the joy he had in telling them. Of all the things she missed, she missed those nights the most.

She looked out beyond the cairn. While the woods were thick down below, the view was still striking. Snow could see the whole of the southern range, with the prominent South Crag taking the most attention. The tree-covered expanse was wild, yet safe for her and her sister.

Maybe I should go out into the woods with Rose. It may help her to have someone to teach, to pass down what Father taught her.

They heard a rustle from the bushes nearby. Snow watched as a figure in a red cloak hurried towards them. It took her a moment to realize that it was her sister, wearing the cloak that The Hunter had brought for her.

Snow smiled, but then her face fell as she saw the worried look on her sister's face. Snow called out, "What's wrong? Why are you running?"

"We have to go!" Rose replied through heavy breaths.

"What?" their mother asked.

"The Hunter said a storm is coming, and we could freeze if we get caught in it."

Snow caught the frightened look in their mother's eyes as she looked north to confirm what Rose had said. Snow turned her gaze north as well. A wall of clouds had appeared behind the mountains. They billowed in a manner that she'd never seen before, and they were moving south faster than Snow thought they should be able to.

And their color. There was something strange about it that Snow couldn't place. Maybe it was the billowing, or perhaps the unsettling hue of blue they had, or -

Her mother put a hand on Snow's shoulder. "Snow White, let's go."

"What is it, Mother?" Snow asked, curious if she knew what was happening.

"I'll tell you when we're back in the cottage." Though she said this as reassuringly as she could, there was clearly fear in their mother's voice.

Snow nodded and quickly gathered up the lunch that they had brought. Rose stayed where she had appeared, eager to waste no time in getting out of the storm's path.

With everything gathered, the three started back towards home. Snow did her best to keep up, wondering what they knew about the clouds that had both of them moving at a pace just shy of running.

What is causing the storm? An even more chilling thought followed on its heels.

What could cause The Hunter to be afraid?

Chapter 5

The longer he waited for The Hunter, the more Roland wished he hadn't let Werner lead the men onward. That chill Roland had sensed was real, and it was emanating from the vast clouds piling up behind the northern range. He hoped they would be nothing more than a rogue storm, but his instincts were convincing him otherwise.

He watched the moment that the storm hit the peaks, like some great wave crashing against a rocky shore. Only this wave was unimpeded, and it consumed the peaks whole. In their absence was a blanket of white that fell from the clouds.

It was snow, yet the weather was too warm for such a thing. If it wasn't some malevolent storm, there was only one reason for the clouds to act in such a way.

For the first time in Roland's life, a roc had flown south of the northern marchlands.

A gust of icy wind rustled his dark brown hair, and Roland adjusted the red scarf around his neck. It was the symbol of a hunter in the north, and Roland was one of the few outsiders who had ever completed their rites. The Hunter had overseen it personally, since Roland was the crown prince, but that status had also made the trial highly scrutinized. Over a dozen of the lesser chiefs had watched the rites as they took place. Because of that, no one could deny that Roland had passed without bias.

Many of those North Hunters had died last year clearing the eyrie. Roland remembered the shock he'd felt when word had reach him, and also the burning desire to have fought the rocs by their side. Perhaps some of them would still be alive if Roland weren't bound by his princely duties.

If that storm is a roc, how many more hunters have died now?

Roland let go of the scarf. He always wore the scarf into the forests as proof of his own prowess, and now he wore it as a reminder of those who died protected them from the northern terrors. The color and pattern were of The Hunter's own tribe, and The Hunter's own grandson had placed the scarf around Roland's neck. The grandson himself was nearly as old as Roland's father.

The knowledge had bewildered Roland. That the Hunter could be so ancient, yet remain so powerful and command such respect was an inspiration. Roland hoped that when the time came for him to assume the throne, he would be even half the leader that The Hunter was.

Yet, despite his love of the north, his princely duties constrained Roland. The prince knew that the fate of his kingdom rested on his shoulders. Any action could bring scandal if he wasn't careful, be that action with a neighboring kingdom, his own people, or the princesses and ladies vying for his attention. In that, he envied Werner. Second sons could withstand the scandals since the throne wouldn't pass to them; or, if it did pass to them, a few years of acting solemnly would make everyone forget the wild days of their youth.

Werner even had a far greater say in his future, as once one of the ladies finally stole his heart, it wouldn't inherently create a diplomatic incident. Roland knew he was destined for a marriage of alliance, to tie his realm to a neighboring kingdom. Anything less, and the high king's court might erupt in an uproar.

Such things didn't worry Roland in the forest. Nor had they created concern in the north. The wilderness didn't care for titles and heritage. It only cared if you had the will and skill to survive.

The storm clouds grew larger, and now the foothills to the north disappeared behind the blanket of snow.

His mind wandered to Fernglen and the manor of Lord Arrenton. If he started running now, he may reach it before the storm struck. The clouds were moving faster than he could have ever predicted. Most royals knew how fast a falcon could fly, but seeing something so massive move with the same speed stirred his excitement at the prospect of hunting a roc.

When the storm did break over them, the nobility that had gathered in Fernglen would remain trapped there for a long time. It wasn't a fate he was looking forward to. A few days Roland could manage, but a week or more? That would drain him.

He chuckled at the two thoughts. As much as he disliked being around the bickering nobles, a leader still needed people to follow him. *Maybe I'll only be a quarter of the leader that The Hunter is.*

As if on cue, Roland caught sight of the ancient man hurrying through the forest. He was still well off in the underbrush, so the prince ran to meet him. "You've made it."

"Forgive my lateness, Prince Roland." The Hunter spoke clearly despite the heavy sweat on his brow and the heaving of his chest. "I had an urgent matter come up concerning a member of my tribe."

This surprised Roland, as it wasn't yet time for the North Hunters to send people south for the winter hunts. "Is it settled, or do you need a hand?"

The Hunter waved him off. "It is settled for now. We must get your people back to Fernglen immediately."

"Unfortunately, I already sent the others on ahead. I think we can reach them before they get to the camp, but only just." Roland tested his theory and jested. "So long as you're not tired."

"I have yet to reach my limits, Prince Roland." As expected, The Hunter bore no amusement at the jest. The threat couldn't be a simple storm, then.

"Good." The prince looked to the man's shoulder, and Roland paled when he noticed something that had escaped him in Fernglen. "You aren't carrying your great bow."

The Hunter inhaled sharply, his eyes betraying anger. "I had left it behind so another could wield it in case a roc arose while I was south."

Roland knew that now was the time to ask. "The chill in the air, is it -"

"Yes." The Hunter said as he started running down the trail Werner and the others had made. "We must hurry."

The pace The Hunter set would make most knights fall in exhaustion after the first mile. The long strides of the North Hunters could endure whatever distance necessary to catch their prey. To Roland, it was a pace he'd forced himself to attain, and thanks to the training needed to pass the rites, there was hardly a sound between the two men. Roland was driven both by pride to stay with the ancient man ahead of him and also by concern to save the others from the coming danger.

Yet the danger posed by the roc was a challenge Roland had dreamed of facing before. If it were only him and The Hunter, he was certain that they would have run towards the heart of the clouds. But without The Hunter's great bow, and with so many lives at stake in the forest, he and The Hunter first had to get the others to safety.

Their pace held for several more miles before Roland heard The Hunter say, "There they are."

Roland looked ahead and saw that the men were already circling towards their ambush positions. The prince searched for any sign of his brother. He finally found Werner on the far right of the circle, settling into cover against a large rock. "We're too late."

"You go to your brother." The Hunter said quickly. "I'll go to the left. We'll join the ambush from both sides and finish this quickly."

Roland cast a glance at The Hunter. There was precious little time to get the company moving back to Fernglen, but this was the only plan they had. "Good luck," he said, then the prince hurried towards his brother.

Chapter 6

"Lord Roxeter, is that where the bandits' camp is?" Werner asked in a hushed tone.

Roxeter nodded and looked to the north. "Not a moment too soon, either."

Werner glanced over his shoulder at the statement. He had lost track of how much time the march into the forest had taken from his enjoyment of the festivities in the manor, but as they got closer to the bandits, his worries turned to excitement. Even if he was more given to the courtly life, he couldn't deny the invigorating allure of combat. He was at once beset by the fear of death and the eagerness to prove himself.

The war of those emotions was at the heart of every warrior. He thought he had encountered it on the tournament field, but now he understood why the older lords put less stock in such things. Facing the battlefield required far more courage to overcome the fear that accompanied it.

Yet that battle ceased once he had looked back for Roland and noticed the billowing clouds. Werner had the superstitious sense that he shouldn't have mocked his brother about a sudden storm. The way the clouds moved was unnatural.

Even Roxeter couldn't place the strangeness of the storm, and he lived along the northern lands. One of Roxeter's men couldn't keep his eyes off of the clouds though. The image stuck in Werner's thoughts, and now that they had neared the camp, Werner pointed to the man. "What is in the clouds?"

"I don't know, my prince. I've never seen anything like that."

"Your eyes say they remind you of something, though," Werner remarked. "What do you think it is?"

The man hesitated, and Werner saw him brace for the ridicule he expected to hear. "I've never seen one, but my grandfather once described a roc storm to me. Those clouds remind me of what he told me."

It was all everyone could do to keep their murmurs quiet. Werner felt the blood drain from his face. *A roc?! Here?* "I thought the North Hunters slayed the rocs last summer. How could another have already arisen and gotten through them?"

"I don't know," Roxeter replied, "but if it is a roc's storm then we cannot wait for Roland and The Hunter to arrive."

"Should we just leave?" Finley asked.

"That storm will hit us before we get back," Arrenton said bluntly, "and several of you are woefully underdressed. Let us capture the bandits and take their supplies. It may be the difference between life and death."

"I agree." Roxeter said as he stepped away from the company. "Everyone to their positions. We attack on my signal."

Werner thought to stop Roxeter and put forward the idea of negotiating with the bandits. He held his tongue, though. There was every chance that the bandits would simply be terrified of a company of nobles and immediately start a fighting retreat into the forest.

It was a risk the prince's company couldn't take, and they had the element of surprise. A swift attack was their best option.

The prince looked over his shoulder again at the billowing clouds. They were close, maybe even blotting out the sun in Fernglen now. His sympathies for the bandits faded, replaced by the desire not to get trapped in the terrible storm headed their way.

A swift attack would also get him back to the manor quicker, back to his beloved intrigues and dancing.

Werner nearly tripped as he thought about these things. He caught himself before he fell on his face, but his pride took a hit from the misstep.

Arrenton chuckled from behind him. "I must say, a tailored suit for the dancing hall is not what most would consider proper forest clothing."

Werner took the taunting heartily, like he always tried to. "Nor will it be good if we get stuck in that storm."

The two grinned at one another in silent laughter as they moved into position. Roxeter had placed Werner next to Arrenton so that their company would know where he stood when the ambush started. Arrenton was a cautious man and wouldn't get drawn down into the camp if the fighting turned into a melee. It was clear

Roxeter expected Werner to stay with the lord on the high ground.

The plan itself was simple. First, they would surround the camp. Roxeter would let out a whistle and they would take the bandits by surprise with minimal casualties, then march home as quickly as possible.

Werner was happy that it was practically the same plan he had proposed, though Arrenton and Roxeter had gone further to determine who would be at each point of the encirclement. The only change since they had arrived was that The Hunter and Roland had to be left out, robbing them of their best archers.

"Werner, you'll be up there." Arrenton pointed. It was an ideal spot for Werner, for there was a large rock that would provide him with cover against any arrows the bandits might send his way. "Are you ready?"

Werner smiled back. "I am. Good luck."

Arrenton nodded and hurried to his position, while Werner crept towards his. Already Werner could imagine the stories he would tell the ladies once they returned from the coming skirmish. The stories would have to be true, of course, lest another call him a liar, but some embellishment was always in order.

His gaze turned towards the camp. It would be a pitifully quick fight. Their company outnumbered the bandits four to one.

Werner leaned against the rock and drew an arrow from his quiver. His fingers were twitching, but he countered the nerves by slowing his breath. This was it. Battle. Something he feared and yet was integral to kingship. If relations with the other kingdoms turned sour, Werner would be called up to lead men into war. This was merely a taste of what to expect.

He exhaled and put more weight against the rock.
Don't worry, there's nothing -

The rock suddenly slid from its resting place, sending both itself and Werner crashing through the underbrush. Werner lost his grip on the bow early in the fall, and at some point, all of his arrows fell out of his quiver. A few bushes tried to catch him on the way down, but they merely spun him around as he fell past them.

When he finally came to rest, it took a moment for him to collect his senses. Then he looked around and found himself in plain view of the bandits. They were all staring right at him, with several reaching for their weapons.

"Who are you?" one of them yelled.

Chapter 7

Roland nearly cursed when he saw Werner tumble out of view. He hurried to the spot where his brother had vanished, reaching it in time to see the rock crash through one of the tents just as its owner dove out of the way.

He looked down to where his brother's fall had ended. It took only a moment to see that Werner, still dazed by the fall, lay completely disarmed and at the mercy of the bandits. One of the bandits cried out, "Who are you?" while others grabbed for their weapons.

The Hunter's concern about the roc's storm echoed in Roland's mind. They had to get back to the manor as quickly as possible, or they would become entombed in the coming snowfall.

Roland made a snap judgment and stood beside where the rock had fallen from. "That one down there would be Prince Werner of Whitehaven," he exclaimed with authority, using his brother's full title and place of birth, as was tradition when within their lands, "and I am

Crown Prince Roland of Thistledown. Our men have you surrounded. You will surrender to me at once, or they will let their arrows fly and you will be food for the wolves."

His sudden appearance had taken the bandits' focus from Werner's accident, and revealing his heritage dumbfounded them. Roland couldn't fault their confused glances towards one another. Princes didn't have a habit of suddenly appearing in the wilds of the forest.

Roland tried to keep his eyes on the entire group, ready for if one of them tried to start a fight, yet even he missed The Hunter's approach into their midst. The man had appeared beside one of their tents, his bow fully drawn and aimed for the heart of their leader. "I would accept his terms if I were you."

If the bandits had any doubts about Roland's claims, the sudden appearance of The Hunter ended them, as did the slow revelation of the rest of the princes' company as they themselves recovered from the sudden turn of events. The leader of the bandits called out to Roland. "The old one speaks of terms, but what promise do we have that you'll not cut us down the moment we lay down our arms?"

"You have my word." Roland said.

"Is that all?"

"That is all you need." Roland wasn't about to make concessions to a group of bandits when he held the advantage, even with the storm at his back. That wouldn't befit a crown prince. To further his own position, Roland raised his bow towards the bandit leader and drew back. "What is your answer?"

The bandits had turned to their leader, and after a few moments, he considered prudence was the better form of valor and tossed his weapon aside. The others soon followed their leader's example.

Roland signaled the company to go forward and take the bandits prisoner. Werner had recovered from his fall and went with Lord Finley to take charge of the prisoners while the other nobles searched the camp for warmer clothing. Roland smirked as he thought of how Werner would try to weave his moment of folly in some stroke of genius.

The worst part about his fall, Roland thought, *is that I may have to let him gloat as much as he wants.*

Roland hurried over to The Hunter, who once again had turned his focus to the north. The prince turned that way as well, and his heart sank. "We were never going to beat it, were we?"

"I doubt anyone could ask for a better outcome, given that no blood was spilled." The Hunter replied. His eyes never wavered from the clouds above them.

Roland watched The Hunter's eyes rather than search the sky himself. They studied the movement for a few seconds, then for the first time in Roland's memory, he saw them widen in fear.

The Hunter turned to Roland. "There was nothing we could have done. You would have been caught by its storm even if you had turned back," he said in a hushed, resigned tone.

"I shouldn't have been so eager to go after the bandits." Roland said as he looked at the clouds again. The white wall was nearly upon them, moving faster than any beast could run. "And neither of us are prepared to hunt a roc."

The Hunter shook his head, and when he spoke, Roland heard the tones of fear and rage in the man's voice. "I should have turned back."

Roland wondered what he meant by that, but his eyes were captive to the wall rushing towards him. One second it was a hundred yards away, the next it was right in front of him. He braced himself.

The storm crashed against them with a furious howl. Roland looked back to see his brother cower at the noise and snow, as did everyone else except The Hunter and himself. The Hunter's eyes remained fixed on the clouds. It was like he was tracking something inside them.

Roland felt fire form in his veins at the sudden rush, a smile creeping across his lips. *This is the power of a roc! No wonder their hunt is so revered among the North Hunters.*

The Hunter shifted his gaze for only a moment to give Roland a nod, then returned his eyes to the heavens. Roland saw the determination setting in on the ancient man's face, but that was the only change in his stature. Roland found himself thoroughly impressed with the steel in the man once again.

Then he followed The Hunter's eyes and saw the massive shadow looming overhead. One look at the shadow made him forget the cold, his hand already touching an arrow's fletching.

He stopped the exhilaration before he foolishly loosed an arrow at the beast. The beast was flying too high for the arrow to do anything more than alert it to their presence, if it even reached the roc. Too many lives were nearby to take such an action.

Even if the roc then landed, I'd have to be right beside it for the winds to not blow my arrow away.

He turned to the others and shouted over the winds, "We need to go, NOW! Form a column and follow me!"

The roc's storm had blown away any animosity which may have existed between their company and the bandits as everyone helped each other into some semblance of a marching line. The bandits had yet to be tied up, but no one cared about that with the sudden change of fate. What cloaks and other warmer bits of clothing that the bandits had quickly got passed around to those who needed them, and several bandits grabbed lanterns. These were hastily lit and passed around the line. Roland then pointed towards Fernglen and urged them onward.

He looked and saw that The Hunter had not joined them. After pointing the way to the noble beside him, Roland returned to The Hunter. "You're going after it, aren't you?"

He nodded. "It will kill many if I allow it to live."

Roland smiled knowingly. "I suppose I would only slow you down if I tagged along?"

In a moment that surprised Roland, The Hunter laughed. "Your face betrays my answer already, and I have only one bow capable of taking a roc down. Get these people to safety. Leave the monster to me."

Roland nodded, then held out his hand. "Good luck, Hunter."

The Hunter shook his hand, then disappeared into the gathering white.

Knowing that they were on their own now, Roland took another glance into the sky, and half convinced himself that a massive wing briefly appeared to beat the clouds before the snow covered it from view.

He exhaled, a wide smile on his face despite the imminent danger. The great rocs rarely flew within sight of Roxeter's lands on the northern marchlands, thanks to the North Hunters' efforts. He knew the stories of hunting the beasts and the reverence the North Hunters had for them. It was likely that Roland would never see another roc again, unless he braved those forsaken lands beyond the North Hunters' villages.

As appealing as the challenge of such a hunt was, it was best left to men like The Hunter. Princes and kings were unfortunately called to other feats of skill.

Grinning at the thought, he turned and hurried to the front of the column. "Follow me, and stay together!"

Chapter 8

Rose kept pushing forward, doing her best to not get blown over by the ferocious winds. The wall of snow had engulfed them far quicker than she could believe, and had she not remembered to bring the lantern, Rose knew that she would have already lost her mother and sister in the oppressive whiteout. As it was, Snow was stumbling every few yards, and her mother slowed to help Snow along.

Rose encouraged them onward. "It won't be much farther."

"How do you know?" Snow asked.

"Trust me." It was a hollow lie, but she hoped they would believe it. She had lost the trail soon after the blizzard began and was navigating mostly by instinct and dead reckoning. Luckily the winds were steadily slowing, allowing her to make out several landmarks along the way. They had to be somewhere close to the cottage.

But in this storm, somewhere close may as well be the other side of the world.

She heard Snow lose her footing again, and then their mother gave a cry and fell beside her sister. Rose hurried back to them. Snow was already trying to get up, so Rose went to her mother. She helped her mother to her feet, but when their eyes met, Rose knew they had to stop. "I can't go on, Rose." her mother said as she nursed her ankle.

Rose tried not to panic. Panicking would only get them all frozen. She needed to think clearly. "Then wait here. I'll look for a place for us to rest," she said and then looked around for a stand of trees that could shield them from the wind. The first patch of green turned out to be next to useless, but the second was a small stand of young pines that would suffice.

Leading Snow and their mother to the trees, she then removed her cloak and tied it between the branches like a lean-to. Snow saw her do this and took her cloak off as well. Soon the makeshift walls were shielding them from the winds, while their mother's cloak serving as a blanket for the three of them.

Yet that was not all they needed. Rose took the bundle of sticks and set a fire, tearing her left sleeve off to catch the sparks from her flint. The fire held, and in its soft glow, their world slowly improved. Their mother and Snow pulled out the food they had brought, and set some snow and pine needles into the wooden cups before placing them beside the fire.

Still, they needed more fuel for the fire if they were to make it through the night. "You two stay here. I'm going to see if I can gather some more wood before the snow soaks everything."

"Be safe." Her mother pleaded.

"I will." She looked at Snow, who returned a fearful gaze. Rose smiled, hoping that any confidence on her part would encourage them, then she went back out into the blizzard.

Immediately, she wished she still had her cloak around her in the biting chill, but Rose ignored the pain as best she could. Already the ground lay hidden under inches of white, but some sticks poked up here and there.

She set to work gathering as many sticks as she could, but it was a long while before she filled her arms. The cold soon became part of her being.

Several times, she thought she saw a pair of red eyes looming out from the snowfall at her. The first time she cried out in terror, and barely withheld a shout the second time. She waited for the wolf to approach, but the eyes wouldn't return until she had gone back to gathering sticks. Eventually Rose convinced herself that it must be her fears playing on her mind.

When she finally made it back to the fire, her family's smiles vanished as they ushered her towards the dying fire. "Your face is turning blue!" her mother exclaimed.

Snow revived the fire, and Rose sat close beside it to absorb its heat. The weak flame did little to pierce through the coldness that had set in.

A hand tapped Rose on the shoulder. As she turned, a charred wooden cup greeted her. She glanced at her mother, then thankfully drank the bitter pine needle tea. The warmth slowly returned to her body.

I must have been almost frozen...

"How are you feeling?" her mother asked.

Rose looked at her mother. "Better. Thank you."

After a reassuring smile, her mother sighed. "We'll have to make do with this until the storm blows over."

"But that could be a week from now!" Snow exclaimed. Both Rose and her mother turned at the sudden outburst. "It's too early for a blizzard like this to be natural. Something must have caused it."

"Snow," their mother started, but her words failed. Rose couldn't muster a reply, either. She only hoped that a great shadow wouldn't pass overhead. There would be little hope for them if that happened.

"Hello, the fire!" The call pierced through the blizzard like an arrow. They turned to see a figure appear out of the driving snow, looking as though he considered the storm nothing more than a small flurry.

Rose perked up at once, recognizing The Hunter's voice. "You are welcomed!" she yelled over the wind.

"Why are you three still out in this godforsaken storm?" The Hunter barked. "Your cottage is back off the hillside."

Rose hung her head. "I'm sorry. I must have missed the turn."

"You're lucky you stopped when you did. Another hundred yards and you three would have gone into the ravine." Rose felt her heart quiver at the thought that she'd nearly led them to a fatal plunge. She'd gotten completely lost in the storm.

Before she could reply, The Hunter turned and motioned for them to follow. "This way."

"Mother's hurt!" Snow called.

The Hunter hurried over to their mother. "What happened?"

"I twisted my ankle in the snow."

"Alright." He held out his arm, and after their mother accepted his hand, he lifted her in his arms and turned away from the fire. "You girls follow us."

The two quickly tore down their makeshift camp. Back in the marginal warmth of her cloak, Rose mimicked the Hunter to help Snow not fall behind.

Rose felt her spirit lift. Everything would be fine now. The Hunter wouldn't let them die.

The trek was still an arduous one, though the hunter made it easier by telling Rose to follow directly in his footsteps.

After what felt like an eternity, a faint light appeared ahead of them. A smile broke on Rose's face as she recognized the outline of the cottage, and it widened as she made out the thin trail of smoke coming from the chimney.

They had made it.

They were home.

Chapter 9

Werner couldn't remember the last time that he had been in a storm as powerful as the blizzard following the roc. The howl of the wind drowned out anything that wasn't a shout directly in his ear, and despite Roland being barely fifteen yards in front of him at the head of the column, there were many times Werner could not see the light from his brother's lantern.

The cold was already starting to numb every part of his body. Werner wanted nothing more than a warm fire by which to curl up and wait out the storm, but no fire would survive long in these winds. Even if they had tried to use the bandits' camp to wait out the storm, its opening gust had blown their tents away.

Their company needed shelter, and the manor was the closest known shelter they would find. Roland had them moving at a good pace. The column was not going so fast as for them to become exhausted, but they were close to that mark.

"How are you holding up?" It was Lord Finley's voice, yet despite his shouting, Werner could barely hear him over the winds. The two of them were at the back of the column, tasked by Roland to make sure no one fell behind.

"Cold." Werner yelled back. "How about you?"

"Same." Finley had his head down and his arms across his chest. It was the first time the pair had spoken in what felt like miles. The young lord appeared miserable.

The prince chuckled to himself, then set his eyes forward again. Werner knew he probably appeared similarly miserable, and most of the men in the column were as well. Only a few had gone out dressed for such a thing. The Hunter and Roland always were ready for whatever nature threw at them, and Lord Roxeter and his three bannermen wore similar warm clothing because of Roxeter's lands being on the northern marches. Beyond them, most were still in some form of summer attire.

Werner tried to see his brother through the snowflakes. It proved impossible until a strange gust whipped the snowflakes upwards. Roland's scarf was clearly visible where his brother had said he would be.

Relieved, Werner's eyes followed the soaring snowflakes for a moment.

Then a moment longer.

Something was above them.

The massive shadow slowly passed overhead. Werner stopped to watch the great wings stir the clouds themselves. It was breathtaking, both in the majesty of such a beast and in the terror it represented.

The storm set in again as the beast traveled on. The onrush of wind knocked Werner to the side, and when he looked at where he thought the others would be, only darkness greeted him.

Oh great! In a panic, Werner tried to run forward. He only managed a few steps before his foot fell through nothing, and for the second time that day, Werner was crashing down the side of a hill. Only this time, no one was there to see it.

Once the tumbling stopped, he tried to get his bearings. This proved difficult as his head was pounding from a bump he'd received on the way down the hillside. Fighting through that, he didn't like his chances. He hadn't been carrying a lantern, so he would have to find his way in the evening darkness of the great blizzard with only his blurred sight.

Think, Werner. What would Roland do?

The prince had no immediate answer, and he cursed himself for it. Roland may be easy to chide at courtly functions, but Werner now realized the mistake he'd made at not mentally preparing for such a crisis like his brother had.

He exhaled slowly to calm himself. "Seek shelter," he whispered. "Get downhill and seek some form of shelter. Maybe a cave or something." Werner got to his feet and continued down the hillside.

The storm roared through the forest, but as Werner made his way further and further downhill, the winds lessened. On the ground, anyway. The constant groans of the trees scared the prince more than the cold that was slowly numbing him. If one of those trees should break over the top of him, Werner knew he would be dead before sunrise.

While progress was slow, he tried to keep himself calm. Rushing after the column had been the reason he'd gone over the edge. Doing so again could lead him into a river or lake that the snowflakes were blinding him to.

Time dragged on, and Werner could hear his teeth chattering together from the cold. His eyes scanned the surrounding forest as best he could. To his left, he saw a spot where the ground dipped away, like there was a stream bed beyond it. Maybe it would provide some shelter from the -

A sound rose above the torrent of the wind. Werner strained to hear it better.

"Stupid fools! Just my luck that a roc flies now!"

Hope stirred in Werner's heart. The voice was coming from the far side of the dip. Perhaps help was near at hand!

He rushed down to the site and froze. Before him was a small fortune in gold and rubies, barely covered by the raging storm. The treasure was so out of place that Werner could barely sense the cold or the howl surrounding him as he marveled at the sight. He knelt down and reached to touch it.

"THIEF!" a shrill voice called angrily.

Werner jumped back and raised his hands. "I'm not a thief. I-" Werner found no more words to say, for the voice belonged to a frost dwarf who stood no taller than the middle of Werner's thigh, wearing a bright red hood over a green tunic and holding an intricately carved staff. All Werner could make out of the little man's face were his beady eyes, for the rest was covered in a white beard that looked longer than the man was tall. Roland and The Hunter had talked of such secretive creatures, but he himself had never seen one.

The dwarf had no such hold on his tongue. "You dare to take *my* treasure!" he yelled as he deftly scooped up the gold and jewels into a sack. "And in this godforsaken storm, no less. I know how to deal with thieves like you."

The dwarf began chanting, and the carvings on the staff glowed an ominous green. Werner realized that his life may be in danger. "Please, I-"

A bluish-green light struck him. Blinded, he fell back on all fours. When his vision finally returned, the dwarf had vanished into the storm along with his treasure.

The prince stared at the spot for a few moments, then he tried to rise. His legs felt strange, and he fell down again. As he tried to get up, he saw that where his hand should be, there was a massive paw. In terror, he looked at himself, and there was no doubt.

The dwarf had cursed Werner, turning him into a bear!

Chapter 10

The Hunter opened the door, and they hurried inside. Once The Hunter had set Rose's mother down, she hobbled over to her chair by the fireplace and collapsed onto it. Within moments, she had slipped into a deep sleep. Rose watched the scene with a guilty heart, knowing that she alone had gotten them lost in the snowstorm.

The Hunter took no notice of this, instead moving to the fire and stoking it into a comforting blaze. He then turned to Rose. "You are lucky I went out again to find you when I discovered you were still out in the storm. If this storm holds through the night, everyone will be forced to stay inside for weeks, if not the entire winter."

Rose felt her heart sink. The kingdom's harvests were still being brought in, and if the people couldn't get what remained, it could be a terrible winter. "But -"

He held up his hand, cutting off her question. "Where is your father's bow?"

Rose didn't reply, instead hurrying to her mother's room where the bow and its quiver stayed and brought them to The Hunter. He gave her his bow and took the arrows out of his quiver, replacing them with the black arrows of her father. A moment later, he took the great bow and strung it in one fluid motion, much to Rose's surprise. Even her father couldn't do that so smoothly.

Though, I suppose he was never in such a hurry, either.

The Hunter exhaled, as though the great man was trying to calm his nerves. "You will stay inside for the night. If they continue into tomorrow, I will have failed; if they have ceased, I will be back for my bow."

"Where are you going?" Rose asked.

"To the South Crag."

Rose felt her jaw drop in shock. The South Crag was the highest peak in the southern range, with its upper slope bare of all but rock and snow for three thousand feet. "But why?! The blizzard will kill you before you get there!"

The hunter's stoicism broke for a moment as a smile touched his lips. "Don't worry. This storm isn't too cold for me. Besides, I need to kill it before its storm sets in too deep."

"Kill what?" Snow asked.

"Kill the roc that is causing the blizzard. The Crag is the only mountain nearby that is suitable for a roc to rest on." The Hunter smiled at the expression of surprise on Snow's face. He then addressed the girls. "Now stay inside with your mother until I get back."

They agreed to, and The Hunter slipped through the door and shut it behind him, leaving them safe inside the cottage.

"A roc! This far south!?" Rose jumped at the excitement in Snow's voice. Her sister's demeanor had instantly turned at the mention of the legendary birds of the north. "I wonder how it made it past the other tribes. Surely, they would have seen it long before it ever reached the northern marchlands."

Rose held a finger to her lips, then glanced towards their mother.

Snow tucked her chin guiltily. When she spoke again, her voice was much softer. "Sorry. But if a roc is causing the storm, what happened in the north?"

"I don't know. I doubt we'll know before The Hunter comes back south again."

"But what could it mean?"

Rose gave her sister a serious look, unsure what fantasy Snow was envisioning. "Such as?"

"If one got through, how many more must have appeared to give it a chance to make it through? And what else may have gotten through if that's the case?"

The thought made Rose's skin turn colder than it had been outside. *Could that wolf have been a direwolf? If Snow's right, how many more are prowling outside?* Her heart thumped violently in her chest. *What if -*

"And why on the anniversary of his burial?"

Snow's words drew Rose back from her fears. "What?"

"Why on the anni-"

"Snow, our father was a great hunter, but that doesn't have any connection to a roc appearing today. It's an unfortunate turn of fate. Nothing more."

The look in Snow's eyes was not one Rose was used to seeing from her sister. There was defiance behind the look. She opened her mouth to speak.

"Girls..."

The argument died as the girls turned to see their mother had woken up. They hurried over to her. "How are you feeling?" Snow asked.

"Tired," she said slowly, "but grateful that you both are safe. Where is he?"

"He went to kill the roc causing the storm." Rose replied. "He took Father's bow and arrows."

"Do you think he'll be able to kill it?" Snow asked.

It was Rose who replied first. "Of course he can. There's never been a greater hunter than him."

"Rose is right," their mother said. "He has hunted rocs by himself before, though the last time was before your father and I met," she sighed with a soft smile on her lips. "When your father came south with me, he insisted on bringing a bow powerful enough to kill a roc in the sky in case something like today happened. To think that his worry would come true now, only for another to have to wield his bow."

Rose moved to pick up a blanket from the neat stack beside the fireplace. "Here, you need to rest. Things will be better in the morning." Their mother accepted the blanket, then fell back asleep almost immediately.

"What should we do now?" Snow asked.

Rose picked up The Hunter's bow and set it on the table along with his arrows. Holding the great bow, she had the temptation to try drawing it back, but she couldn't bring herself to do so without his permission. "We should rest, too. The next couple of weeks could be pretty busy if the storm continues through the night."

Snow nodded. "I'll sleep by the fire tonight. You were the one who was out the most today."

"I'll stay out here, too." Rose smiled at her sister's offer to have their bedroom to herself, but while she was sure Snow could maintain the fire, Rose could also see the exhaustion written on her sister's face. "We should all be together tonight."

Her sister smiled, then took a blanket from the stack behind their mother's chair and curled up in front of the fire. Rose took another and set herself on the padded seat by the southern windows. The timbers had a slight chill to the touch from the freezing snow outside, and Rose silently doubted how The Hunter could weather such a storm unscathed.

She closed her eyes and fell into a light sleep.

Chapter 11

It was slow progress, but Roland kept the men moving. The snow was blinding enough that he couldn't rightly tell who was next to him at any point as he gave commands. But they were still on course. He was certain of that, if nothing else.

Roland's mind fought between his constant search for familiar signs and the roc flying somewhere nearby. The storm had weakened and intensified depending on how near the bird was, and fortunately, the snow had been gradually weakening for a while now. The bird was somewhere to the northeast. The company was safe from a swooping death from above. Roland only had to worry about the biting cold gripping them.

Yet there was still the desire to send everyone on ahead and go fight the monster alongside The Hunter. He'd dreamed of such a struggle many times, despite knowing how dangerous it was.

A voice in his head continued to tell him he may never get such an opportunity again. Killing the roc would break the storm, after all. They would have to deal with an early winter, but if the warm autumn held after the storm, the people may salvage some of their crops.

I don't know if my bow can kill it, though. If not, I don't like my chances with a knife.

Once more, his eyes drifted up to see if the storm was still weakening. A gust of wind cleared the wall of white for a moment. Above them, Roland heard the groans of overburdened limbs as the gust pushed them beyond their breaking point. One tree snapped in half and crashed towards them. "LOOK OUT!"

The men near him had time to leap away, but the mass of limbs fell into the middle of their column. Roland heard cries of pain from several men trapped beneath. He hurried to their rescue with the others beside him. "Get them out of there, now!"

He saw a hand trying to lift the branch pinning its owner down. Roland wasted no time and lifted the branches while others pulled Lord Mauvelin free. Three others who had been standing beside him followed the young lord out.

Roland and the others continued around until they thought they could account for everyone under the broken tree. One bandit was dead, while nine of their company bore injuries. Lord Mauvelin's were the worst, followed by the tailor from Middleton. Time was not on either man's side.

Roland tried to stay calm, hoping that it would inspire the others. "The four of you carry Lord Mauvelin and Jack; the rest of you help the other injured men keep up. We must keep going. Sanctuary is not far off."

"How far is that?" a voice asked.

"About two miles that way," Roland said with certainty. "Keep moving and we'll be safe and warm in no time." A few cheers rose from the company, yet Roland saw that the resolve of many was close to breaking.

He counted the shadows to make sure they had everyone ready to march. But even after going through three times, he found they were still one man short. After a fourth time through, horror gripped his heart as he realized who was missing. "Where is Werner?"

The men tried to remember, but no one knew where or when Werner had disappeared. "He was in the back with us, but I haven't spoken to him for a while now." Finley's voice betrayed the guilt of losing track of the prince. A quick glance at the others from the rear of the column told Roland the same story.

At some unknown point, Werner had simply vanished.

Roland felt his heart tear in two. Werner would have to be exceptionally lucky to survive in the storm by himself, but if Roland abandoned the others, it was likely that they would die instead. At least Lord Mauvelin and Jack would certainly die. Roland was the only one in their company who could find his way through the blizzard.

But can Werner survive until I make it back?

"We keep moving." His lips spoke without his input, as if his very soul wanted to convince Roland of the right action as much as everyone else.

"But Roland, what about -"

"I don't know how far back he is, Lord Finley, and the longer we stay out here, the sooner our injured will start dying." Roland turned towards their course. "I'll get you to Fernglen, then I'll return for him myself."

"But Roland, -"

"Enough, Lord Finley!" his voice roared. "We don't have time for you to argue. We move now!" Roland then began a quick march through the driving snow. The shock of the decision on the nobles quickly faded as the peasants and bandits moved to follow Roland, carrying those who couldn't walk.

Their pace was brisk, with each following in Roland's tracks as best they could. He tried to stay focused on reaching Fernglen, but his mind constantly wandered to his brother.

Hold on, Werner. I'll find you.

Roland found a new energy in the fear for his brother's life. He used it to work up and down the line to make sure that no one else got separated from the group. It was a grueling task, but soon the lights of the manor came into view. The men gave a cheer and hurried for the doors.

Several guards who had been on watch kept them from entering until Lord Arrenton confronted them. "You will let us in *now!*" With that, the chill of the storm disappeared as the warm halls greeted them.

But the prince was determined not to stay long. He first turned to the castellan of the manor. "Have these bandits taken to a secure room and detained. Keep them there until I return."

"What's this?" one bandit asked. "After carrying these men through that storm, you're still going to lock us away?"

"You are still my prisoners," Roland replied, "and I will deal with your sentencing once I return."

The bandit opened his mouth to speak again, but their leader silenced him with a wave of his hand. The leader then looked at Roland. "You intend to go out there again?"

Roland nodded. "I have to find my brother."

The leader smiled at Roland's determination. "Very well. We will wait for you to return."

"But Alaric, -"

"Hold your tongue, you fool," he said, and the bandit went quiet.

Among the nobility, though, dissent ran rampant. Every one of them tried to convince Roland that it was a fool's errand for him to go back out, that it was inviting death, but Roland shrugged at their words as he hurriedly threw on warmer clothes and turned back into the night. There was no time for arguing.

"Neither I nor Werner is going to die tonight! Not if I have any say in it." He said, then returned to the blinding storm.

With a single-mindedness bordering on obsession, Roland retraced the steps he had taken. The howling wind returned in greater force than before, but he pushed on.

Already he was beyond the broken tree again, his eyes scanning the quickly disappearing tracks for any sign of where Werner had left the column. Roland had reached this point as fast as any could have hoped to. He might still find Werner before it was too late.

Roland was glad that he didn't have to spare any concern for other searchers. No one else had been foolish enough to leave the safety of the manor, and thinking on it now as he looked into the wall of snow, Roland couldn't argue that going back into the roc's storm was perhaps beyond foolish. If anything happened, he would be stuck out here as well, with little to no hope of rescue.

Both of us could die tonight if I'm not careful.

That very sentiment had risen before he left the manor. His thinking had been brash, even reckless, but now that boast rang in his mind as the fitting last words of a tragic hero.

Stay focused, he told himself. *Waxing lyrically won't save either of us out here.*

He continued on, another mile disappearing into the white abyss. The cold was burning what little exposed skin it could find. His lantern threatened to go out at several points as the wind forced its door open. But the trail was still visible, and Roland kept his gaze fixed on it.

Then he found it, a set of nearly filled tracks that veered away from their course and disappeared over the side of the hill.

It could only be Werner!

Rejuvenated, Roland made his way down to where the streaks of a falling man stopped, then followed the disoriented trail for as long as he could. It looked to Roland as though Werner had gotten turned around in his fall and was following the slope down instead of trying to regain the top of the hillside they had trekked across.

Maybe it would have been wise at another time, but the slope was leading him away from the manor and into the heart of the forest. Werner was going even farther from help with each step.

The tracks turned to a dip in the forest. Roland hurried after them. He was maybe an hour behind Werner now, judging by the snow within the tracks. There was still a chance he could drag his brother back to the warm manor tonight before the snow got too deep to walk out of in the darkness. Time was perhaps still on Roland's side.

But when he crossed into the dip, he was at once terrified and bewildered by what he saw. Werner's tracks disappeared beneath those of a massive bear. The bear was thrashing around, breaking everything in its path, but there was no sign of blood, nor any sign that Werner had continued beyond that point.

After the moment of panic, Roland searched beyond the signs of the bear, hoping that Werner had been long gone by the time the bear had crossed his path. The prince searched for as long as his warm clothing would permit, but there was no sign of his brother's tracks.

Werner had simply vanished without a trace.

Chapter 12

Werner couldn't rightly remember the last minutes or even hours of his life. He'd lost all sense of reason upon realizing that the dwarf had turned him into a bear and had charged around the forest like a terrified rabbit, hoping that it was some sort of nightmare.

Only now had Werner regained control of himself, but he wasn't sure that was an improvement. The mania had at least felt like it was purposeful, to wake him from this troubled dream; now that he knew the dream was real, he found himself deep in the forest with no clue of what he could do to help himself.

Taking a calming breath, he tried to collect his thoughts. There was always the chance that the curse was not permanent, that it was merely a temporary change like one might read about in the old stories. Then again, he knew that there were permanent changes in those accounts as well, and he had never given them enough credence to know what the differences may be.

In either case, there was no way he would be allowed to enter the manor in his current state. Even getting close to Fernglen may lead to Werner being filled with arrows. He would have to find some other form of shelter from the storm. Once the storm had passed, he could try to figure out what to do next.

Thankfully, the thick fur that now covered him was excelling at keeping the chill away from his body. Only the bare pads on his paws felt the cold, and even then, it was not terrible. *I suppose this is a small blessing.*

He tried to laugh, but a menacing sound startled him. Werner spun around to face whatever had made such a noise, and it was a few seconds before he realized the sound had come from his own throat. He tried to talk, but only unfamiliar noises growled into the night. *Seems I'll have to get used to how I sound, too.*

The prince walked through the forest, though this time he found that his fear of the storm had subsided. The winds had died down some more, but Werner knew the calm feeling was more to do with the cold being defeated by the thick fur than anything else.

Again, he thought of the unexpected blessing of the curse. Werner was now better dressed than anyone in their company had been, even The Hunter himself. As a bear, he probably could sleep anywhere and survive the storm if the roc didn't decide to hunt him during the night.

Despite this, Werner wanted to find better shelter than simply beneath some tree. Because of princely pride or not, he justified the thought by reasoning that even if his fur worked now, that it didn't mean that it would hold up for the duration of the storm, however long that may be. He would look for a cave or some abandoned structure to hide in, like he had planned to do before crossing paths with the dwarf.

And so, he slowly plodded through the storm looking for such a place. The forest floor rolled beneath him for miles as the snow piled onto his back. Whenever he felt the land sloping into a hill, Werner chose not to expend his energy climbing. Civilization would be in the flatlands, not the hills.

Yet the hilly ground became more prevalent, and Werner wondered if his mania had led him into the southern range, or if he was crossing the spur of hills into the royal forest to the southwest of Fernglen. He stood and looked for any mountains that may be looming through the darkening storm, but found none.

Hopefully that means there are none, and I am passing through the spur hills. Werner moved on, putting any remaining concerns to the side. In time, to his delight, the hilly ground flattened out.

The storm lifted, accompanied by the moonlit shadow of the roc flying overhead. Werner stopped and watched the magnificent display. The bird flew in a lazy circle with its wings at their full extent. It must have been nearly a hundred feet from wingtip to wingtip. Its massive blue eyes were searching the land. Werner quickly moved to hide beneath the trees.

Hoping that the roc hadn't seen him, Werner took the opportunity presented by the break in the storm to look around. He saw snowy hills in the moonlight back along his trail, but he couldn't tell which hills they were on account of the storm still raging in a ring around them. All he knew was that they didn't extend long enough to be the spur hills, or the foothills to the southern range.

He was somewhere deep in the forest.

Werner tried to recall the maps he had seen of these lands. It didn't calm him when he remembered the numerous stands of hills dotted the map, though he took solace in knowing that he hadn't crossed a river yet.

At least, I don't think a river could have frozen over so quickly...

The prince looked at the hills again. They may be hiding the mountains from the southern range, or those of the northern range. The moon was high enough that Werner couldn't tell east from west, and he didn't know the constellations well enough to get their help. He could be anywhere in the forest.

An ear-rending screech shook the trees. Werner dropped to the ground and stared at the circling roc. Its eyes had fixed on something in the distance. The roc turned towards the hills, and Werner watched as the storm collapsed back to the roc. The howling winds and snow returned, and Werner marveled at the power the beast possessed. *How can anyone hope to hunt a roc when it can do that?*

Werner waited for a few minutes to make sure that the roc didn't return. Once he satisfied his fears, he turned away from the now unseen hills. *I suppose I'd better not head that way.*

The prince continued plodding on in his search for shelter. Though he had felt a rush of energy after seeing the roc, his massive body was starting to struggle as fatigue set in. More than once, the thought about just resting beneath a tree or in some bush rose in his mind, but arrogant pride pushed him onward.

Then Werner stepped into a clearing in the forest. He could barely make out a light coming from further into the clearing. Werner was so tired by this point that he didn't care if someone saw him. He lumbered over to it, finding that the light was escaping from the shuttered windows of a robust cottage. Given the late hour, it was likely that all inside the cottage were asleep.

Werner quietly tried to make his way to the door in order to hide under the eaves, but he stumbled in exhaustion and accidentally bumped his shoulder hard against the door. He waited a moment to hear if anyone inside stirred, worried that they may come out and chase him away, or even worse, attempt to kill him for the threat a bear would understandably pose.

A few seconds passed, and Werner heard nothing. He exhaled in relief and sank to the ground. There was enough heat coming through to make the night a little more tolerable. Werner gave a sigh, then tried to get some sleep.

Chapter 13

A thump against the door roused Rose from her sleep. As she gathered her senses, she could hear the wind beating against the timbers of the cottage, so the roc must still be alive. She wondered what time of the night it was, then she heard a second thump near the door, as if something had fallen beside it.

A dreadful thought struck her. Perhaps someone else had lost their way in the storm and had stumbled upon their cottage. Whoever it may be could freeze within reach of sanctuary like her family would have. Wrapping her blanket around her, she rose and hurried over to the door.

As she reached for the latch, she hesitated. What if whoever was on the other side wasn't a friend? What if they tried to harm her and her family in some fit of madness created by the storm?

What if... it's another wolf?

Rose slowly let out her breath. If that was what awaited her, she would have to defend her mother and sister. Her feet moved swiftly to the cabinets, and she took out one of the long knives. Then she slowly made her way to the door.

I'll likely only get one chance. Rose let out a slow breath, then reached up and undid the latch.

The door swung open as though propelled by some unseen force. Rose found herself thrown back and nearly lost her balance. She kept her footing though, yet when she turned to the door again and saw the culprit, she leapt back in fright.

A massive black bear lay across the threshold. It was unlike any she had seen in the woods before. Fear held her in place. Would it attack her like the wolf had? Would it not heed the magical bond?

The bear stirred, and it began slowly waking from its slumber.

Rose was unsure what to do. The bear had rolled onto the threshold, so she couldn't shut the door again. Not only that, but the cold of the storm was robbing the heat of the cottage. Could she push the bear back outside before it finished waking up?

She took a step towards the bear, but then the massive head turned to look right at her. In desperation, she tried to use the magic bond, but a moment later she knew the bond wouldn't work. The fear turned to terror. *Another one?*

"Rose," she heard from behind her. It was her mother's voice. "Why is the door - Oh my!" Rose turned to see her mother rising from the chair, wrapping the blanket around her. Snow, meanwhile, was only now stirring from their mother's outburst.

Rose looked back at the black bear. The bear stared at her, its eyes glancing between the knife and her as if understanding the terror that she was in. It made a gruff noise at her, as though it thought she might understand it, then it lowered its head as if asking her to put the knife down.

Rose let out a bewildered chuckle at the idea, but then the bear repeated the gesture. Curious, she slowly lowered the knife and placed it on the floor, though her hand hovered over it in case the bear started to attack.

The bear glanced between her and the knife, then it slowly got to its feet. She felt her heart quiver as its shoulders nearly reached her full height, showing how large the bear truly was.

The bear looked her over for a moment, then it lumbered past her to the fire. It lay down beside the flames with a huff, coming to rest right beside where Snow had been sleeping.

Snow looked at the visitor with a gleam of wonder in her eyes. When she turned to Rose, there was a wide smile on her lips. "What do we do with him?"

Rose didn't have an answer. *What are we supposed to do with a giant bear?*

Their mother spoke up in Rose's silence. "First, shut the door, Rose. Quit letting the cold in. Snow, find a broom to beat the snow off of him so he can warm up quicker."

"But -" Rose began, fearful of what would happen if the bear attacked like the wolf from the afternoon. The bear didn't respond to the magic bond. Even if their father's bond still somehow protected Rose and Snow from the bear, the magic didn't protect their mother and the bear could turn on her for any reason.

Her mother wasn't about to hear any of Rose's concerns, however. Rose saw her eyes were glistening at the bear, a look similar to when Snow was daydreaming. "We will worry about it in the morning. Until then, let's keep him comfortable."

With a sigh, Rose shut the door and latched it. Snow had already taken the broom for cleaning the fireplace and was removing the snow from the bear's fur, laughing as the bear first watched her curiously and then would move to help her reach the snow better.

Rose felt a pang of jealousy watching them. Her sister hadn't experienced the horror of seeing an animal turn on her. Rose silently hoped that Snow would never experience it.

"Rose, go help your sister while I put something together for us to eat." Her mother then chuckled to herself. "I can't believe I fell asleep feeling so hungry."

Rose smiled at her, then helped her sister by beating the snow off with her hands. Soon the black fur was clear of any lingering ice. The bear gave a satisfied grunt and looked like he would fall asleep by the fire. However, when their mother came by to put a pot over the fire, he gently got up and moved out of her way.

"Well, you seem to have some manners." She said happily.

"He's beautiful with this golden coat." Snow remarked. "I've never seen a bear like this."

Confused, Rose turned to her sister. "Golden?"

"Yes. Look." she pulled back the fur where Rose and their mother could see. Sure enough, beneath the outer fur lay a short golden coat. Rose glanced around the bear, and her eyes caught several spots where the gold was barely visible through the black.

"I've never seen a bear like this, either." Their mother said, shaking her head with a smile that told of other wonders in her mind. "I'm curious where he is from."

Where he is from... The statement became stuck in Rose's mind. The bear was the second beast not to heed her bond, and both had appeared at the same time as a roc had flown south. *Perhaps all three are connected. Maybe he's a North Beast.*

One beast stood out from all the others from that thought. The spirit bear, the only North Beast that was revered rather than feared among her father's people. Rose pulled back the black fur to stare at the hidden gold beneath. *It's not the right colored fur at all, but maybe...*

She shook her head. *Now I'm sounding like Snow.* The bear's behavior raised plenty of questions, but Rose decided she would ask The Hunter about it when he returned from the South Crag. If anyone knew what the strange bear was, it would be him.

Until then, Rose would have to trust her mother's judgment that they would be fine keeping the bear inside until morning.

Soon their mother had the porridge ready, giving the first portion to their unexpected guest. The bear devoured it with a furious appetite while she gave Snow and Rose their bowls, and soon he had eaten all the extra that their mother had made as well.

His appetite amused the three women, and shortly after their laughter had died down, the bear laid beside the fire and fell into a deep sleep.

"He's a strange one, isn't he?" Rose asked.

Snow chuckled. "He acts like one of those spirit bears Father would tell us about."

"I had thought that, too," their mother replied as she studied the bear, "but then, I suppose I've only heard of them having pure white coats."

That's what I had thought as well. Rose finished her food. "We can ask The Hunter when he gets back from fighting the roc."

"I suppose that will have to do." Their mother said as Rose took their empty bowls into the kitchen. "Now, I think we'll take after our guest's example and get some more rest."

"Could you tell us a story, like you usually do?" Snow asked sweetly.

Their mother hesitated for a moment, then smiled and went to the bookshelf, reaching for one of the large books. "What kind of story would you like to hear?"

"One I haven't heard before." Snow replied.

Their mother laughed softly and put the book back. Their mother examined the other books there for a few moments until she pulled out the thin one with the red cover.

She smiled as she held it. "I haven't read these stories in a long time." Then she moved her chair close to the fire and sat down. The girls wrapped themselves in their blankets and gathered beside her as she told an old fairy tale from her youth.

Chapter 14

The heavy oaken doors swung wide with a resounding thud against the walls. Roland saw that all across the room, people spun towards him. Then they hurried over as the prince reentered the great hall, his clothing freezing around him. Despite it being well past midnight, it surprised Roland to see so many of the nobles still awake.

Lord Finley was the first to speak. "Did you find anything?"

Roland nodded, rubbing his hands together to get some warmth back in them. "I found where he slid down the hill. It was around a mile or so behind the tree, so we didn't lose Werner too long before we noticed he was missing. The fall looked like it disoriented him, and his trail started going downhill. I wasn't able to follow them after he took another slide into a hollow."

"You couldn't find anything else?" One lady asked. Roland was unsure of her name at the moment, but he knew she was one of Werner's frequent pursuits.

The prince hesitated for a second, worried about telling them of what he'd found. If they heard about the bear tracks, they would all lose hope. There was no reason for that to happen yet. After all, the bear had spread no blood along its path. Surely that meant that Werner had gone off somewhere just beyond where the storm had forced Roland to give up the search. "I lost his tracks and wasn't able to find any further signs of him. I'll go out again when it is light."

"You're shivering." The elderly feminine voice instantly put him on edge. More than anyone else, Lady Harken was a bane of his existence. Though she was among his mother's most trusted ladies-in-waiting, the old hag liked to act as Roland's unwanted matchmaker when he engaged in social gatherings. This time though, he was welcome to her suggestion of "Let's get you by the fire."

He nodded to her, then didn't object when two young ladies took him by the arms and led him to the warmth. Roland knew he should recall their names, but like before, he couldn't place them. *The cold must be robbing me of my memory.*

A servant then brought him a bowl of soup, and he slowly let the broth warm him from the inside. He heard many questions from the nobles, but he could hardly remember them after he gave an answer. His focus was inward on his own thoughts. Werner was gone, and Roland couldn't help but accept that it was his fault.

"Prince Roland?"

Roland looked up at Lord Roxeter. He saw that Lord Finley was standing to the lord's left. Both were quiet, a silent invitation for him to speak his mind.

The pair put a sad grin on the prince's face. If anyone could be as worried as Roland, it would be Finley, and Roland had gone on many hunts with Roxeter. Perhaps they could understand the turmoil within Roland.

He exhaled and gathered himself. "If I hadn't allowed Werner to come, he wouldn't be out there now. Or, if I hadn't sent you on ahead, we may have returned before the storm struck."

"True," Roxeter said bluntly, "he wouldn't be out there."

"Percy!" Finley exclaimed, but Roxeter raised a hand to cut him off. Roland appreciated how calmly Roxeter kept his demeanor compared to Finley and the others.

Roxeter continued. "That being said, if he hadn't come, he wouldn't have surprised the bandits as he did, and we may have had some of our number killed in the skirmish. None of us would have made it back if we had been wounded at the bandits' camp. Even those that were struck by the tree barely survived. As for us turning back, that would have doomed the lives of those bandits. Even with them being outlaws, you and Werner allowed us to save more lives by your actions."

"I don't think that sentiment helps that Werner is still out there, Lord Roxeter," Finley remarked.

"True," Roland said, "but Lord Roxeter is right. Our good fortune was Werner's doing." He rose from his seat, convincing himself that the warmth had worked itself fully through his body. "Maybe that fortune will smile on me now."

"You're not going out again, are you?" one of the ladies who'd brought him to the fire asked fearfully.

"You barely made it back alive as it is." Lord Finley added.

"He's still out there," Roland said, "and I know where I have to start looking."

"My prince," Roxeter spoke sternly, "I know you wish to continue the search, but it will be best to wait until morning. Werner will have found shelter by now if he's still alive. You needn't kill yourself needlessly."

"Allow me to convince him, Percy." Lady Harken slid back into view. "Roland, it is best that you get some rest. You can lead everyone with fresh spirits in the morning. You know your mother and father would advise you to do the same if they were here."

Roland gave a thin smile. Despite his will to venture forth again, he knew that what they were saying to him was right. Two winter excursions had worn his body to the point of exhaustion; even though he knew where to look, he didn't have energy to overcome the storm. "Very well. But please have a servant wake me when the sun rises. I'll go out again in the morning."

"But Prince Roland, the storm is still raging," one of the young ladies said.

"It won't be when the dawn comes." Roland remarked, knowing that The Hunter wouldn't wait until morning to deal with the roc. It was likely that their battle was currently being waged on a dark mountaintop, the victor to be determined well before anyone in the manor arose in the morning. "Even if it hasn't, I must keep looking."

"We can't lose two princes to the same storm." Lady Harken said.

Roland let his anger slip through as he growled, "Werner will not die out there! Not if I have anything to say about it." Then, without another word, he retired to his bedchamber and to a fitful rest. Too often he awoke thinking he heard Werner's cry, only to be met with the howl of the wind instead.

He awoke once more to the siren call, only this time he found the air was still. He nearly sprang out of his bed in delight. The roc was dead, and that meant he could get back to the search.

A quick glance outside told him it was still the dead of night, and while many snowflakes kept falling from the sky, the raging winds had died with their maker.

With a wide grin, he ran to the door and ordered the servant stationed there to wake as many of the men as he could and tell them to get ready to leave at once. The prince then returned to his room and hurried to dress for the calm snowscape that he would search through.

"Stay safe, brother." Roland prayed. "I'm coming."

Chapter 15

The first rays of sunlight peeked through the shutters, stirring Rose from her slumber. She resisted the light as long as she could, clinging to a dream where the previous day had not happened, but it was to no avail.

With a sigh, she stretched her arms over her head and looked around. Snow was still sleeping by the fireplace next to where they'd listened to the story, and her mother was curled up in the big chair. The black and gold bear had remained dutifully by the fireplace all night. The air was calm and peaceful, as if this was how things should be.

She cast her gaze to the window, then hurried over to it and threw open the shutters. Her spirit rose as the clear blue sky greeted her. The battle was over. The Hunter had killed the roc, or at least driven it away. There was nothing to fear from the beast anymore.

Memories of the day before tried to rush in, but she willed them into the depths of her mind. There was nothing she could gain by dwelling on them right now. Once The Hunter had returned, they could plan what to do in the aftermath of the storm.

Until then, she would try to cook a proper breakfast for once.

With practiced silence, she readied a brass pot with barley and water, then added some honey and dried berries from the cellar below as Snow had done yesterday. She also added a dash of cinnamon spice that The Hunter had brought during one of his visits over the summer. Rose set asides her usual thoughts of this being excessive. They had survived the roc's storm; that was reason enough to make a special breakfast.

Carefully, she carried the pot past the sleeping bear and set it on its peg. Only then did she remember that Snow mixed in the flavoring ingredients after the barley reached some unknown texture. It was too late now to correct that mistake.

Rose took another glance at the bear. Seeing that it hadn't shifted, she smiled and built up the fire. Once the flames were hot enough, Rose took a quick look around the room. It told her that her activity had gone unnoticed by anyone.

Satisfied, she turned to the bookshelf. Picking one of the large books that suited her fancy, she sat by the open window with her blanket draped around her and let the words distract her until the porridge was ready.

Several times she glanced up from the tale of knights and monsters to look at the bear, but it never moved so much as a hair. His breathing was heavy, like her father's would be when he had overworked himself. *Could the bear have been even more tired from the storm than we were?*

Whatever the bear's story, Rose found she was glad they had crossed paths. The potential danger such a creature possessed still concerned her, yet the bear provided an intriguing twist in life she could never have expected. She had no doubts that her sister had already created fantasies about what the bear heralded, and Rose couldn't keep herself from doing the same.

It was sometime later that her mother stirred in her chair. Rose set the book down and moved to get a bowl of porridge for her mother. It was stickier than Snow's had been, but at least it smelled good. Rose reached her mother as she was opening her eyes. "Good morning."

Her mother nodded, saying nothing as her voice was still asleep. She took the bowl from Rose with a grateful smile and had a few mouthfuls. The food appeared to drive away the last remnants of sleep. "Thank you, Rose. When did the storm break?"

"I don't know. It was clear when I woke up."

Her mother nodded. "Good. Then he succeeded."

Rose smiled. She could hear more stirring behind her and stepped to the side as the bear stretched its legs towards her. It made an odd groaning sound as it did so, much like when an old man stretches before standing, causing Rose to chuckle.

"Get him some breakfast as well." Her mother said with a laugh.

Rose swiftly got a large bowl ready for their guest. When she set it on the ground beside his head, the bear's eyes fixed on her with a look of thanks before he ate the offering. She was curious about what was going through the bear's mind. He must have found the whole situation strange that three women would let him in and care for him.

It is strange, she thought with a smile. *It's like we're in one of Mother's fairy tales.*

Rose left to get two more bowls ready, sitting down to eat hers after she set the other beside her still-sleeping sister. The smell soon caused Snow to wake up as well, and all four enjoyed their breakfast together.

"What are we going to do with Goldie?" Snow asked as she finished her food.

Rose and her mother smiled at Snow's nickname for the bear, then laughed when the bear reacted by turning to Snow and tilting his head as though he couldn't decide if he liked the name. "I don't know," their mother replied. "What does he want to do?"

Surprisingly, the bear dipped his head as though he was in thought, then he stood up and motioned his head towards the door.

"You're leaving already?" Snow asked, her voice filled with disappointment.

Goldie turned to Snow with what Rose could only describe as a sheepish look in his eyes. He glanced away for a second, then looked back at her and nodded. Rose saw her sister start to tear up and couldn't deny that she felt a bit of sadness as well. Though he'd only stayed the night, there was something about the bear that was comforting despite the threat he posed.

Snow reached out and scratched the bear behind his ears. At first he appeared unsure how to react to this, but he let Snow continue for a few seconds more before he turned his head towards the door again.

Rose got up and opened the door. He strolled out into the white landscape, his shoulders barely squeezing through the doorway. Wherever it caught, the golden undercoat glistened in the morning light.

"Stay safe, Goldie!" Snow called out to him.

The bear turned and slowly bowed his head, then lumbered off into the woods. The three women watched him go, and then stared at the place he disappeared from sight for a while longer before their mother said, "Well, I suppose we should get the place in order for winter."

"Yes, Mother," the two replied. For the next couple of hours, they set about their winter routines. Rose went to her place chopping wood for the fire from the pile stored in the lean-to behind the cottage. The state of the pile produced a sigh when she first assessed it. They had stored plenty, but only a pitiful amount from two summers ago had been cut. The rest was in a messy heap.

Quietly, Rose berated herself. She'd done well to bring more wood in after her father had died, but she'd chosen to wait to get it in order. The warm summer had promised more time to prepare, and she had accepted the promise. Now Rose would spend most of the next week just getting the pile into a manageable state.

She put a hand on her face and groaned. *I should have spent less time wandering the woods looking for peace.* Rose then picked up the ax and started swinging.

For the first while, she worked as she always had, but as time dragged on, she caught herself looking more and more towards the tree line. It wasn't to see Goldie come walking back again; Rose was afraid that another pair of red eyes might be watching her.

She ran through the past day again and again, trying to calm her fears. The wolf had died, and she was safe. That's all that should have mattered, and yet she couldn't shake that look in the wolf's red eyes.

She should have died yesterday.

She would have died.

"Hello, the house!" the familiar voice called from inside the tree line.

At once, the spell of the wolf broke. Rose hurried out of the lean-to and around the cottage to greet The Hunter. Upon seeing him, though, she gasped. Her hand covered her mouth in disbelief at the sight she saw.

The Hunter's face was awash in dried blood. His left eye had almost swollen shut. His once pristine clothing now looked like it had been dyed crimson, with what looked like the work of a hundred blades cutting back and forth across it. Three large gashes had nearly split his cloak from side to side. Only the pack he carried appeared to have escaped the struggle with no visible marks.

And yet the man moved as though he felt none of the pain.

Her mother stepped out to greet him with a hug. "You made it," she said calmly, as though such a sight were commonplace to her.

"It was hard-fought, but the beast has fallen." His voice was weary, but the grand smile on his face betrayed the pride he felt. As if to confirm his words, he took off the pack that hung over his shoulder and produced a trove of massive feathers and several large talons.

Rose gasped at the size of the talons. They were nearly as long as her arm. She pictured how big the roc must have been to have such weapons. That a single man could kill such a thing in the middle of their storm was truly a feat to behold.

"What now?" her mother asked.

The Hunter sighed. "I wish I could rest, but I've already found several other North Beasts that followed the roc south. I need to head north to see what the roc did to our people, then we will probably spend the winter clearing the lowlands of the roc's followers. Speaking of," The Hunter turned to the cottage door. "Snow White, I have a question for you."

Rose looked to see that Snow was standing in the doorway, her face even paler than usual at the sight The Hunter presented. "Yes?"

"There was a bear here last night, wasn't there?"

The three looked at each other. "There was," Snow replied, "but the only thing he did was lay down by the fire and eat with us."

"Is that so?" The Hunter glanced between them curiously. "What did this bear look like?"

"It was black all over, but his undercoat was golden." Snow replied. "His shoulders are as tall as I am when he was on his paws. I never saw him stand on his hind legs, but he may be over ten feet tall if he did. I called him Goldie, and he seemed to answer to it."

"It definitely wasn't a normal black bear," their mother added. "He seemed to understand even me without much effort."

The Hunter had no immediate reply to this. Rose had never seen his face have any measure of confusion on it, and she was certain she saw confusion slipping through now. *Is it possible that Goldie is something even The Hunter has never come across? Is such a thing even possible with him?*

Eventually, the look on his face returned to its normal features. He turned to Rose. "What do you think, Rose Red?"

She waited a moment before replying to collect her thoughts. "He doesn't respond to the bond, but the bear didn't make any movement that was threatening. He also understood what we were saying, and he left as though he had a plan in mind."

"Hmm." The Hunter stroked his beard. "The coloring doesn't match, but from its size and habits, it sounds like a spirit bear visited you last night."

Rose glanced towards Snow. Her sister's eyes lit up like she had rarely seen before. There was little imagination about why. If Goldie truly was a spirit bear like they'd suspected, her sister would doubtlessly add it to the roc's appearance and conclude that something fanciful was happening to them.

Though, even if Goldie isn't a spirit bear, can I still doubt that this all seems like a fantasy?

"I had thought that he might be a spirit bear," their mother answered before Snow could voice her fantasies, "but I realized later that the bear appeared after we were safe. Even so, its arrival and behavior were so similar to what I've heard of theirs. Do you think it was just a normal bear that was caught in the storm?"

"No, not if it would not heed the bond," he said slowly, running his fingers through his beard, "and that this bear would listen to you is interesting, to say the least. I wish I could figure it out myself."

"You're leaving right now, aren't you?" Rose asked.

"I must. Time is of the essence." He gave them a nod. "If I happen upon Goldie, I will see if he is a spirit bear or not. Now," he took their father's bow and quiver from his side, "I leave these with you and will take mine back. There should be no more rocs before I return to our lands, and the bow deserves to remain here with you."

Their mother took the two in hand. "Of course. Rose Red, get The Hunter's things from where he left them last night."

"Yes, Mother." Rose hurriedly went inside to get the bow and quiver from the table and grab a few provisions for The Hunter's journey back home. He was still asking a few questions about the bear when she returned, but once he had his kit, he was ready to leave. He left the three with five feathers each, then he hurried off into the woods.

Rose went back to her woodcutting, and it wasn't long before the wolf took control once again. There had been nothing she could do, and now The Hunter wouldn't be around to save her.

Her bond couldn't save her.

What can I do?

Chapter 16

A gentle breeze brushed against Werner's face as he moved through the forest. He knew he had to find some way to break his curse, but he had no ideas about how to even start looking for one.

The only thing that came to mind was to return to the hollow where he had seen the dwarf and his treasure. Perhaps that could provide an answer, but the raging storm had covered his tracks. The only clue he had was in the rising sun and the hills to his right. Thanks to the position of the sun, he knew the mountains to his left had to belong to the northern range. The other hills, meanwhile, looked like the ones he'd seen when the roc cleared its storm last night.

Because of that, he knew he was well north of Fernglen, and therefore even farther north of where the dwarf must have been. If Werner couldn't even see the tracks of his massive paws from last night, what hope did he have to find such tiny footprints as the dwarf's?

A dark thought loomed over him as he trudged through the fresh snow. *Am I going to be stuck like this forever?*

He was fortunate to have found the cottage last night, and that the three had let him in. Werner knew that he would have tried to drive away any bear that showed up at his door.

Well, Roland would have done that. Werner breathed a laugh as he pictured himself running at the sight of a bear in the doorway, more of a coward than any of the three women.

His thoughts drifted to the two green-eyed girls. Snow had taken to him immediately, entirely unafraid of him and treating him as an honored guest. Rose, meanwhile, seemed the more practical one, since she regarded Werner with caution throughout the night. She'd even answered the door with a knife in hand. That girl had some bravery in her. Werner had seen the fear in her eyes when he had rolled into their doorway, but Rose kept a firm hold on that knife.

Even though he was a bear, Werner couldn't stop the thought of what the two thought of him. He silenced it a moment later. He held no doubt that they thought of him as a simple bear with strange black and gold fur.

Goldie. Werner shook his head in mild amusement at Snow's name for him. He'd always enjoyed the attention of the court and had gained his reputation as a golden child while trying to stand out from Roland's shadow. Now it was the only name his saviors knew him by.

Werner kept plodding through the fresh snow. He again marveled at how he barely felt the cold thanks to his thick fur. So long as he didn't push himself too hard, he would be fine as he meandered along.

The thought again reminded him of the warm cottage, and he looked over his shoulder towards where it lay. Though the structure itself had long disappeared into the trees, Werner took a mental note of the hills near it in case another storm blew in.

A soft pain in his heart formed as he thought of how remote their cottage was from the rest of the kingdom. *Yet they seem so happy being out here. Maybe Roland does know something about what's good in life.*

The breeze shifted, and a scent reached his nose. Ever since he had become a bear, Werner had noticed that his sense of smell had grown far more acute, but this scent was familiar. It came from the direction of the girls' cottage, but it wasn't one of their scents. Curious, Werner turned back to get a look at what this scent belonged to.

Why does it seem so familiar?

It was only a few moments later that Werner saw him. A figure dressed in bloodied white appeared from behind the trees. He carried a bow in his hands, with the arrow nocked.

Werner froze for a moment before panic overtook him, and he turned to flee. A ranger was after him.

He was being hunted!

He needed to -

"Hold!"

Werner skidded to a stop, sending up a wave of fresh snow. That was The Hunter's voice!

Werner looked at him with whatever passed for joy on a bear's face. Surely, the old man would have some answer for what Werner needed to do to get back to his human body.

"Well, you certainly are a strange one." The old man approached, but with a measure of uncertainty that Werner had never seen before.

Not that Werner could blame him, given the circumstances. Judging by the state of his clothing, The Hunter had fought a brutal battle against the roc. The man had to be exhausted despite how he carried himself.

Werner tried to speak, hoping that perhaps among The Hunter's many gifts was the ability to understand the tongues of bears. Apparently, he did not possess such a gift, but the grunts Werner produced seemed to give the old man an idea.

The Hunter reached inside his cloak and pulled out a silver amulet. After a brief incantation in a language that Werner didn't understand, the charm glowed with the same bluish-green hue as last night.

"Dwarven magic. So, you are not what you seem. You're cursed with this form." The Hunter returned the charm and cast a sympathetic gaze on Werner. "I can't free you from this magic, and unfortunately, I must head north to deal with the roc's followers. I can tell you this about the magic used to do this to you: if you kill the one who cursed you, the spell will be broken."

The Hunter then turned to the north. "I wish you well on your hunt, and I ask that you take care to not harm those women you stayed with. They belong to my old tribe and are very dear to me. Good hunting, 'Goldie'." With a wave, the Hunter hurried into the forest. Werner tried to call out to him, but to no avail. The man simply disappeared into the snow. Werner was alone again.

The prince stood in the snow for a long time, lost in his thoughts. There was disappointment that The Hunter couldn't provide him with more help. That meant that he was truly on his own. Werner would have to make his own path.

There was fear in that path as well. Werner was no tracker, and he hadn't the slightest idea where he'd crossed the dwarf and gotten cursed because of the mania last night. It was also going to be a long winter. Could he even get close to where the dwarf's domain was? Would he have to wait until spring to get his chance to break his curse?

Yet Werner also felt the fire of determination take hold, even as despair was building inside him. He wasn't entirely alone. The girls in the cottage had given him shelter during the storm, and The Hunter had provided him with clarity, provided him with a purpose.

The plan was simple. Hunt down that dwarf, kill him, and break the curse.

That was all that Werner could do now. He'd have to take after Roland's example and become a hunter. He would have to learn on his feet and rely on the pieces of wisdom his brother had tried to give him in the past. Once the hunt was over and Werner was human again, he would find some way to reward the girls and their mother for the kindness they'd shown him.

Werner took his first steps on the path of revenge. *If I have to hunt all winter, I will.*

That fire of resolve held for most of the day, but by the evening it became completely drowned by the thunder in his belly. Werner had trekked dozens of miles through the snow and found not a single trace of the dwarf or of the bandits' camp. For all he knew, he was on the far side of the forest from Fernglen.

Werner's belly growled again, even louder than before. His eyes glanced towards the hills to the north, and he saw he was near where he started that morning. He huffed as he realized he'd gone in a circle.

Still, that put him close to the cottage. They had already taken him in once, and Snow had shed a tear that he had left. He didn't doubt that they would let him back in; the primary fear he held was that he would eat them out of all their stored food and get forced out as an unwelcome guest.

I'll need to learn to hunt for myself, if only to ease the burden of feeding this body from the girls and their mother. He set his feet towards the cottage and lumbered back to his newfound sanctuary.

Chapter 17

It had been a long day in the cottage after Goldie and The Hunter had left, and the girls had spent much of the afternoon helping their mother rearrange the place for winter while she took stock of their food stores. They were lucky in one respect; her mother's decision to buy a large store of the early barley harvest meant they would have plenty until spring.

The rest of their stores would run low if the roc's storm induced an early winter and cut them off from the villages. Their garden being ruined by the sudden blanket of ice worsened that aspect. She salvaged what she could, but it would be plain porridge for the last month of winter if the real snowstorms coated the land as they usually did.

There should be plenty of berries still on the briars. Snow grinned as she thought of the rare last fruits before winter. When an early winter struck, the freeze would concentrate the berry's sweetness, making them her favorite for juices and desserts. Now would be the perfect time to go see what the nearby briars still held.

Excited at the prospect, Snow grabbed two bowls and went out to find Rose. Her sister was still in the lean-to, chopping away at the pile. "Rose, do you have a moment?"

Rose jumped and spun around, then forced a laugh and set the ax down. "What is it?"

"Do you want to go with me to check the briars for ice berries?"

Her sister's eyes widened in fright, and Snow was certain that Rose's skin lost some of its color. It only lasted for a moment, though. "Sure. Let me get my bow first and we'll go look."

Snow nodded, but her concern grew. *Why do you want your bow?* The question remained unasked even after Rose returned. Snow decided to watch her sister for a while, in case Rose's reactions were simply the lingering effects of the roc's storm.

The girls didn't have to go far beyond the tree line to find the first briar. They found some berries were perfect for Snow's purposes, while the rest could be on the vine a while longer. Snow eagerly filled her bowl, yet she noticed Rose kept looking into the woods. "Are you looking for Goldie?"

A look of embarrassment swept across Rose's face. "I... suppose I was."

Why is she lying? There was something wrong with her sister. Snow opened her mouth to speak, but the memory of Rose freezing up at the question about peace jumped into her mind. *If she's worried about something, I should wait to ask once we are back in the cottage.*

"I think that will be enough for today, don't you?" Rose asked.

Snow looked at Rose's bowl and saw that it was already full. It caused her to laugh. "You filled yours up a lot faster than I remember."

Rose chuckled, and this time the act was genuine. "Well, I have gotten plenty of practice this year." She then stepped back from the briar and turned for the cottage. "You coming?"

Snow looked down at her bowl. It was about two-thirds of what her sister had, but together they would be enough to occupy her for the rest of the afternoon. "Yes, I'm coming."

"Good." Rose hurried back to the cottage, and once they had taken the berries inside, Rose quickly went back to the lean-to.

Snow set to work readying the berries, but her mind was on her sister. She didn't yet know how she wanted to ask about Rose's strange hesitancies today. While it was possible that they were simply lingering stress from the prior evening, that answer did not convince Snow. Something else had to be the problem.

She resolved to confront Rose at sunset and concocted a plan to do so. Instead of Snow cooking the evening meal as would be normal, she would ask if their mother could. It would surely let on that something was bothering Snow, but that was the idea. Rose would be more willing to speak with her in order to help Snow, then Snow would turn the tables and try to understand what the matter with her sister was.

That was the simplest plan she could think of, and it gave Snow the rest of the day to string together a list of questions.

The afternoon progressed as best it could, given the circumstances of the sudden winter. By the time the scarlet evening sky appeared, they had put the cottage in perfect condition, and brought inside anything that had survived the storm.

Snow watched the sunset from beside her rose tree, getting the last of her questions for Rose ready. But as the sun touched the far tree line, her eyes caught a black coat lumbering out of the woods.

It was the bear again, heading right for their cottage. She turned and called inside, "Mother! Rose! Goldie is back!"

The two hurried to the door, and they watched as the bear slowly made its way to them. Snow could tell that Goldie was exhausted. She walked out to him and stroked the fur behind his ear. "You poor thing. Do you need a place to stay tonight as well?"

The bear looked at her for a moment, as though considering the proposal. Then he nodded, and Snow led him into the cottage. She and Rose again beat away any snow that clung to the bear's fur, and their mother took it upon herself to cook a larger meal than they had expected.

Once they were done, Snow went to the stack of blankets, took the thickest quilt from the stack, and laid it out by the fire. Goldie gave her a look, then seemed to smile at her and set himself down on the quilt. She laughed and scratched the bear behind his ears. "Are you going to go out again in the morning?"

Goldie huffed and gave a slight nod.

Intrigued, Snow leaned closer to him. "Will you come back again in the evening?"

He glanced towards the fire as if mulling it over. Then he huffed and nodded again.

Snow laughed and turned to her mother. "Can we let him stay?"

Her mother smiled. "I think we can let him stay for now. At least until he finds what he's looking for."

Goldie grunted in what Snow took to be appreciation. Snow put her arms around his neck and gave him a hug. "I'll take that as a yes."

Soon afterwards, their mother had the porridge ready. They ate their meal and then settled down beside their mother to read another story before bed, with Snow taking a blanket and lying down beside Goldie. The bear tried to push her away, but she merely laughed at him and eventually settled herself just out of his reach. Goldie rolled his eyes at her before closing them and drifting off to sleep.

The story was one that Rose had asked for. It was one of their father's favorite stories, the one where he and The Hunter had hunted a roc. Their father had asked The Hunter to join him so that he could benefit from the man's knowledge. After two weeks of tracking the bird, their father had finally caught it in an ambush. His first two arrows had missed as the bird wheeled through the snowy air, but with The Hunter at the ready nearby, their father kept evading the roc and finally killed it with his third arrow.

It had always been a fascinating tale to Snow, given how unreal the rocs sounded in those stories, but now having lived through the storm and seeing The Hunter after facing one alone, she was in awe that her father had returned without a single scar, much less survived.

Once the story was over, their mother said that she would sleep in her own bed that night. Snow said she'd like to stay by the fire again, and Rose replied that she'd sleep by the window as she had before. Their mother said good night to them and disappeared into her room.

"Do you trust the bear?" Rose asked softly after their mother had shut her door.

"Why not?" Snow replied. "Goldie understands us and answers in his own way. No normal bear would do that."

"But the bond..." Rose didn't finish her sentence, and waved her hand before Snow could reply. "Never mind. I'll see you in the morning."

Her sister settled into her seat and seemed to fall asleep almost immediately. Her breathing wasn't right, though. The faint breaths were nothing like the deep ones that accompanied Rose's dreams. Snow knew her sister was pretending to be asleep. Clearly, Rose didn't want to discuss the day any further.

Only when Snow closed her eyes did she remember the questions she had prepared for Rose.

I'll ask in the morning. She then fell into a pleasant sleep.

Chapter 18

Already a week had passed, and Werner had yet to find any sign of the dwarf. Each morning, he had eaten with the girls and then headed out, and each evening he had returned to the cottage right as the sun was setting and the girls had welcomed him in. Rose had finally come around to liking him, while Snow was as affectionate as ever.

That affection came with concern on Werner's part. Snow believed that he was a simple bear and treated him as such, even resting against him by the fireplace. How would she react if she knew he was a prince? Or even that he was human to begin with?

Those concerns would amount to nothing if he didn't find the dwarf. Werner was getting better about making a dedicated pattern to his search, but a natural snowstorm had once again returned the land to a white canvas. He'd spent most of the morning going back over yesterday's trail to see if the dwarf had made an appearance, to no avail.

His belly rumbled as the sun reached its highest point. Werner had been trying not to take as much from the family, but he had yet to find success in hunting any small animals he'd happened upon. It was an exhausting trial of restraint.

Soon he happened upon a gentle stream. He'd already crossed a few during the last week and had found that his paws didn't mind the freezing water, so he decided he would cross to the other side.

He got about a third of the way when he saw a flash of silver in the water. When he stared at it, his spirit rose immediately. It was a fish, and it was lazily swimming towards him.

Werner stood waiting for the fish to reach him, one paw in the air. He planned to smack the fish into the air towards the shore. Not knowing the danger that lay ahead, the fish came right up to him.

The prince swung his paw into the water and lifted it. He felt something hit the side of his paw, but only water came up with it. The flashing silver swam away furiously.

Werner stared in shock. He had swung right where the fish had been. How had he missed? It seemed impossible for him to have missed when it was right in front of him.

Exhaling his frustration, he watched as other flashes swam up the stream. Thrice more, one of the fish came up to him, and all three times, he came away with nothing. After the last one, he smashed his paw through the water in a show of his temper.

Why is this so hard?

Werner took several breaths to calm himself. After his anger cleared, he took a step forward, and then stopped. His paw didn't land where his eyes told him it should be.

The water was distorting his paw.

If that's true...

Werner waited for another fish to swim up to him. This time he aimed further back and not as deep, and when he swung his paw, he caught the fish full on its side. The fish flew into the air and landed on the shore. Before it could flop its way back to the water, Werner had rushed out of the stream and batted it further inland.

Once he reached the fish a second time, his impulses took hold and instead of eating the fish bite by bite, Werner swallowed the fish whole. It was a strange feeling as the fish wasn't yet dead, but his belly was no longer growling.

The prince laughed to himself. *Now I won't starve, at any rate.* He caught another fish for good measure, this time making sure it was dead before he swallowed it.

With his hunger satisfied, he crossed the stream and continued into the forest.

About an hour later, his nose caught a scent. He immediately reviled it, yet it was strangely familiar. Remembering the one scent that became The Hunter, Werner followed his nose into the forest.

It was miles before he caught sight of the source of the scent. A tiny man with a white beard and a red hood over a green tunic was walking on top of the snow, leaving no tracks. On his back was the same sack from that fateful night. The only thing missing was the dwarf's staff.

It's him! Werner roared and charged the dwarf. The little man spun around in a panic, but easily sidestepped the charge. "AH! What are you doing still awake, you stupid bear?! Leave me alone!"

Werner tumbled into a bush as he tried to turn too sharply. The dwarf laughed. "HAHAHA! What's the matter with you, you klutz?" The dwarf had taken his eyes off of Werner as he doubled over in laughter, and when he looked up again, Werner was nearly on top of him. "AHHH!"

Werner barely missed the dwarf with his claws, but one claw ripped the sack that the little man was carrying. Gold coins and rubies fell into the snow, like the ones Werner had seen on the day he was cursed.

"No, no, no! Give those back!" The dwarf began hopping between Werner's paws as he scooped up the lost treasure. Werner nearly smashed him once, but all he ended up doing was tripping over himself again. He landed on the remaining treasure, pushing it deep into the snow.

"Ah! You foolish bear! What do you think you're doing?" The dwarf said as he hopped around out of range of Werner's paws.

Shaking himself up, Werner again rushed after the dwarf. The little man weaved his way into the brush and slipped out of Werner's sight for a split second. It took several more seconds for Werner to find him again, picking up the rest of the treasure from where Werner had embedded it in the snow. By the time the prince had closed the distance, the dwarf had already gathered the last gem, and he slipped away into the undergrowth.

Werner huffed. The dwarf had outsmarted him, and it stung to admit it. In fact, it was infuriating. He could already picture Roland and the others laughing at the way the dwarf had given him the slip.

He also pictured Roland trying to explain how to catch the dwarf. Werner attempted to reason out what Roland might say to him. That answer was obvious; the small dwarf would be difficult to catch on the run. Werner would have a better chance if he could get the dwarf in an ambush where the little man couldn't hide or run away.

There was also that he now knew that the vile scent belonged to the dwarf. Werner could find the dwarf with no need to rely on his eyes. Like he'd seen Roland do, Werner could stalk the dwarf until the right moment to strike.

For the first time since he had been turned into a bear, Werner had options to choose from.

He chuckled. Even in his failure, he'd gained an advantage over his foe.

Now the hunt truly begins.

Chapter 19

It had been a month since the roc's storm ushered in the early winter. Goldie had gone off on his daily routine a few hours before, and Rose was in the lean-to cutting more wood for the fire. In the past, this was an activity that allowed her time to clear her mind, but her thoughts kept returning to the wolf.

She tried to shake the memory and bring back happier ones from before her father had gone north the last time, when the woods were never any concern. When she and Snow could sleep out under the stars and not worry about any danger.

But those red eyes kept staring at her. Sometimes it was simply a memory, but other times she was sure she'd caught them gleaming at her from the trees. Waiting for her to make a mistake.

Or waiting for Snow to wander off, unaware of their presence.

Rose heard the quivering of her breath. She had kept the knowledge secret so that neither her mother nor Snow would worry, but how long could she do so? Surely the nightmare wasn't over. The Hunter had said the roc had brought many followers south. How many wolves were a part of that group? Or what other North Beasts were making a home in her woods now?

What could Rose do? She wasn't a huntress yet. She knew a couple of traps that might catch another wolf, but she had never built one. Even if she tried, would they even work on a direwolf from the north?

And there was also how her mother would react. Would she decide to abandon their cottage and live in one of the villages, or maybe go back to her childhood home?

Would Rose be forced to leave her woods, rather than choosing to?

She swung the ax, splitting the round in two. Rose grinned in satisfaction and channeled her frustrations into the cutting. It only took a few more swings for her to imagine the wolf's head where the round was. The first time she did this, she struck a knot and the ax bounced, but soon she had found her placement and was cleaving through with each stroke.

Rose continued on until she realized that an entire row of rounds lay split at her feet. She stepped out of the lean-to and looked to the sky. The sun was already past noon. She'd never even heard her mother call her in to eat.

Rose chuckled and looked down at the ax. *If nothing else, maybe I could kill a wolf with this.* She exhaled and set the ax down. She'd rather never have to use an ax against such a beast; hitting it at a distance would be much better.

An idea formed in her mind. One that her mother probably wouldn't approve of, but Rose was determined to try it in her moment of inspiration.

She picked up a large round from the next row and carried it some thirty paces past the lean-to. Her eyes darted around the tree line to make sure no red eyes were watching her. Unsure but willing to risk it, she set the round down on its side and hurried back to the cottage.

Quietly, Rose went inside and found that both their mother and Snow were taking a nap. Their mother had been feeling sick the past couple of days and Snow looked like she was about to become ill as well. They had enough herbs on hand to treat the illness several times over should it come upon Rose as well, but for now, the two were taking it easy and resting.

This was all fine for Rose. Silently, she slipped into her parents' room and grabbed her father's bow and arrows. While she had that old training bow, it had already proven to be useless against one of the red-eyed wolves. Taking the bow carefully in hand, she then hurried outside.

Rose only paused once she set the arrows down and went to string the bow. A feeling of irreverence built within her. Could she claim to be worthy of wielding it, even in such a circumstance? What would The Hunter say if he learned of this? What would her father have thought of it?

Can I even string the bow?

Gingerly, she tried to string the bow. Then more forcefully. The bow resisted with all the power stored within its strong limbs.

She had witnessed how easily The Hunter had strung it, as well as the numerous times her father had won the struggle. Even with all her might, the bow refused to yield to her.

With a tear forming in her eyes, she retrieved the arrows and went back inside the cottage. Her family was still asleep. Rose was thankful that they wouldn't know what she had attempted.

She hurriedly stored her father's bow and went to stack the newly split wood. It was without the joy that had come when cutting as she re-lived the failure with the bow.

She couldn't protect her family from the wolf.

She couldn't even protect herself.

Stop it! Rose thought as she threw an armful of wood. That wolf was dead. The Hunter had killed it. If any others followed the roc, surely the rangers would hunt them down while the North Hunters kept any more of their kind from coming south. It was foolish to be afraid of something that may not exist.

Yet, it had existed. And it had nearly cost Rose her life. She didn't know if that was the only wolf or if it had been a member of a pack. If there was a pack, where would they be now?

Rose gathered the thrown wood and stacked it, then finished the pile before picking another armful to take inside. At the door, she looked at the trails that Goldie had left throughout the month.

Seeing the well-worn groove in the snow made Rose envy the bear. No sane creature would try to attack Goldie. Even a pack of those blue-gray wolves would struggle to take down such a beast as Goldie. One angry swipe of those massive paws and most creatures would find themselves tumbling away, either stunned or dead.

Is there anything that scares you, Goldie?

Exhaling, she went inside and set the wood in its place. She glanced at the table and saw that her food was sitting there. It was cold now, but Rose took it by the fire and set the bowl near enough to be heated without the flames burning it.

Rose watched the flames for a while. The fire was dancing without a care. She'd always loved being entranced by the dance of a gentle blaze. Despite having no song, the flames moved to a slowly shifting rhythm that only they knew, never quite touching the wood they burned but gliding over it.

She thought again of her father, and his promise that she would soon have a bow of her own. It was his last promise to her, and it also felt like an unanswered calling. Rose would get a proper bow one day and learn to wield it. Maybe someday she would even be strong enough to wield her father's bow.

When winter ends, she told herself.

Rose knew that when the snow melted, she would go gather the plants for her mother's dyes, and then Rose could use some of the money they made from the sale of the dyes to buy a bow.

It wasn't what she should do as a North Hunter; the bow had to be carved from one specific kind of tree in the north to be considered a true hunter's bow. But it wouldn't be difficult to convince her mother that Rose should have one.

If nothing else, The Hunter would surely take her side after the wolf attack. He may even bring a hunter's bow south with him, just before he took them north.

The reminder of that outcome stung, for she knew her woods would be abandoned. This might be her last year that she called the woods home. If so, she'd make sure

that the aedelis and menulia plants she cut before The
Hunter returned would make the finest dyes. A final gift
to her mother if that future was Rose's fate.

But that in itself would require her to go into the
woods alone to get those plants. Rose felt her heart quiver
at the thought.

She sighed and put the thoughts to the side. *Spring
is still a few months away. Maybe I can prepare myself
before then.*

Chapter 20

Midwinter's night had come and gone, and Snow was once again staring out at the track leading into the woods. She had told her mother that she wanted to read in the branches of the oak tree while it was sunny, but her eyes never stayed long on the pages.

Goldie had once again surprised the family last night by bringing in a catch of fish that he gingerly carried home in his mouth, and their mother made the fish into the best meal they'd shared all winter. It had been a wonderful celebration, but Snow's one regret was that they didn't have a gift to give the bear in return. What could they even give him?

Rose had said that a roof over his head was probably a gift enough for the bear, and her mother agreed. While that was true, and Goldie was clearly pleased with the arrangement, Snow's heart wanted to do something more for the bear.

She had woken up early to play with Goldie before he headed out again. He had grown used to her and enjoyed the way she scratched his ears, but there was still a sheepishness to him whenever she tried to lie down beside him in front of the fire. It was like it embarrassed him to have her be that close to him. Snow never pushed him too far, but she found she enjoyed embarrassing Goldie in that way.

The bear's routine once he disappeared into the woods remained a mystery to her, and as the winter dragged on, Snow found she wanted more and more to sneak away one day and watch the bear from afar.

She'd gone through her books a dozen times by now, reading how the old heroes and her father had stalked their prey. Snow had even practiced sneaking up on her mother and sister, with growing success. There was no way she thought Goldie would catch her.

Snow also knew that beneath the mystery of Goldie was the growing wonder of the wilderness that she had never felt before. Sure, she had dreams of going north, or south, or many other places. She'd never lacked curiosity. Yet this winter had taught her that having the stories of what lay beyond the woods told to her was one thing; the places themselves had to be experienced to fully know what they were like.

Having surviving the roc's storm brought her father's tales from the North into vivid detail, and having a bear living with them while he was on some unknown quest was like living in one of her mother's fairy tales.

Yes, they had nearly died in that storm, but by grace, they had survived.

She glanced out across the white meadow to the trees. What else could the winter be hiding from Snow? What else did it have in store for her?

These questions drew her to the woods, and she decided that today would be the day she got some answers.

At first, Snow thought to ask Rose to join her in her little escapade, but Rose's continued caution towards going into the woods told Snow that her sister remained trapped in the memory of whatever had happened to her before the roc's storm. Snow had never gotten around to asking her sister what that had been, and now it had been long enough that Snow felt shame for not asking sooner. What would her sister think if she learned Snow hadn't asked those questions yet?

That said, Rose was the best equipped of the two to follow Goldie if the trail should vanish. After all, Rose had real experience going out during the winter, while Snow had merely the knowledge she'd learned from her father's stories.

But if I ask, she might tell me not to go...

Snow glanced down at Goldie's tracks. If she didn't leave soon, he would get too far away, and she would be without his protection. Besides, maybe he needed help to finish whatever quest he was on.

Snow leapt down from the branch. *Here I go.*

She was about halfway across the clearing before Rose's voice reached her. "Snow!" When she turned, her sister was hurrying towards her. "What are you doing?"

The look in her sister's eyes scared Snow. Rose was at once furious and terrified. Concerned about what caused the reaction, Snow decided she should keep her plan hidden. "I thought I saw something in the trees and was going to look for it."

"Don't! You don't know what's out there!"

Rose's demeanor startled Snow. This wasn't like her sister at all. She looked into the woods. "What is it? What's out there?"

A few moments of silence followed before she looked back at Rose. Her sister's lips hung on the unspoken words. Finally, she sighed and said, "You remember The Hunter told us that other North Beasts came south with the roc? I don't want any of them to find you."

Snow stared hard into her sister's eyes. "Do you think there are any in our woods?"

Rose hesitated and glanced away, towards the tree line. "... I'm not sure. Just... come back inside and we'll find something to do."

A pang struck Snow's heart as she watched Rose's reaction. In hiding her intent, Snow knew she had inadvertently dug up the terror that stalked her sister. Something had scared Rose before the blizzard struck, and whatever it was, it didn't react to the bond. *Is that why she was so nervous around Goldie at first? Could that be why she always stays in the room where he is? To try and protect us?*

Snow realized she couldn't wait any longer to ask those questions. "Rose?"

"Yes?"

"What... happened before you met us at the cairn?"

A memory flashed behind Rose's eyes, and her face paled. "I don't feel like talking about it right now."

"Rose, whatever it was, it made you afraid of the woods. I can see that plainly."

Rose tucked her chin and glanced away. "I'd hoped you and Mother wouldn't notice."

"You haven't gone out of sight from the meadow except for when we gathered ice berries. You've never gone so long without doing that before. Even after Father's passing." Snow put a hand on her sister's shoulder. "Stop carrying your burden alone, Rose. What was it?"

Her sister turned her face away. "It's nothing. The Hunter took care of the wolf already."

"The wolf?"

Rose stiffened, then gave a sigh. "I ran into a wolf that wasn't affected by the bond. The Hunter found me just as it was about to attack and killed it, but I'm worried that others may be out there."

At first, Snow didn't know what to say. That she was being drawn into the woods while Rose fled inside seemed a cruel twist of fate. Yet, there must be something about the wolf Rose had noticed. "What did it look like?"

She saw the fear in Rose's eyes, but her sister kept the rest of herself calm. "I'll tell you in the lean-to. Just promise me you won't tell Mother. I'd like her to hear it from me."

Snow nodded and followed her sister to the lean-to. After making sure their mother wouldn't hear them, Rose told Snow the full story of the wolf attack and the roc's storm.

Several times during the story, Snow felt her heart stop beating, especially when the wolf seemed unaffected by Rose's arrow. From what Rose described, the encounter sounded like one of their father's direwolf hunts she'd recently read again. Direwolves were rarely a threat to their father, but then again, the roc was far more menacing in person than the stories have ever made them out to be. Against such a force, a mere direwolf would hardly seem like a threat to their father.

Hearing Rose's tale also caused concern for Snow's plan. She would have to leave almost as soon as Goldie did, not hours later as she was now. It would also help to know about all the North Beasts that could be out in the woods.

I suppose answers will have to wait a few days more.

When Rose had finished her story, Snow said, "I never imagined that could happen in our woods."

"Neither could I, but it has." Rose stared into her sister's eyes. "That's why I don't want you going into the woods alone. At least until I know that the wolf was alone."

"But what if I was with Goldie?" Snow asked without thinking.

Rose didn't have an immediate response to that. Snow could see the conflicted thoughts playing out on her face. "I... I guess you would be fine then, but I don't know what he does during the day or how far he goes into the woods."

"Neither do I, and I'd like to know. Don't you?"

Rose hesitated, then nodded slowly. "I've thought of it, but it doesn't concern us."

"Is that all?" Snow's reply was more accusatory than she meant it to be. "You're not curious why he doesn't respond to the bond? Maybe the answer is in following him. He's not that far off. We can easily -"

"Stop it!" Rose snapped.

Both girls dropped their heads in guilt. Snow couldn't blame her sister for the outburst. Snow had let her wonder blind her from how Rose would see her request. The direwolf attack would have terrified Snow to no end, and the woods had been the domain that Rose had shared with their father. To be deprived of her sanctuary because of North Beasts...

"I'm sorry; I shouldn't have snapped like that," Rose said.

"No, I shouldn't have spoken like I did." Snow then moved to appease Rose by walking back to the cottage. "Let's go inside and see if Mother will read us a story before lunch."

Rose didn't question the idea, clearly glad that Snow had willingly given up following Goldie into the woods. But in the back of Snow's mind, she kept the plan alive.

Rose won't go, and she'll try to keep me from going. I don't know if the direwolf had friends, but Goldie will protect me. I just have to be close to him and everything will be fine.

And I have to do it when neither my mother nor my sister are able to follow me.

Chapter 21

From what Werner could remember, there was less than a month until spring set in. At this point, Werner was waiting for that day with more anticipation than he had for any festival or banquet as his former self.

Aside from that chance encounter a week after he'd been cursed, Werner had not seen hide nor hair of the dwarf. Many times, he had caught the scent of the foul thing, but the dwarf had continued to elude him.

It wasn't as though Werner had failed to search nearly every corner of the forest that was within a day's trip of the cottage. Only a few days ago, he had caught sight of Arrenton's Manor in Fernglen. He'd found no sign of the dwarf, and being so near the last place he'd visited before being cursed brought forth conflicting feelings.

On the one hand, he wished to have returned with the others and enjoyed the long, cozy nights in the manor. On the other, he would never have met Snow if he hadn't gotten himself lost.

The prince wondered if they were still looking for him, or had they already gone on with their lives. Though that thought pained him, Werner couldn't hold it against anyone who had given up on him. *As much as I hate to admit it, the dwarf's curse is the only reason I'm alive.*

Pushing the memory away, Werner continued on his current path. After finding himself near Arrenton's Manor, he focused his search south of the manor. He'd found what remained of the bandit camp, but what traces of the dwarf scent he could find had been faint. All floated towards the northeast, so that was the direction he would keep searching.

Midday found Werner along the shore of the reedy lake. It was a better fishing spot than the streams on most days and provided a clear view that was unrivaled on this side of the forest. Today was no different. Three trout served as his lunch and the thin clouds above kept the glare of the snow from being overpowering.

Now if only I could catch a scent...

Werner had a few options to check from here. The stand of low hills south of the cottage could be hiding any number of caves, as could the northern mountains. He could start with that cairn with the two rings and granite capstone as his reference point. Or he could explore the flat lands on this side of the stream. The trees were thinner on this side and he had caught a few whiffs of the dwarf, though the last had been what eventually led him back to Fernglen.

It had also been many weeks since Werner had wandered to the far side of the lake. That side was the wildest part of the forest, thick with trees and underbrush. Even the rangers, who were spreading farther and farther afield as the winter wore on, rarely left any prints heading towards that area.

They had more reason not to than just its remoteness. Years ago, Werner's father had instructed these forests to be unhunted. That edict would end in the coming summer. Werner had never placed much thought into the edict, but now he wondered if perhaps it had to do with Snow's family. They were from The Hunter's old tribe, after all; perhaps the edict was as a favor to the northern high chief.

Whatever the reason, the forests here held many unexplored places. There was every possibility that the dwarf was hiding in that dark corner across the river, and therefore most of it lay beyond where he could get back to the cottage before night encircled him.

He'd thought about staying a night in the snow, but his princely pride remained and he had a warm place to sleep every night. Besides, the girls expected his return now. It felt cruel to have them worrying about him.

Though, that may make it the best place to try searching again.

The prince bounced between these choices before he decided he would follow the main stream from the lake. Along the way, he spotted several herds of deer meandering about, as well as other prey animals coming to drink from the waters. Most of the time, they took one look at Werner and moved away.

His eyes caught sight of gray fur coming out of the underbrush. Up ahead and oblivious to him appeared a family of wolves, the four large cubs prancing through the snow while their parents followed. The father saw Werner and immediately dropped its tail and flattened its ears. The mother and the cubs hurried back out of sight while the father made a fearful show of protection.

Werner had no reason to fear the wolf, nor a reason to provoke it. He huffed and turned into the stream as though he were going to take a drink. The father watched him go, then hurried off after his family.

The prince considered the encounter as he left the water. In particular, he thought of how the wolf stood against a foe so much greater than itself to protect those under its care. Werner had rarely dwelled on the matter, at least in the realm of physical combat. He was well accustomed to verbal sparring, covering for wrong words spoken or turning the tables on his courtly foes. But to stand against a massive bear like the wolf had done was something Werner doubted he would have had the courage to do.

Of course, Roland would do it, and The Hunter went even further than that by going after the roc alone and slaying it by himself.

Werner thought to the other lords of the land. Some, he decided, would make such a stand, others not so much. He doubted Finley and Mauvelin would stand in the way. Arrenton was older and might simply remain frozen in place by duty to those around him. Roxeter and his men most certainly would. The men of the marchlands had a sterner disposition than the men of the interior.

Throughout the morning, the wind had been coming from the direction of Fernglen, but as was its custom, the wind shifted to come from the east as the sun began its downward descent. A gust ruffled his fur, and Werner caught the vile scent clinging to it. There was another scent too, only slightly different, but Werner dismissed it.

It's him!

He plunged into the frigid waters and made for the far side of the forest. The cold water froze in his undercoat, but Werner didn't notice or care. He plowed through the snow with abandon, only stopping when the thought finally broke through that the dwarf would easily hear him coming and disappear before Werner ever caught sight of him.

Werner crept along until he got under the tall pine trees. The snow here wasn't as deep as in other parts of the forest. One glance up at the heavily laden boughs was enough to answer why. All along the ground were signs of game animals, and Werner followed the trails they'd cut as he made his way deeper towards the dwarf's scent.

The voice reached him before Werner ever caught sight of the dwarf. "I won't have it together until after the snow melts."

"You promised to have it ready before winter." Another small voice said.

"Is it *my* fault that a roc flew south so early, hmm?"

Wondering if he could glimpse the dwarves, Werner raised up cautiously. He immediately dropped to the ground.

"What was that!?" the dwarf called out.

"What was what?"

"I could have sworn I saw a bear's head up ahead."

"HA! A bear this time of year!?"

There was the sound of something solid striking someone. "How dare you laugh at me! One attacked me not a week after the roc's storm."

"The stupid thing probably hadn't figured out where to hibernate yet."

"Then what of the bear prints I keep finding, huh?"

"Ah, pish-posh. You worry too much. And even if there is one, you have that staff with you."

The voices were getting closer, and Werner couldn't believe his luck. The dwarf and his companion were walking down the game trail he had been following. And even though the dwarves had seen him, the absurdity of a bear walking in winter hadn't alarmed them enough to change their course.

Now Werner needed to find a place for his ambush.

He backtracked the game trail until he reached a point where it weaved between a berry bush and a large rock. The prince chuckled as the plan came into being. He would hide behind the bush, then when the dwarf passed him, he would smack him against the rock. That would leave his foe dazed and with nowhere to hide. Then Werner would get his revenge.

He heard the dwarf's voice on the wind. "Even though that blasted roc set me back, once the spring comes, I'll have it all gathered and ready for you."

"You're sure?" a second voice asked in jest.

"When have I ever failed on a deal? Now get going, and we'll burn this place come the spring." Werner then heard whistling making its way merrily towards him. Werner's excitement grew. The prince slipped behind the bush and waited.

It was a brief wait. The whistling grew louder as the dwarf followed it, completely unaware of Werner's presence. *The fool isn't even looking at the ground to see my prints.*

A little red hood came into view, and that was all the signal the prince needed. Werner struck at once, knocking the dwarf against the rock. The little man was stunned by the impact, and before he could recover,

Werner had pinned the dwarf's legs under one massive paw.

Two beady eyes looked up at him in horror as he yelled through his thick black beard. "Help! Help!"

Werner's other paw raised up to strike the killing blow, but he paused. *A black beard? But ...*

Slowly, he realized his mistake, and Werner took his paw off the dwarf. The little man was the right height and had the same clothes, but it was not the one he was after.

He sniffed the air and immediately caught the vile scent behind him. *He's still close, I can -*

A pulse of bluish-green energy struck him on his left shoulder as he turned. The dwarf must have thrown another curse at him. Werner looked down to see what had become of him now, but there was no change. He was still a bear.

Werner shifted his gaze and saw the white bearded dwarf staring at him with wide eyes. "What!? Why didn't that work?"

Werner growled and advanced towards the dwarf menacingly. The dwarf made another incantation and the energy from the staff lanced towards him. Werner didn't bother to dodge it, and the energy again dispelled as it hit his body.

The prince felt his smile grow as he saw the dwarf's face pale. The dwarf took a step back. "WHAT? What manner of devil beast are you?"

One you already cursed. Werner roared as he lunged forward. *You're mine!*

He charged at his foe, and the dwarf was hard pressed to flee him. Even in the tangle of brush that the dwarf tried to dodge through, the prince maintained his chase. Werner had grown used to his bear form and was no longer as clumsy on the run as he had been that first week.

"You fool demon! Stop chasing me!" The dwarf yelled out curses and tried to cast a few more incantations at Werner, but nothing worked to slow him down. Twice he came within an inch of catching the dwarf's cloak in his claws. The dwarf cried out something in terror and ran towards the gap between the bush and the rock.

Werner had nearly caught the dwarf when they reached the ambush point. *Only a few more steps, then -*

His paw snagged on something, and Werner fell flat on his face. He heard the blackbeard dwarf call, "I got him!" and the whitebeard replied, "Then get lost!" By the time Werner got back to his feet, the dwarves had disappeared from sight.

Werner caught the scent of the whitebeard and tried to follow it. The dwarf was moving too swiftly and through too thick of underbrush for Werner to track him down effectively, though. His foe had even doubled back over the blackbeard's trail and gotten Werner to follow that scent trail for a few precious seconds.

The prince kept up the chase for as long as he could, but after a few miles, his frustrations boiled over.

If only that other dwarf hadn't been there. Werner roared loudly. *I had him!*

Chapter 22

It was a dreary morning, which thankfully there had been few of this winter. Snow looked out at the dark sky with its flurry of snowflakes. Sometimes they fell gently towards her, other times a sudden gust of wind would stir them into chaos. Though she enjoyed watching the ever-changing pattern, it heralded a day that one should stay inside unless they had something urgent to deal with.

Snow shuttered the window, then went to sit at the foot of her mother's bed alongside Rose. Their mother was bedridden with a cold, while Rose had become more and more depressed as the winter dragged on. Snow hoped that her sister would return to her usual self once the winter was over, but feared that the incident with the direwolf would haunt Rose for the rest of her life.

I pray not. Snow didn't think she could manage seeing Rose so listless.

Rose put her hand up to their mother's forehead again. "You seem to be over the worst of it."

Their mother nodded weakly. "I do feel a little better this morning."

"Would you like anything?" Snow asked.

"Another bowl of soup would be nice."

A big sneeze erupted, startling them all. Snow turned to see Goldie looking into the doorway. She got off the bed and gently rubbed behind his ear. "Is it time to go out again?"

He nodded his head and grunted. Snow's heart ached for the bear. It was clear for all to see that he was sick as well, yet he continued his daily routine of going out at dawn and returning in the evening.

Snow smiled and tapped him on his nose. "Alright. How about something to eat first before you leave?"

Goldie shook his head with a huff, as though he'd guessed that she hoped he might take a day to rest. His eyes even appeared to sparkle for a moment. But the bear still tossed his head to the side in his usual habit.

"Very well, then." Snow turned to Rose. "I'll let him out, then I'll be back with some soup."

She and Goldie walked through the cottage slowly; Snow tried to delay his departure so that he could think more about her suggestion, while the bear fought against the exhaustion of his illness.

When they reached the door, she glanced over at him. "Are you sure you have to go out today?"

He nodded without hesitation.

Snow sighed. "You know that we're fine with you staying in here during the day as well, right?"

Goldie gave a slow nod, then pressed his head against the door.

"Fine, but don't get yourself any more ill than you already are." Snow opened the door and Goldie lumbered slowly into the flurries for a dozen steps.

He looked back for a moment, as though he was considering her proposal one last time. Snow smiled at him, and he appeared to smile back. Then he turned and went out on his enigmatic routine.

The idea which had taken root weeks ago finally reached its full bloom. Snow decided that today was the day she would follow Goldie. She would wait until after she'd taken over watching their mother from Rose. Her mother was on the mend, as Rose had said, and it wasn't like Goldie could go that far into the woods with his own cold and all the fresh snow on the ground.

The one concern that ate at Snow's conscience was Rose's warning about the direwolf that attacked her. Ever since she had first had the idea, Snow had read the stories of her father's hunts constantly. Now that she knew direwolves had made it this far south, she studied every word and tried to remember the night she had heard the tale.

The book she had bought the last day her father was home, which had laid empty ever since, now had many of its pages filled with details of every beast her father had encountered. Once she had finished the book, Snow found only a few beasts that she believed would be a threat to Goldie. The roc of course was a threat to anything that lived, but she also noted the nathair and the silverwing, two serpents that her father had said could swallow a man whole, and perhaps the farroclaw, a monstrous cat twenty feet from nose to tail and wearing a speckled white coat.

Beyond these, and perhaps an entire pack of direwolves, Snow was confident that Goldie could protect her as long as she stayed close to the bear.

Everything will be fine.

Snow slowly shut the door, then hurried to get the soup for her mother. She brought it in, only to find that her mother had drifted back to sleep while she was away. Setting the soup to the side, she put a hand over her mother's forehead.

"How is she?" Rose asked.

"I think she could be back on her feet by tonight. She's always healed quickly once her fever breaks." Snow turned to her sister. "Best to let her rest for now to help it along."

Nodding, Rose followed her back into the main room. Snow tried to keep her face from showing the excitement welling up inside of her. Their mother was going to be fine, and Goldie would be as slow as he'd ever been.

Now for the last piece to fall into place.

She glanced over at her sister. Rose was staring into the fire, her thoughts hidden behind a similarly stoic face.

There was always the chance that Rose would allow Snow to follow Goldie if Snow asked, but that wasn't likely. Her sister was still nervous to even approach the tree line, to say nothing about letting Snow go off by herself. Even if Snow suggested they go together, she knew that someone should be home with their mother, in case her illness took a bad turn.

No, I have to go alone, and without Rose knowing. She sat down beside her sister and added a piece to the fire. "Rose, you look tired. How about you get some rest while Mother is asleep?"

Rose tried to object, but a yawn interrupted her.

Snow smiled at the sign of good fortune. "See? Go lay down. I'll get you when I'm ready to sleep."

Rose breathed a laugh. "Fine. Keep the soup warm for when I wake up." Her sister then stood up and went to their room. Snow stayed and stared at the fire, silently counting to a hundred. Then she snuck to their doorway and peered in. Rose was facing away from her, but she had her blanket firmly bundled around her.

Just a little longer.

Snow waited until she heard her sister's breathing change. Any noise, no matter how loud, and her sister might still wake up. Once she reached the point of deep breathing, however, Rose would be so deep in sleep that she wouldn't know if a thunderstorm was overhead.

There it was.

Rose was truly asleep now. Snow gave a smile as she silently closed the door to their room. Hopefully, she'd be out and back before either of them woke up.

Though, depending on how far Goldie went, Rose may still wake to find Snow missing.

Snow listened to the deep breaths on the other side of the door. *Even if she does, I don't think she'll be awake for a few hours. I should be fine.*

She took the parcel of food from its hiding place, firmly tied her cloak around her, then she slipped out into the morning air to follow Goldie. Snow even had the notion that the winter was on her side, with the snowfall now drifting in soft flurries.

She smiled triumphantly. *Now to see what you've been up to.*

Chapter 23

Another sneeze shattered the quiet of the late winter morning. Werner stopped in his tracks and mumbled at his luck. So far, it had been a miserable week for the prince while he tried to find the dwarf without the help of his nose. Between that and the sheer sound of his sneezes, there was little hope of surprising anything out in the forest.

It was as if the dwarf's failed magic had an unintended side effect, for he had been sick since the day after the failed ambush. Werner knew that probably wasn't the cause, though. It was more likely to do with the ice in his fur from plunging into the stream when he'd caught the dwarf's scent.

Regardless of that, Werner had always gotten some sort of illness during the winter months, so why not this winter as well? Perhaps he'd hoped that as a bear he would be immune from whatever his seasonal affliction was, but as with many things this winter, he'd had no such luck.

I still have plenty to be thankful for, Werner reminded himself. Even with his lack of success in hunting the dwarf, he had food and shelter every night and none of the courtly intrigue. While he had once loved the intrigues, the sheer simplicity of life in the girls' cottage was an alluring peace that he was finding himself drawn to.

While the latest snowfall continued to settle and become easier to walk through, Werner felt like today was the hardest trek he'd had in weeks. His body was telling him to rest, to take several days to recover. There was no harm in such a thing.

Yet Werner had persisted. In the back of his mind, he had the belief that the one day he didn't venture out would be the day the dwarf finally made a fatal mistake. Or the dwarf would finish gathering his treasure like he had told his friend. Werner didn't know what that outcome would lead to; whether the dwarf would then flee to some dwarven stronghold or if he would remain in the forest once the treasure went wherever it was going.

If the truth was the latter, Werner had nothing to worry about. If it was the former, ...

Werner shook his head. *I can't dwell on that. Kill the dwarf and that outcome won't even matter.*

Werner couldn't deny that he was wavering in his quest for revenge. If he hadn't gotten cursed by the dwarf, he would have never met Snow and her family. He wouldn't have overcome the challenges of trekking through the forest every day hunting his prey.

True, if he hadn't gazed at the roc instead of marching, the dwarf wouldn't have cursed him, but he would also still be in the dark about what drew Roland to this untamed world.

With all that, could he actually kill the dwarf?

The question had been heavy on him since the last encounter. For all Werner knew, the dwarf had cursed him over a misunderstanding in the heat of the moment. It had been during the greatest storm anyone could remember, after all, and he had been about to take hold of the treasure.

Still, the dwarf had called him a thief and cursed him before Werner could say anything in his defense. Such unrestrained power was a threat. What if the dwarf crossed paths with someone else and had a similar misunderstanding?

How many has that already happened to?

He looked at the gray sky, barely able to make out where the sun hid in the clouds. It was only mid-morning, and Werner felt like he had been out all day. Sighing, he started to move forward again. *Perhaps, -*

Behind him, a twig snapped. He spun towards the sound, frightened that it may be a ranger looking for a large kill. To his shock, he glimpsed Snow trying to hide in the bushes beside a stand of pine trees.

How she got there he didn't know, but Werner laughed as best a bear could, then motioned with his head for her to come over.

Snow hurried over with a wide smile on her face. "Did you know I was following you?"

Werner blinked in surprise. *Following me?* He hadn't caught a whiff of Snow's scent, nor had he heard anything until now. He hung his head. If she'd snuck up on him so easily, what hope could he have of surprising the dwarf in his current state?

Another large sneeze escaped from him. Snow giggled at him for it. Werner huffed. *Maybe I should -*

"Maybe you should rest for a while until that cold goes away," Snow said sweetly. "Then you can get back to looking for whatever you are after."

Werner's eyes met hers as he tilted his head. He loved looking into those caring green eyes.

She smiled as she stroked the side of his face. "You look surprised. Did I say something important?"

Werner huffed, hoping that she wouldn't ask many more questions. He wasn't in the right mind or body to communicate his feelings at any rate. His thoughts wandered to her safety. She may have surprised him, but what if she happened upon the dwarf?

The mere notion of the idea lit a fire within him. Snow could never cross paths with that being. Not if he had any say in it. *It's probably best that I lead her back home, even if that means I have to cut my search short.*

"Why are you going out this way?" Snow looked up, perhaps trying to see what he was looking for. Werner leaned out and gently pushed her with his shoulder before he started walking again. Snow chuckled, then walked beside him, her hand resting gently on his shoulder.

It was a strange sensation. Werner had walked through many halls with a lady in his company, but never like this. In the halls, slipping away with a lady was a game of the court, with him teasing the ladies to decide which he would prefer having future encounters with and the ladies gossiping about who his eventual match would be.

Out here in the forest, Snow expected nothing of the sort from him; she only wanted to learn about what he was up to.

Yet that was a dangerous thing for her. Like it or not, Werner's bear form could easily survive in the forest.

The cold had little effect on him, and he could come and go as he pleased with no challenge from the local wildlife.

Snow? Snow would be easy prey for a predator.

Again, his protectiveness roused into flames. The dwarf could wait for a day. He didn't want Snow to be seen by the dwarf and possibly share his fate. *I'll just continue to walk with her. Maybe that will satisfy her curiosity, and I won't have to worry about her safety.*

They walked through the woods for a while. Werner pretended to be going in a set direction, but in truth, his path would make a slow circle back to the cottage.

Snow stopped for a moment and yawned. Werner looked into her eyes as she lowered her arms. Clearly, Snow was tired. After thinking about it for a moment, he couldn't blame her. Snow was not the one walking all over the world every day. From what the girls had said during the evenings, going out into the forest to find sustenance was Rose's role in the family.

"Sorry," she smiled sweetly. Her eyes then glistened in mischief, and a few seconds later, she asked, "Can I get a ride for a while?"

Werner chuckled at the request, then dipped his shoulder. She then hopped up onto Werner's back, and the bear prince carried her through the woods as the snowflakes began swirling around them. He tried to picture it from another's view and chuckled again.

We must seem like something out of one of those bedtime stories.

Chapter 24

With a yawn and a stretch, Rose woke up from her nap and walked into the main room. The fire was still going, but it was much lower than it should be. She sighed, thinking that Snow must have also fallen asleep instead of watching over their mother.

"Snow?" she whispered, hoping not to wake her mother if she was still sleeping. There was no reply.

Where is she? First, she looked in their room again, but she wasn't there. Nor was she in their parents' room tending to their mother. Concerned, Rose checked anywhere that Snow could have hidden from view. She was nowhere to be found.

Rose looked again at the low fire. Her heartbeat slowed at the sight as she thought of a plausible idea. *Maybe she's just getting more wood from the lean-to.*

Gingerly, she opened the door. A flurry was starting outside, but the tracks going out from the cottage were still visible. One set was Goldie's great paws, but following them were human prints that were already several hours old.

Rose's breath caught in her throat. Snow had slipped out into the woods, alone.

Panicking, Rose returned to her room and threw her cloak around her shoulders. She then hurried to the door. Already her fears were casting illusions of finding Snow laying out in the woods somewhere, her pale skin already blue from the cold that had nearly claimed Rose during the roc's blizzard.

The memory of Rose's encounter with the strange wolf returned in force. The beast was always creeping in the back of her mind. Rose couldn't shake the blue-gray form and the red eyes that seemed to glow. Even though she had seen The Hunter kill the wolf, there was this unshakeable fear that her woods were no longer safe.

Rose stepped out of the door.

Then she paused, and she instead walked back to look at her sleeping mother. If her mother saw that both of them were gone, she would surely chase after them. In her weakened state, she would have less of a chance than Snow did. Rose would have to make sure that didn't happen, either. How to manage that was another matter.

In time, an idea formed. One that her mother would both have thought of herself and also vehemently opposed, but it was for her mother's own good.

Rose went down into the cellar. Quickly, she found the stash of dried menulia blooms. The petals had little in the way of taste, but they made a powerful sleeping tea if mixed properly. Her father had requested it many times after a hard day in the woods.

Smiling, Rose took the blooms and a few other ingredients back into the kitchen. It was a quick process to get them all mixed into an herbal tea that her mother would mistake as simply helping her with her cold. The other ingredients would, but the menulia would keep her from following Snow and Rose into the woods.

With the tea in hand, Rose went to her mother's room. As if sensing her approach, her mother opened her eyes and went to sit up. Rose put a hand on her shoulder. "Easy, easy. No need to spring up."

"How is Snow?" her mother asked.

"She's off in one of her fantasies." Rose said, then offered her mother the tea. "Now take this and rest some more while I get some lunch ready. I think you're through the worst of it."

Her mother nodded her head and drank. Rose spoke with her for a little while as the menulia took effect, then once her mother had fallen back asleep, she made for the door. Saying a quick prayer for protection, she hurried off into the snow-covered landscape. Cold or no cold, she would find her sister.

You better be all right when I find you!

Her sister left a simple trail, following alongside the tracks of Goldie. Rose felt fear welling in her chest as the trail confirmed what Snow was up to. *Doesn't she know -*

Rose stopped herself. Snow knew. She had listened to Rose tell her the story of the wolf attack. And yet her sister had still gone carefree into a realm now filled with perils. The wolf may be dead, but what else could be out there now?

Fearfully, Rose gathered her cloak around her and followed the trail as fast as she could. Thankfully, Snow was not Rose, who had learned from their father to at least try to mask her trail in case someone should happen upon it and learn about their secret places in the woods. Her sister's tracks, meanwhile, were as clear as the summer sky. There was no chance Rose would lose her.

It was a half hour later when Rose followed the trail into a stand of oak trees, and Snow's tracks suddenly changed. They were about as old as Goldie's, telling Rose that Snow may have caught sight of the bear. But Snow was now moving sideways into cover beneath the trees.

It's like she's hiding from something...

More fears flooded her mind. Had Snow spotted something like the strange wolf? Was that why she was no longer following Goldie's prints? Rose followed her trail into the bushes. The tracks continued to move as though Snow was watching something, and then...

Her sister's prints simply vanished.

She looked all over the ground, but there was nothing to be found. The falling snowflakes weren't nearly enough to have covered any tracks, and such a thought was absurd, since Rose could clearly see the older prints behind her.

Maybe she jumped through the bushes? Rose moved outside of the bushes to look around. There was no sign of prints.

Snow was gone.

Could a small roc have taken her, one that's not large enough to create a storm? Thoughts like this flooded into Rose's mind. *How could she even track such a thing if it were true? Was Snow already dead? Would she ever see her sister again?*

"Snow!" she called into the flurry, hoping that perhaps her sister might be nearby. She ran in the direction that the trail had ended.

"SNOW!"

Chapter 25

The late flurry of snow had continued for the past couple of hours, and Roland slowly admitted the snow wouldn't cease today. If anything, the snow had grown stronger throughout the day.

It wasn't for fear of getting stuck in a coming storm; he'd survived more than his fair share already this winter. One last mild storm before spring wouldn't kill him now. No, his frustration lay more in that the flakes limited his vision. Werner could be just past the trees a hundred feet away, and Roland would not have noticed.

His hunt had been like this for far too many days. The voices in his head, and from the nobles still in the manor, kept saying that it was futile to continue the search. Roland would have probably died by now if he was in Werner's place, and Werner was ill-prepared for the task when the storm had hit.

That truth had become even more accepted once the original search party had seen Werner's tracks merging with a bear's. Most had simply given up after the first day.

The remaining lords had only joined in the search for a few days before they had left to tend to their own homes. Roxeter had left with them, as reports of his lands being overrun with North Beasts reached Fernglen. Finley had forced himself to follow Roland for a week before he was bedridden with illness and left for his warmer shoreline domain. Arrenton and his men roamed the forests beside Roland for nearly a month, but eventually the older lord had given up as well.

The king's own rangers had turned their attention to the hunting forays needed to feed the people during the long winter. Most had to deal with some sort of rationing now, even among the nobility, and the rangers of Fernglen had to sojourn farther and farther along the southern range to look for anything to hunt.

It was now only the prince, and Roland had slowly expanded his search northward and to the unhunted side of the forest. This was one of the few places in the kingdom he was unfamiliar with, and the late winter months had been determined to keep him from learning more about the deep forest. More storms had followed the roc's, and as fit for the challenge as Roland was, he couldn't stay out in such storms all day.

All this should have made it obvious that Werner was dead.

Yet, his heart told him that Werner had somehow survived. It was perhaps the forlorn hope of a brother, but he refused to let that ember go out until he'd seen the evidence. While the winter had deterred him many times, it also had yet to confirm any of the suspicions of the court. Werner hadn't died where the bear tracks were, and there was no sign that he'd died anywhere nearby.

Roland wished The Hunter could come south again. If anyone could help, it would be him. Unfortunately, there had been more than one roc, and while only the one had gotten past the North Hunters, so many North Beasts had ventured south and past the North Hunters settlements that the ancient man could not venture south to bring his own eyes on the scene.

Roland exhaled, adjusting his scarf to better withstand the cold. Winter had nearly run its course. The spring would bring fresh growth and the means to recover from this disaster. The fields would sprout again, the North Beasts would retreat north along with the cold, and then more people could join the search again. *Maybe then-*

What was that? Something had caught his ear. He strained to listen for it. It was faint, but it sounded like a -

"Snow!" a voice called in the distance. It was a woman's voice, and it carried the tenor of stress with it.

Roland looked at where the sound had come from. His mind made the quick decision. Any detour would derail the hopes he had of finding his brother today, but the voice was clearly in need of some help. Praying that Werner would hold on a little longer, Roland turned to the siren call.

When she appeared out of the flurry, her appearance struck Roland. The maiden wasn't much younger than him, with beautiful dark red locks of hair seeping out from the bright red hood of her cloak. Her green eyes were wide with surprise and fear upon seeing him appear out of the snow, and her mouth was barely open, as if unsure whether to cry out or run.

He held up a hand and smiled, hoping it may calm her fear. "Were you the one calling out in the storm?" The maiden in the red cloak nodded, but didn't respond. "Well then, what can I do to help you? This isn't a normal setting for a lady to be alone in the woods."

Her lips briefly turned to a smile, her cheeks reddening at the compliment. "I'm looking for my sister."

The irony made Roland chuckle. "Oh? Then we have a common concern. I am looking for my brother."

The maiden tilted her head. "You are?"

Roland nodded. "He's been missing for some time, and I haven't seen a trace of him. What about your sister? How long has she been missing?"

"She disappeared sometime this morning from our cottage. I only noticed a few hours ago and then lost her tracks in the snow."

"Where did you last see them?" When the maiden pointed, he started walking that way. As he passed her, Roland felt a passing notion and offered her his hand awkwardly. She stood looking at his hand in silence. Roland gave a chuckle at his apparent misstep. "Would you go with me? I'm afraid I don't know what your sister looks like."

His attempt at humor seemed to put the maiden at ease. She accepted his hand, though not daintily like the ladies of court. Hers was a firm grasp more similar to how he greeted his knights and the noblemen.

The maiden noticed this at once and pulled her hand away so that she could offer it again in a more ladylike manner.

Roland smiled, feeling reassured by the gesture. As awkward as he'd been in offering his hand, the maiden clearly had the same grasp of courtly manners as he did. "Let's go."

The trek was quiet as they walked side by side. Roland didn't know what to say, and neither did the maiden. He knew the simplest way to break the silence was to introduce himself. It was customary, after all.

Yet, he couldn't quite keep the mischief in him from trying to emulate the mystique of The Hunter for the maiden. The number of tales that spoke of The Hunter appearing out of nowhere and aiding people were countless. This was Roland's chance to do the same.

Whatever the forest maiden thought of the circumstance they found themselves in, she kept it to herself. Roland didn't blame her. The two were strangers, and though he had offered his help and she had accepted, she was clearly still on edge about an unfamiliar face.

And so, the silence persisted as the two walked back over her tracks, hand-in-hand and tongue-tied either in mischief or uncertainty.

Once they got to a small stand of oak trees, the forest maiden spoke. "Those bushes are where I lost her tracks."

"Alright. Let me see what I can find." Roland let go of her hand and made his way over to the bushes. Sure enough, there was a broken set of tracks that were partially filled in by the flurry. He sighed with pity towards the maiden.

I can think of a few people who would have lost these tracks, he thought. Yet then the mystery increased when he found that the maiden's footprints now joined them. *If she could follow the tracks into here, then...*

With renewed focus, he examined the trail. The sister's tracks were short and side-stepping, as though she were trying to hide from something to the north yet still keep her eyes on it. He followed the tracks until they reached a pine tree that had several low branches. After a few muddled steps, the trail ended.

"Are you lost here, too?"

He chuckled at the tone in her voice. It was at once curious and smug. She must have found some satisfaction at the sight of him also being unable to make sense of the trail.

Roland's eyes didn't linger on her, though. On a hunch, they followed the trunk of the pine to its low branches. A smile formed as he noticed small wet marks along the bark, and the snow looked to be crushed down on one of the larger branches at something of a regular interval. He pointed to the marks. "She climbed up onto that branch, and ..."

Without looking for a reaction, he climbed up the tree and followed the steps. The maiden gasped at first, then she walked along the ground beneath him.

Roland had to admit that this was an entertaining trail. The sister clearly enjoyed being in trees and was making her trail confounding enough to make an old stag jealous, but Roland was on to her now.

Twice she had jumped to a separate tree, and he'd followed. Finally, he reached the end of the snow marks and leapt to the ground beside where a new track had appeared. He noticed a hidden branch had snapped where she'd landed.

The maiden had already moved beside the prints. Roland couldn't withhold a cocky grin. "And here is where she came down."

The maiden smiled at him. "I'm impressed."

"Thank you," he said, then he noticed her cheeks were turning red from the cold. Roland removed his scarf and handed it to her. "Here, take this. I wouldn't want you to freeze out here."

She gasped and retreated half a step. He'd seen that reaction before. Something traumatic must have happened to her in the past regarding what he'd just said or done. Roland silently hoped that the maiden hadn't had a former love offer her a scarf once, then he chastised his mental lapse in decorum.

After that moment of hesitation, she took the scarf and put it around her neck. "Thank you."

He smiled. "Let's follow the trail." Now that they were out in the open, Roland could get a better grasp on the sister from her tracks. They told him she was about the maiden's height and build, but she had a habit of dragging her feet that the maiden didn't have. Her clothes were also ill-suited for the deep snow as the hem of her dress kept getting caught by the dragging feet.

He lifted his eyes to look further along the trail, and he froze.

A second set of tracks appeared ahead, not thirty yards from where they were standing. His breath caught in his throat as he recognized the tracks of a massive bear joining the sister's path.

"What do you see?" the maiden asked.

Roland instantly remembered how the nobles had reacted when they learned he had hidden Werner's encounter with a bear during the roc's storm and decided not to hide the truth from the maiden. It would save her the terror if they found the aftermath of what would happen if the bear attacked her sister. "I don't wish to alarm you, but there are bear tracks joining with your sister's."

"Goldie!" the maiden exclaimed.

Roland jumped at the sudden outburst of joy. The prince had braced for the maiden to experience several emotions, but joy wasn't one of them. "Who's Goldie?"

She quickly composed herself, though that smile didn't fade. "Goldie is a bear that has been in our cottage the entire winter. He goes out in the morning but returns in the evening to sleep by the fire. Sometimes he brings fish back with him, but other than that, I don't know what he does during the day."

Roland couldn't stop the confused look taking over his face. He'd never heard of such a tale beyond the pages of the old histories and fables, yet the maiden's green eyes told him she wasn't lying. A bear was truly spending the winter in their cottage.

If nothing else, the prints he'd found told him a bear was not hibernating like it should be.

His curiosity piqued, Roland followed the trails for another twenty yards beyond where the two had crossed. There he found the bear and the woman's prints intermingling as they were moving around one another. They then moved on to the northeast, walking side by side.

He reached down and touched the prints. The sister's prints were on top of the bears, not the other way around. It led him to one conclusion; the sister must have been following the bear.

The prince and the maiden continued along the trail, looking into the distance to see what the trail could tell them. About two hundred yards on, the sister's prints came to a stop, then she made two deep prints as though she were jumping right beside the bear. Beyond that, only the bear's tracks appeared in the snow.

As if she were riding on top of the bear.

"I'm sorry," the maiden's voice interrupted his thinking. "I must sound like I'm out of my mind."

He looked up into her eyes again. They were the same as before, confirming his belief. "I admit it does unbelievable, but my eyes rarely lie to me."

"About the prints? What do they say?"

He chuckled again and pointed. "The prints tell me that your sister is most likely riding on the back of the bear after catching up to him at this point. Furthermore," Roland said as he looked back at her and pointed, "the look in your eyes tells me you believe every word I just said."

She tilted her head and gave a hesitant smile. "Do they?"

Roland nodded. "I have met many young maidens around our age. In that time, I've learned that their eyes can reveal much about what they are thinking. Sometimes the eyes say she is lying, others say she is crazy. Sometimes the eyes say both. Your eyes," he said with a slight grin, "say that you are neither crazy nor lying, and that the news about this 'Goldie' finding your sister is the best thing you've heard since I met you."

He stood up, chuckling to himself. Nothing he had said was a lie, but the sheer difference between the typical lives of the ladies from court and the fanciful world of this maiden was astonishing. "The tracks will be easy to follow from here, but it is getting late. If you trust Goldie to get your sister home, may I ask to walk you home as well?"

She gasped at the proposal, though the new shade of red on her cheeks told him she was at least pleased by the idea. After considering it for several seconds, she shook her head. "I hardly know you. Besides, I can follow my own tracks home." Her body stiffened as she realized that this also meant he could follow her home by the same means.

Roland smiled as disarmingly as he could. "I'll accept your wish then, though my brother may call me a fool for doing so."

"Oh?" she asked with a curious grin. "And why would that be?"

Now it was Roland's turn for his cheeks to show a little red from his thoughts. "Well, I'd be letting a beautiful maiden disappear back into the forest without a trace." The maiden blushed at this, and Roland found he liked the way she tucked her chin at the complement. "But, if it is to be the case, I hope to cross paths with you again. Preferably under better conditions." He said this as he glanced around at the falling snow.

She smiled at him. "So would I."

Roland gave her a courteous bow. "Until we meet again." With a last smile, he turned and retired back into the forest.

In his mind, he berated himself for the suggestion. *Why would she have let you walk back to her home? She clearly was trying to keep that a secret. As far as she knows, you're a tracker looking for his idiot brother. She doesn't know you're the crown prince.*

She made the right choice, regardless of that knowledge.

But you could have done far better than you did. You're lucky she wants to see you again.

That's if what she said wasn't a simple platitude to get me to leave.

You know she was telling the truth, oh powerful viewer into the windows of the soul.

Roland chuckled at himself and set his course to the southwest. He could wax lyrically once he got back to the manor.

For now, he kept his focus on seeing if any other prints appeared in the snow. The dismay of the storm was now firmly behind him. He'd just had a chance encounter with a beautiful maiden in the forest and left her on amiable terms. Such things were rare. Perhaps fortune would continue to smile on him, and he'd find some sign of his brother.

It took a moment before his thoughts turned to the sister's prints. The spot where they met the bear gave him pause, and he wanted to examine them further. By now, the forest maiden had vanished. Roland could see which way she'd gone, but honored his word about following her. His curiosity about the bear had to be satisfied first.

He watched how the bear moved next to the sister, then focused on the prints size. His breathing slowed, but his heartbeat increased in delight. Unless he was mistaken, the bear was the same size as the one that crossed paths with Werner.

Roland thought about what the maiden had said about the bear. No normal bear would act in the way she had described. With the sudden appearance of so many magical creatures from the north, was it possible that a spirit bear had come south and saved Werner? He'd heard stories of such things, but did he dare to believe one had followed the roc so closely that it had reached them within mere hours?

Maybe I should have followed her home.

It was then that he realized he had never asked for the maiden's name. He was still for a moment, then laughed. *Fool of a prince.*

Roland rubbed his neck and sighed, then he started laughing as he felt the skin of his neck. He had forgotten that he had given her his scarf and hadn't asked for it back.

Now I'm doubly the fool. Guess it'll be a cold walk home.

Chapter 26

The journey with Goldie had been beautiful, with the snowflakes falling gently and the woods perfectly quiet aside from the bear's steps and the occasional sneeze. It felt surreal, and Snow wished she had thought to do it earlier in the winter.

Even so, she was getting the sneaking suspicion that Goldie had changed his routine the moment he had spotted her. His pace was slower, and he was taking care to go under the trees where she wouldn't get as many snowflakes piling on her.

She leaned down to whisper into the bear's ear. "Goldie, is this all you do during the day besides catching fish?"

Goldie shrugged at her question, the motion lifting her higher as she sat behind his shoulders. Snow laughed. "Is that all you're going to tell me?"

He huffed, though it sounded like a laugh to her. She had spent enough time with the bear in the evenings to know what a few of the sounds he made meant. Joining his laughter, she replied, "Well, it has been an enchanting morning with you. What do you plan to stop for lunch?"

The bear shifted his body so that he could look at her, then pointed a paw into the distance. Snow turned eagerly towards it.

Her mouth fell open in shock. "Is that...?" Snow stood up on Goldie's back as the trees thinned out in front of them. The bear stopped his motion so that she wouldn't fall off of his shoulders.

Sure enough, the outline of their cottage was now in view. A glance skyward told her that evening was still some time off, but it was well into the afternoon. A shiver ran down her spine as she realized how long she had been out. *Hopefully, Mother and Rose slept through the whole day.*

She leapt down alongside Goldie and nearly lost her balance. Once she'd caught herself, Snow eyed the bear. "Did you just make a big circle, hoping I wouldn't notice?"

Goldie made an exaggerated glance away from her. It caused Snow to laugh as she reached over to scratch behind his ears. "Well, it worked. I suppose you don't want me following you on your little quest."

He nodded.

"Why?"

The bear paused for a few moments as he tried to think of a way to communicate with her. Snow enjoyed seeing the small twitches in his eyes as thoughts unknown to her bounced around.

She tried to use the bond again, knowing that it would fail. Snow had tried many times over the winter to sway Goldie. Not once had Snow felt like she came close to succeeding. His mind was a barrier to her; not as though he were resisting her as some larger animals could, but as though she couldn't comprehend the thoughts within.

Goldie turned away and moved to a tree. He then extended his right paw to her.

"Me," she replied.

He nodded and swung his paw at the tree. His claws cut deep gashes into it, leaving behind sappy wounds.

Snow inhaled sharply at the action, and one hand went over her heart. She took a few steadying breaths as she understood what he was saying. "Danger?"

He huffed and bowed his head again.

"What... kind of danger?"

Goldie hesitated for a moment, then merely shook his head. Whatever it was, he couldn't explain it to her.

She took a deep breath, thinking about her sister's fears of direwolves and other things. "Is it from the north?"

That question confused Goldie, and the only answer he provided was a shrug.

It gave her the idea to ask one more question. "Are you from the north?"

The bear shook his head, instead pointing to the southwest.

"Oh?" Initially, Snow felt disappointed by the answer, but then curiosity took hold. If he wasn't from the north, then why had he appeared during the roc's storm? Were there other bears like him in those lands? How far had he come? Did spirit bears exist outside of the north?

She had to stop herself, though. Goldie could talk with her in simple terms. What she wanted to know required some way of actual speech, and Snow knew of no way to make that happen. "I wish you could talk."

He huffed in agreement, and Snow laughed. Whatever this strange bear was, he seemed almost human. She thought of some of the old tales where animals could talk and wondered if there was a way to use the bond to allow Goldie to speak with her.

The thought was fleeting. Goldie wasn't affected by the bond at any rate, and Snow had never come across such a use in any of her father's stories. Snow laughed softly at the idea, then pointed to the cottage. "Let's go inside and warm up. Try not to wake Mother and Rose."

Goldie nodded, and they walked across the meadow and entered the cottage quietly. The fire was low, giving Snow the hope that Rose hadn't yet woken up. She took her cloak out and shook the snowflakes off to maintain the illusion that she hadn't left, then took a peek into her mother's room.

Snow exhaled with a smile. Her mother looked like she had slept the whole time she had been away. Chuckling to herself, Snow then looked into their room.

Her sister's bed was empty.

"Rose?" she whispered, as if her eyes were lying to her. She left the doorway and hurried past Goldie to look outside.

Her heart skipped a beat. A third trail was leading away from the cottage, and there was no sign that it had returned.

A twinge of fear struck her heart, but it passed quickly. Rose was used to the woods, even in the winter. This weather was nothing she hadn't experienced before.

And she was worried about another wolf, so I doubt she'd go out unprepared.

... then again, her bow isn't strong enough to kill a direwolf...

Goldie had followed her to the doorway. When she looked at him, she could see the concern in his eyes. His warning about danger came roaring back to her. The fear showed in her voice. "Do you think we should go after Rose?"

The bear looked at her, then looked out again. There was an attempt to sniff the air, but it ended in another eruption of a sneeze.

Without his nose, Goldie would have to rely on following the trail. Snow could see the paradox it presented. There was every chance that Rose had come across some trouble and needed help, but equally, she might follow their trails back here while they were out again. An endless loop of chasing one another.

"Do you think she's alright? Do you think that danger is near us?"

Goldie glanced between her and the woods several times, then stamped one paw before the other.

Snow laughed despite herself. "I'll ask again. Do you think the danger is near us?" He shook his head with certainty. "Do you think she's alright?" The affirming nod was less certain. She knew it was simply to reassure her, but Snow appreciated the gesture. At least her sister was safe from whatever Goldie was looking for. "Then what do you think we should do for now?"

"He's back already?" The two spun as her mother entered the room, a blanket firmly wrapped around her.

"You're awake!" Snow replied cheerily. "How are you feeling?"

"Much better, though I'm still a bit tired."

Snow breathed a laugh. "It will probably be a day or so before that goes away. What else do you feel?" She led her mother to her chair by the fireplace and stoked the fire into a comforting blaze. Goldie lumbered over and laid beside the chair to provide an additional distraction.

The informal plan worked for a while, as Snow asked other questions related to the illness. But such things couldn't hold out forever. Soon, the dreaded question was asked. "Snow, where is your sister? Is she asleep?"

I wish that was the case. "She decided to go look for some things in the woods."

"What things?"

"She didn't tell me."

"How long ago was it? The fire is much lower than you know to keep it at."

Snow tried to think of a way to say what had happened without making her mother worry. "I suppose it was after lunch."

"Well, of course. She gave me some tea before lunch." Her mother chided, then her eyes narrowed as she saw Snow's reaction. "Were you here when she ga

ve me the tea?"

Snow smiled sheepishly, and Goldie put his head all the way to the floor. "Actually, I followed Goldie after we checked on you this morning." Her mother made no comment, though her eyes widened in surprise. Snow continued, "I had thought that I'd be back before Rose woke up, but... we just got back."

There was a painful silence. "Did you tell Rose you were leaving?" her mother asked.

Snow dropped her gaze. "No."

At this, her mother rose to her feet, as did Goldie. "So, Rose went out after you two and is still not back? And you don't know when she left, only that she has?" Snow could only nod in reply. Her mother took off the blanket and started to her room. "We should follow your trail back to look for her."

Snow placed a hand on her mother's arm. "You are still recovering, Mother. Don't go getting yourself sick again. The two of us can go get her." She turned to Goldie. "Are you fine going out again?"

The bear nodded emphatically, and her mother relented. "I suppose you're right, even if I'd rather go with you. At least let me see you off, though."

Snow nodded as she put on her cloak again, and the three turned to go out the door.

Chapter 27

There was a strange spring in Rose's step as she made her way back to the cottage. Thoughts of the ranger quelled her anger at Snow. It had been such a strange encounter, having him appear to help her find Snow and then vanish back into the woods with hardly a trace.

Rose couldn't deny that the encounter had been frightful at first. She had worried that the man could be a bandit or some other outlaw, though his mannerisms quickly quelled that notion. She also considered herself lucky that the ranger chose to divert from his own search for his brother to help her find Snow. Rose hoped that he would find his brother now that Snow was safe.

The only blight on the experience was that Rose had never learned his name. Now she knew that there would be no end to the grief from her sister should Snow learn that the chance meeting had left her hero nameless.

But surely that wasn't too unusual, right? *Well, The Hunter's name is forgotten, so why can't my ranger be nameless as well?*

My ranger...

When he had first taken her hand, Rose found herself puzzled by the young man's appearance. That he was a ranger she had little doubt, though she'd never seen a ranger that wore such a fine cloak before, nor once who wore a coat of chain mail underneath his surcoat. Perhaps he had some connection with the king. A king's ranger, perhaps? The personal hunter for the king's banquet table?

Rose chuckled as she remembered the thoughts, thinking of how she chose not to reason it out any further. If the ranger could help her find Snow, that was all she needed to care about.

Once they had found where Snow had caught up to Goldie, that belief changed. Rose couldn't keep her eyes from studying the ranger. The discerning brown eyes, the amused smile, the firm yet gentle hand. There was also the way he moved through the woods, calm yet alert to everything.

The ranger had said they were about the same age, and unlike the one hunter who'd gone north with her father, the ranger had a presence about him. Being near him had made Rose feel safe.

He also cared little about the cold. Little enough to have forgotten to reclaim his scarf, at least.

His scarf! How was she going to explain it to Snow and her mother? Surely, they would know that she had never worn it before.

Rose caught the end of the scarf and looked at it. Despite its plain colorations, the scarf showed expert craftsmanship, which agreed with her belief that the ranger must have some connection to the king or at least to a patron with some wealth to provide such a gift.

She puzzled over it as she continued on through the falling snow. There was little chance her mother or sister would believe it belonged to The Hunter. His clothing bore no patterns save those that signified his status. A better option was to claim that she found it in the snow, but that might sound even more like a lie. Who else would be in their forests at this time of year?

I know. I'll hide it before I go in. Then whenever we go outside again, I can claim to find it then, or let Snow discover it and... Rose paused at that outcome. If Snow found it, then Snow would say she had the right to keep it, and any protest Rose made would make it even more suspicious.

Rose sighed and reached her hand under her hood to scratch her head. As she did so, she noticed the hood's color was eerily similar to the scarf. She held them next to each other and gasped.

The colors were exactly the same!

Is he also from the North? Does he know The Hunter? She didn't know any patterns from the north that looked like the one on the scarf, but the only place she knew of where that shade of red could be found was from the shellfish hiding under the icy lakes of the north.

A more alarming thought came to her. *Is he from our father's tribe and this pattern is some personal mark he's earned? Did he give me the scarf as a proposal when he saw my cloak?*

Did I just accept his proposal?

Rose had no means to answer these questions, but the revelation provided her with the answer she needed regarding the scarf. Since it was the same workmanship as the cloaks The Hunter had given her and Snow, then if either her mother or Snow asked about the scarf, she would simply say that The Hunter must have left it behind when he'd left in his hurry to fight the roc, perhaps as an undelivered grave gift for her father. That would hopefully be believable enough for now.

The meadow opened up to her, and Rose was nearly to the cottage when Snow and her mother stepped through the doorway, with Goldie poking his head out just before the three caught sight of Rose.

Rose waved to them, and she could see the relief in her mother's eyes. "You made it back already?" her mother asked.

"Yes." Rose looked past her towards Snow. "I woke up to find Snow had gone after Goldie, so I followed them. I found where you started riding on his back and knew he would bring you home, so I just came straight here."

Snow sighed in relief as their mother's eyes settled on her. Clearly, Snow and Goldie had returned before she had woken up. Goldie decided that this conversation was one he didn't need to be part of, and pulled his head back inside the cottage.

Her mother then turned her eyes back to Rose. "And was she gone when I asked you where she was?"

Rose bit her tongue. She had hoped that the revelation would only bring ire down upon Snow. Apparently, she was mistaken. "I didn't want you to worry about both of us being gone while you were still feeling ill."

Her mother let the moment linger uncomfortably, then she smiled. "At least you both made it back. Now come inside and let's see how your day-long soup tastes."

Her mother followed Goldie inside, but Snow waited outside for a moment to speak with Rose. Rose whispered first. "What were you thinking?"

"I wanted to see what he does all day."

"And you didn't think I'd come looking for you?"

"I was hoping it wouldn't be that far away and that you would sleep a little longer than normal."

"And when it turned out he was going far away? You didn't think to turn around then?"

"I got lost in the moment, okay?" Snow replied before eyeing Rose. "Why did *you* stay out so long? He didn't move that quickly, both before and after I caught up with him."

She bit her tongue again. "I... lost your trail for a while."

"Really?" Snow said with a triumphant smile. "When?"

"Girls, come inside." The two ended their conversation and went in. Goldie was already eating his dinner portion while their mother set the table.

After praying over the food, they ate while Snow talked about her day with Goldie. Soon, they heard a deep snore emanating from beside the fire. All three turned to see that Goldie had already fallen asleep.

"He sure knows how to fall asleep quickly," Rose remarked.

"I can't blame him." Snow said with a laugh. "I'm tired from following him, and I don't have nearly as much weight to carry around."

"Speaking of your excursions today," her mother turned to Rose and pointed, "where did you get that scarf?"

This was it. The moment Rose was worried about. "I found it by where The Hunter set down his bow before going after the roc. I think it was supposed to be for Father's grave."

Neither her mother nor Snow bought the lie. "Rose Red, The Hunter wouldn't have left that scarf here."

Her heart sank. "Really?"

"Yes." Snow replied smugly as she leaned in closer. "He'd already left a gift when we'd reached the cairn. Besides, that pattern doesn't resemble the ones from our tribe. Or any tribe that I know of. The color matches your hood though, so at least its color has to be from the north."

Rose silently berating herself for thinking such a claim would work. *I should have thought more about pretending it was a grave gift.*

"Where did you get that scarf?" her mother asked again.

Rose exhaled slowly. *Guess there's no hiding it now.* "I met a ranger while I was out looking for Snow. He gave it to me because he thought I was getting cold, then he forgot to ask for it back when he left."

Her mother looked at her quizzically, unsure of what to make of the story. Snow, meanwhile, went into a fanciful frenzy at the revelation and immediately forgot how she had discerned the scarf wasn't from The Hunter. "You met another North Hunter? What was he like? Was he tall? Did he tell you his name? Wha-"

"Snow!" their mother said sternly as she put up her hand. "Give your sister a chance to answer." Returning her attention to Rose, she asked, "How was he dressed?"

Rose took a moment before answering, trying to bring every detail she could to the front of her memory. "He had a long black cloak, but he never had the hood over his head. He wore leather gloves and a leather jerkin over a coat of mail, but I didn't recognize the pattern on his jerkin." As she said this, Rose glanced at the scarf's pattern again. It was a match for what the ranger bore on his jerkin.

"Describe the pattern to me." Her mother said. Rose merely held up the scarf to her mother, and she gently took it from Rose's hand.

"What did he look like?" Snow asked while their mother studied the pattern.

"He had dark brown hair and brown eyes." Rose tried not to reveal too much more about the ranger, in case Snow dreamed up even more fantasies than had already formed in her head.

Their mother nodded slowly. "Did he tell you his name?"

"No, he didn't."

"Really?" Snow asked.

Rose nodded. "And he didn't ask for mine, either."

Her mother smiled. "I doubt he's from the north, then. He doesn't sound like any hunter who would be around your age."

"How do you know?" Snow asked before Rose could.

Their mother looked at them with loving eyes. "I asked The Hunter to give you your cloaks because I intended to take you north after the harvest season. Several of the hunters were asking to introduce you to their sons, and I met a few of your potential suitors over the summer."

"You did?" the girls asked in unison, though Snow was noticeably more enchanted by the notion.

"Yes, and such an outfit as Rose described would not be becoming of a North Hunter. It would seem that Rose's ranger is from our kingdom, or at least from somewhere in the lowlands, given what this pattern reminds me of."

"Have you seen it before?" Snow asked.

She shook her head as she rubbed the scarf in her hands. "I'm not certain, but it looks similar to a quilt my mother owned long ago. I think it was from either Dunvale or Thistledown near the coast. But this scarf had to be woven in the north. I can tell by the craftsmanship."

Rose frowned. "How would the scarf have this pattern if he's from so far away?"

Their mother shrugged, but Snow responded, "Maybe he went through the rites as well. Is that possible, Mother?"

She thought for a moment. "Your father mentioned a young man who had completed the rites a few years ago, though his hunts were at the behest of both King Harald and The Hunter. I doubt a commoner could attain such patronage, and I never heard of such a noble living near our woods."

"Did Father say who he was?" Snow asked before Rose could open her mouth.

"No, he never told me his name. Just that The Hunter had spoken for the man."

Rose thought for a moment. "So, how would he have our tribe's color?"

"It's possible that it's a gift from another member of our tribe. Such things have occurred in the past."

"Or it's the same man who Father spoke of," Snow exclaimed. There was quiet afterwards, and Snow settled back in her seat. "I suppose not."

While their mother gave a dismissive look at the notion, Rose quietly held on to the idea. It appealed to her. "So, he may not know what the scarf really signifies?"

"Yes," her mother replied.

Rose exhaled and leaned back. "Well, that's a relief."

"Why?" Snow asked. Rose didn't plan to answer, but she saw her mother was grinning. Snow saw it, too. "Mother, why did she say that?"

Their mother chuckled. "You were worried you'd accepted his proposal, weren't you?"

Rose didn't need to reply, her burning cheeks being an obvious proof of her mother's claim. The two laughed, and Rose turned away, both from embarrassment and to try to not laugh at herself. "It's not that funny."

Snow looked at Rose with mischief in her eyes. "He must have left quite an impression on you if you were considering a proposal."

Rose felt the burning spread across her face. She couldn't refute the claim, though.

It had been quite the encounter in the snow.

Chapter 28

Roland was still in high spirits when he got back to the manor. With how dour the winter had been with Werner missing, the maiden had chosen the perfect opportunity to meet him.

He tried to tell himself that it was little more than a chance encounter. He'd wandered far enough and long enough in the snow-covered forests that meeting anyone out there was more than likely. Then again, such a beautiful maiden with such an equally fascinating tale would never have entered the thought of the court bards.

However, Roland forced the thoughts of the maiden from his mind when he saw the crest on the soldiers near the door. It could only mean one thing. He greeted the familiar faces, then hurried into the library.

Sure enough, Roland found his father seated by the fire, reading one of the old books. The king looked up from the pages and rose slowly to his feet. "Have you found anything?"

"Nothing for certain, Father." Roland said as he hurried over and embraced him. "How is Mother?"

"She's holding on to hope like you, but frankly, I doubt Werner is still alive."

"Stranger things have happened. A roc never flies this far south, and we've seen many North Beasts that followed in its wake." Roland pulled back and put his hands on his father's shoulders. "One could have saved him."

The statement brought a twinkle to his father's eyes. "You mean a spirit bear? You saw one?"

Roland shook his head. "No, I haven't. But a maiden I met in the forest told me that a spirit bear has been living with them. Or, at least a bear that behaves similar to one from everything I've heard. It has gone out from their home every day near dawn and returns every night near evening. No normal bear acts like that."

The king considered the matter for a moment. "And how does that connect to Werner?"

"Remember when I followed Werner's tracks until they disappeared beneath those of a bear? That I could find where the bear wandered off but never found Werner's tracks, nor did I find any blood from an attack?"

"Go on."

"Well, the maiden was looking for her sister, and we found her tracks mingling with a bear's before hers disappeared and the bear's continued. I'm certain that her sister was riding on the back of the bear. The maiden believed so, too. I can think of no other conclusion from what I saw. Perhaps that also happened to Werner."

"Can you prove it?" The voice of his father filled with hope. It had been far too long since Roland had heard anything beyond sorrow in that voice.

"Maybe. I would need to see the bear first."

"I suppose you must. If only The Hunter was south again." His father's eyes lowered in thought for a few seconds, but then they turned to mischief. "What's this maiden's name?"

Roland shrugged, feeling his cheeks burn a little. His father's interests had clearly turned to Roland's recent encounter. "I failed to ask for her name. I know her sister's name is Snow, but I forgot to ask for her name, nor did she ask for mine."

The king grinned. "She's beautiful, isn't she?" Roland felt his face twitch, and his father laughed. "I don't need you to answer after that! She must have left quite the impression on you to garner that reaction."

Roland smiled. "You don't meet a maiden striding through the snow as though it's nothing every day."

"A peasant, no doubt?" The tone wasn't dismissive, as Roland had often heard when Werner's socializing at court came up. Rather, the king was keen on hearing about the sudden appearance of this maiden.

Roland couldn't deny that the interest was mutual. "I've never seen her before, so I'm certain she isn't a member of the nobility." He thought for a moment. "Her cloak was of a fur I've never seen in the forest, though, and it had a red hood."

"A huntress from the north?" his father asked with intrigue.

Roland shook his head. "She lives nearby; near enough that her family's cottage is within half a day's journey. Maybe she's a relative of a hunter, but she herself is probably just a peasant living in the woods."

The king chuckled, his eyes alight with mischief. "It would make a lot of the ladies of court very upset to learn that a peasant girl has outdone them in competing for the crown prince's eyes, not to mention those of the other kingdoms."

A wide grin spread across Roland's face. "That is usually more of a Werner concern."

"I suppose it is." The king then turned and walked to the fire. His voice became serious again. "Roland, I had come here intending to tell you that you should return to court. Most gave up hope long ago that Werner may have survived. Not only that, but there is talk of war in the south once the snows melt. Nothing is certain, but we may need to muster our banners to defend our allies."

"Any princesses involved yet?" Roland asked before he could hold his tongue. The time-honored tradition of the marriage alliance was what Roland had always expected would be his fate, but the forest maiden had shaken that resigned belief. He felt his heart fall a little in his chest as he waited for his father to answer him.

His father did not miss the worry that slipped into Roland's voice. The king chuckled. "Not yet. I would guess you have a few more months to win a forest maiden's heart before such... intimate discussions begin in force."

"Father..."

"Roland," the king walked over and put his hands on the prince's shoulders, "I want you to think of something. If there is a spirit bear protecting Werner, you will find him after the snow melts. I've heard enough of them from the North Hunters to know that to be the most likely case. He'll be in some cave that is only accessible by the greatest of efforts. So once the snows melt, I'll allow you three more weeks to look for your brother. After that, we will have to prepare for the future."

Roland hesitated. "And if I don't find him?"

"If anyone can find Werner, it's you. Or The Hunter, but he's still busy ridding the frontier of all the North Beasts that followed the roc south. If you can't find Werner, no one will."

Roland nodded. "I understand."

His father patted him on the shoulder. "And if you happen to find this forest maiden again, let me know if the second impression is as good as the first."

Roland chuckled. "It will be hard to surpass, but I'll let you know what she does." The king laughed, and Roland remembered the many times their family had laughed together before the roc came. He hoped he would hear it again soon. "So then, should I keep searching, or do you want me to return home until spring?"

The king waited a few seconds before answering. "If you believe you can find Werner or the forest maiden before then, I will not hinder you. I know no one has ever spent more energy looking for his missing brother than you have. Just stay safe."

He nodded. "I will, Father."

The king patted Roland on the back. "Well then, let us join the others at the banquet table. You must be hungry after a long day in the woods."

It was Roland's turn to laugh. "Normally yes, but meeting the maiden seems to have made me forget my appetite until now."

The king raised an eyebrow. "You met her today?"

"Yes." Roland said with a boyish grin. "Did I fail to mention that?"

His father's next question was asked slowly. "Where did you find her?"

Roland hesitated, wondering if his father might take offence at the edict being broken by the maiden.

"Roland?"

The prince exhaled. "Northeast of here, beyond the stream and hills."

His father looked at him carefully, as if considering things that Roland knew nothing about. They were at the entrance to the banquet hall before his father spoke again. "I look forward to hearing how your search plays out, both for your brother and for the forest maiden."

The words carried the cryptic tone that told Roland any further discussion would gain no new knowledge. It intrigued the prince, not just that his father was now in a scheming mood upon hearing of the maiden, but that it also seemed as if his father knew who the maiden might be.

Knowing that he wouldn't get anything more out of his father when he entered such a state, Roland followed him to the banquet hall. It was easy to see how out of practice he had become from the months in the snow, and only about halfway through the meal before he'd become comfortable in the setting again.

But throughout the night, the maiden played in his thoughts. Every idle moment found his mind being drawn to her.

It only strengthened Roland's resolve to see her again.

By the time he retired to his room, he had a second goal for the morning. The first was still searching for any sign of Werner; the second was to find the maiden again, and perhaps the strange bear that was staying with her.

Until we meet again.

Chapter 29

Werner took a deep breath of the early morning air. The myriad scents of spring filled his nostrils even with stubborn patches of snow still on the ground. He tried to pick out all the new scents as he stood beyond the tree line of the meadow. Animals were moving around more than ever, and the early blooms were clouding everything in rich aromas.

It would take a while for him to adjust to the spring's challenges, but there was little hiding his excitement. The evenings were warming, and the nights were now tolerable without the fire of the cottage.

I'll get used to it soon enough, being out here day and night.

It was a decision that Werner had been preparing to make for weeks now. The snow had melted to where he could sleep outside in relative comfort. He no longer needed to return to the cottage every night for warmth. That meant he could stay on the hunt for the dwarf, sleeping close to the last scent and pursuing from there instead of spending hours lumbering out from the cottage and back.

The sooner he's dead, the sooner I can repay Snow and her family's kindness. He glanced back through the trees at the cottage. The girls were already on their morning routines, likely assuming that he would return tonight as he always did.

What would they do when he didn't return? Would they worry about him, as the kingdom likely had after he disappeared in the roc's storm? Would they think he had died?

Werner had gone through these questions countless times, but how could he say goodbye?

The bear took a few steps closer to the tree line, though he stayed hidden as best he could. Both Snow and Rose were outside and looked to be laughing. Snow had always been the cheerier of the two, but Werner was glad to see that her sister had brightened considerably since she had run into that ranger in the woods. He'd overheard plenty of gossip about the man, mostly guessing at what his name might be.

Werner chuckled at the memories. *The man sounds like he's spent one too many hunts with The Hunter. Maybe Roland knows who he is.*

That was the best Werner could hope to do in helping Rose in finding this ranger again. The only memento that she had was a scarf from the man, but Werner had only glimpsed it when Rose had first come home. He'd thought nothing of it at the time since it matched her hood, and Rose had inadvertently kept it hidden from him in the girls' room ever since.

Despite that, he thought he could remember the scent. He sniffed the air. There was something that smelled similar. It was faint, but maybe Werner could follow it...

No. A ranger is more likely to kill me on sight rather than follow me back to their cottage. Best to leave finding him to the girls, or to Roland after I kill the dwarf.

Setting the thought of helping Rose aside, he watched the girls for a while. It pleased Werner to see them smiling so brightly. All winter, they had struggled with anxious energy; this was most blatantly shown on Rose's part, while Snow hid hers behind a pleasant mask. Only in the last couple of weeks had they both fed on each other's joy.

Could he truly go back and ruin that happiness? If he slipped away, then they may never know. Their lives could continue on this path, and he could return once the dwarf was dead.

But what if instead they worried about him long after he was gone? What if they went out looking for him and ran across the dwarf?

The thought of the dwarf cursing the girls sealed the decision. He made a low growl as he thought about that fate. *No, I can't let them worry about me. Not if it will lead to that outcome.* He stepped out of the tree line and back towards the cottage.

Werner was halfway to the oak tree before Rose spotted him. Her face showed surprise, then shifted to worry. Snow was overjoyed to see him come back and called his name so loudly that their mother soon appeared through the doorway. Snow was halfway to him by that point. Werner kept his eyes on the other two. They seemed to know instinctively that he was leaving for good.

"Goldie!" Snow called to him. Werner made a playful hop towards Snow before she threw her arms around his neck. "What are you doing back already?"

He saw that their mother stayed back a bit while Rose walked to be beside her sister. A hundred thoughts filled his mind, but he had to find some way to communicate what he was planning to do.

The tight hug disappeared as Snow looked him in the eyes. Her smile turned to a frown, finally sharing the worry. "What's wrong?"

Werner looked towards the forest, then back at Snow and Rose.

"You want us to follow you?" Snow asked hopefully.

No, Snow... Werner extended his paw towards her, then stamped it into the ground. He then tucked his head, then extended his paw towards the southwest.

He watched Snow as the sadness welled in her eyes. She stared at him for several seconds more before she spoke. "You're leaving?" she asked softly.

He nodded, feeling his heart ache at the look in her eyes.

She was quiet for a moment. A tear streaked down her cheek. "Will you ever come back?"

Werner looked away, not wanting to upset her further but knowing that he likely wouldn't see the girls again before he'd finally tracked down the dwarf. They wouldn't recognize him after that.

After a moment, he turned back to her and shrugged his shoulders.

"Oh." Another tear ran down Snow's cheek, and she tucked her chin. "I understand."

Rose stepped forward and put a hand on Werner's head. "Is it because of what you spent all winter looking for?"

Werner huffed and nodded his head in agreement.

Rose smiled weakly. "Alright then." She then opened her arms towards him. He stepped forward and put his head against her shoulder. Rose wrapped her arms around him and gave him one last hug. "Good luck, Goldie."

Werner silently thanked her for the encouragement, then he tried to repeat the gesture to Snow. She practically leapt around his neck and cried into his fur. Snow didn't loosen her grip until their mother approached and touched Snow's shoulder.

Snow moved her lips to be right beside his ear and whispered. "Is it safe from danger?"

He inhaled deeply, trying to catch any scent of the dwarf. None was there, so he nodded. *I won't let him come near your cottage if I can help it. I promise.*

She pulled away and wiped her eyes. "Make sure you come back, okay?"

Werner felt he was on the verge of tears himself. How could he make that promise when he would hopefully be human when he saw her again? Would any of them even believe his story?

But Werner wanted to help Snow stop crying, so he nodded his head. *I hope to see you again soon, Snow White.* He slowly turned and walked into the forest, his heart heavy at the tearful parting.

The morning soon turned to the familiar routine, though now it was much easier to make his way through the forest without fighting the snowbanks. He looked to the east. That dark corner of the forest, where he had last run into the dwarf, was now well within reach.

Werner spent the rest of the morning trying to find the dwarf's scent. Faint traces lingered here and there, but a few times the similar scent of the other dwarf crossed his nose as well and took him on a wild goose chase.

Werner resolved to see this through to the end. He'd chase all the geese in the world if they led to the dwarf. He'd be himself again and the girls would be safe.

Soon, Snow White. Soon.

Chapter 30

Rose smiled at the early morning sunbeams breaking through the clouds to the east. The snow had completely melted away in the week since Goldie had left, letting the green grass return for its long hibernation.

She let out a happy sigh at the thought. With the snow gone, it would be easier to move around the woods. It would also bring out all the animals that belonged in her lands. Maybe she could call on them with the bond to act as a protective guard against any more of those wolves.

That is, if the rangers haven't already dealt with them. The thought brought a pleasant feeling with it, and Rose turned to see her sister in the doorway. Snow was gazing at the far tree line, her eyes still searching for a sign that Goldie might return.

Rose felt the same sorrow at not having Goldie around anymore, though she knew it wasn't nearly the same degree as Snow. He had become part of the family over the winter, always looked for as the sun touched the horizon. Rose couldn't deny the feeling of going out to look for the bear, and she knew her sister felt that even more strongly.

Yet it was what the bear had wished. He had even turned around in order to tell them goodbye. Goldie was off on his own adventure now, and they would have to continue on with their lives without him.

"It's good to see the trees budding already." Their mother said with a smile as she looked at Rose's tree. "It makes me want to get out my kettle and get my dyes prepared again."

"Mother, we can go out and gather the plants for you." Both Rose and their mother turned to look at Snow, who tucked her chin sheepishly. "I mean, The Hunter told us the bandits he'd found got captured by the princes and their company, so there's no reason for us to be afraid."

Rose maintained her silence. On the one hand, this was exactly what she herself had been thinking of, to get back to the way things used to be. To be out in the woods again. Though she was still worried about the possibility of more wolves, she'd also dismissed their danger for the first time that she could recall.

Even so, this was Snow asking to go help gather the menulia and aedelis plants. Rose supposed that she should have known that her sister might want to leave the cottage now that spring had bloomed; Snow had snuck out to spend that one day with Goldie, after all. Still, it was a wild change from how things used to be.

Snow glanced between Rose and their mother. "Did I say something wrong?"

"No, dear," their mother replied. "I just didn't expect you to volunteer to go out with your sister. You usually like to stay here with me."

Snow smiled. "I thought I might try something new."

Like following a bear into a snow flurry? Rose thought, though she too was smiling. Goldie had brought Snow into a world beyond her books, although the strangeness of it all had Rose questioning if the roc's storm had transported them to one of those ancient fairy realms. Snow had her spirit bear, and then Rose had her encounter with the ranger.

Their mother smiled at Snow's answer. "I suppose that should be fine. Rose?"

Rose nodded. "We'll have to get started now."

"Why?" Snow asked. Their mother simply smiled and went inside to pack some food for their day of gathering. Snow turned to Rose, but Rose likewise smiled at her sister before following her mother inside. Rose knew that Snow would be slower than her in the woods. Every moment they waited to leave the cottage would be at least two that they would lose to gather the plants.

Her satchel and cutting blade hadn't moved all winter, making the preparation a quick affair. She glanced across their room to where Snow was trying to pick which satchel she wanted to take. Her sister had a small collection of them, depending on what Snow and her mother were taking to market.

Rose thought about taking her bow so that she could practice in the woods as well. A shiver ran down her spine as the specter of the wolf chased the thought. She knew the bow couldn't harm the beast unless it was impossibly close, but she would have to protect Snow if one appeared again.

I have to take it. Rose tied the quiver to her hip and put the bow over her shoulder. She also slipped into their parents' room and took their father's long hunting knife. She hoped the knife would be unnecessary, but at least she knew the knife had the edge to kill the wolf if her bow failed to harm it.

After Rose made sure that they had everything they'd need, she led her sister into the woods. The first part of the journey was quiet as the girls listened to the song of the birds and saw the smaller animals running across the ground. When they reached a crossing downstream of the fork, Rose used her bond to sway a chorus of songbirds to sing to them as they waded through the water, much to Snow's amusement.

"I hope that's not the only magic we run into today," Snow said.

Rose stopped in her tracks. "What do you mean by that?"

Snow turned to face her, excitement radiating from her face. "If your ranger is still looking for his brother, we might run into him."

"You don't think he is still looking for his brother, do you?" Rose said incredulously. "It's been weeks since we met. His brother is probably home by now."

"His brother could have hidden in a cave or something," Snow said as she looked up into the trees. "Rangers can survive the winters easily enough. The Hunter never had a problem in our woods."

"The Hunter is hardly human," Rose replied with amusement. She'd always respected the high chieftain, but seeing him after his battle with the roc made The Hunter incomparable to any mortal. "He can survive things that would kill everyone else that tried."

"Well, maybe he's related to The Hunter." Snow said with a grin as she held out her hand to catch the squirrel she'd swayed.

Rose now knew that Snow was stuck in another fantasy. "And who are you to say that the brother was a ranger as well? He could have wandered off like you did and gotten lost."

"Well..." her sister paused as she thought of a reply, "perhaps we'll find his brother. And then you can be the one to reunite them and he'll owe you a favor."

Laughter was Rose's response. "Now you really are just dreaming!"

The two girls continued into the woods, laughing about the whole idea as they practiced their bonds. They were still in joyous spirits as they came to the first aedelis patch. The plants had weathered the long winter exceptionally well, and Rose found plenty of new growth that was ready for their mother to turn into yellow dye.

Rose took Snow to one part of the patch and showed her where to cut the plants in order to encourage new growth. She also reminded her not to take too many cuttings from one spot or it could kill off the entire patch. The two then set to work making their piles.

It was long, tiring, and joyful work for Rose. For one, it was good to have someone with her in the woods again. She didn't realize how much she had missed the shared company. And seeing Snow enjoy the work despite her pile falling well behind Rose's brought cheer to Rose's soul. Maybe this could become a regular outing for them until they went north.

Though, if Snow isn't home, who will keep it spotless? Rose breathed a laugh at the thought and continued gathering.

The morning went by with little fanfare, and finally they'd cut two piles that Rose was happy with. "That's good enough for the two of us. Let's eat and then head for home."

Snow nodded and wiped her forehead. "And here I thought I had the hard work back home."

Rose laughed. "You do, but you don't have the sun beating down on you the whole time." Snow joined her laughter. Then the two ate their lunch, filled their satchels with aedelis cuttings, and turned for home.

It was a few miles from the patch when they heard a voice in the distance. It was frantic, as if someone was in trouble. Rose and Snow shared a brief look, then they hurried towards the sound.

Once they approached, they both gasped in surprise. The voice they heard was not a man, but it belonged to a frantic dwarf. It didn't take more than a glance to see the reason for his yelling, for his beard had snagged in the cleft of a fallen log. The beard was longer than the dwarf was tall, and he had both his hands pulling furiously to free it. "Stupid, useless piece of lumber! Let go of my beard!"

Snow was the first to speak. "Excuse me, -"

The dwarf leapt in surprise, and nearly fell on his wizened face as the log kept a firm grasp on his beard. "Ow! Stupid girl! Don't surprise someone with their beard caught in a jam." He then turned back to his attempts at freeing his beard. "Let go, let go!"

The two watched him for a little while, bemused by the sight of the dwarf jumping around like a grasshopper. Rose heard Snow giggle softly, and so did the dwarf. He faced them with fiery little eyes. "What are you doing standing there? Just going to gawk at a fellow trapped in a tree all day? Come and help me out."

Rose stepped forward. "We can try, but what were you doing to get caught like that?"

"Stupid, inquisitive goose!" The dwarf remarked. "I was trying to split the tree in order to get chips to put in my fires. I'd gotten my wedge in all well and good, but as I struck the blasted thing, the wood slipped and closed upon my beautiful white beard." The dwarf's voice noticeably slowed as he vainly stroked the long hairs. "And now the poor thing is stuck while you silly, smooth-faced milkmaids just stand there and laugh."

Despite feeling bad for laughing, Rose could hardly contain herself at the dwarf's exaggerated demeanor. "Alright, alright. We'll try to help."

At first, they tried to roll the log, but the dwarf shouted as though in pain. Then Rose tried to help him pull the beard straight out, but it was no use.

Snow then picked up the dwarf's hatchet and was about to chop away at the log, but the dwarf protested. "Not that, you stupid girl! You may miss and mangle the grand hairs of my beard! How could you think of doing such a thing?"

She put the hatchet down and left that idea to the side, but after several other unsuccessful or protested efforts, both Rose and Snow were at a loss for what to do.

Rose stepped back to think. The dwarf didn't take kindly to them just standing around and went back to his tugging and jumping from when they'd first seen him. "Useless girls..." he muttered.

"Any ideas?" Snow asked.

Rose shook her head. "I suppose we could go get Mother."

"Oh sure, go get your mother!" The dwarf exclaimed. "What's the point of getting more people when you two are already too much for me and the day is getting away? Is there nothing else that occurs to you?"

"How about this?" Snow said as she took their father's knife from Rose's hip.

The dwarf snarled at the sight of the knife. "You would cut my beard in two?! Are you such a wretch as to think that is the best idea?"

"I'll only cut from where it's caught." Snow replied. "It's barely more than a few inches."

"A few inches!? BAH!" The dwarf puffed up his chest. "What self-respecting creature would maim such a lovely thing?"

Rose was now losing patience with the dwarf. "I'll hold him for you."

Snow nodded and Rose grabbed the dwarf at his waist, but the dwarf began violently tossing his head back and forth. "Don't cut it, you hussies!"

"Hold still," Rose said.

"DON'T -" but before he could continue, Snow had clipped the beard free with a swish of the knife. Only a small tuft remained stuck in the log.

But that was entirely too much for the dwarf. He spun out of Rose's hands and held up the slightly shortened beard. "You wretched girls! You cut my lovely beard! What ill-mannered mother raised you?"

The remark sparked Rose's anger. "How else were we going to -"

"DON'T give me that excuse." The dwarf replied curtly, while Snow handed the knife back to Rose. "Oh, my poor beard. You two are almost as much of a pain in my side as that demon bear is."

"Demon bear?" Rose and Snow asked in unison, though their tones couldn't have been more different. It was clear from her voice that Snow wanted to hear more; Rose wanted nothing more than to run home. In all their father's stories, Rose had never heard of such a thing. She felt her heart beat faster at what such a thing could be.

"Yes. That blasted demon keeps trying to steal my treasure." He then hopped over to the side of the log and dug beneath where he had been chopping. "Should have done this first," he muttered to himself.

Soon the dwarf had pulled out a small bag, but he pulled with such force that some of its contents spilled on the ground. Brilliant golden coins shone in the late sunlight.

Rose glanced at Snow, who asked the dwarf, "Where did those coins -"

"It matters not, you hussies! They're mine now and that's that. Your help doesn't warrant payment, if that's what you're thinking. I've never met worse people in all my years."

There was a small sound behind the girls. Rose saw the dwarf's eyes look that way and go wide with fright. "AH! Direwolves! An even worse turn of events!"

Rose and Snow turned to see a pack of four blue-gray wolves had crept up on them. Upon realizing that they no longer held the element of surprise, the four stood at full height and bared their yellow fangs.

The memory from last autumn rushed back as Rose saw their blue-gray pelts and red eyes. Rose took Snow and pulled her sister behind her protectively.

"What's wrong with them?" Snow asked fearfully. Snow had noticed what Rose already knew. Their magical bond had no effect on the wolves, just like the wolf from autumn. They were at the beasts' mercy.

Rose tried to keep her voice calm, but she heard the fear quiver in her words. "I... don't know,"

The dwarf cried out again, but his voice was fainter. "Eat them, you fiends! Eat them!" Rose realized with horror that the dwarf had abandoned them to the wolves.

Instinct told her to run like The Hunter had warned her to do, but she would easily outrun Snow. If that happened, the rabid beasts would catch her sister and kill her. Rose couldn't allow that to happen.

Her eyes caught a glint near her feet. She glanced down and saw the dwarf's small ax laying where Snow had set it down. She picked it up and faced the direwolves, ax in one hand, the knife in the other. "Snow, stay behind me."

The wolves started fanning out to encircle them. Rose could hear Snow trying to stifle her terrified sobs behind her, but she didn't dare to look behind to give a reassuring look to her sister. Rose's arms were already tired from the hours of collecting aedelis and trying to help the dwarf, and her voice had a raspiness to it as she yelled at the wolves to stay back.

In her heart, she knew she couldn't stop the four of them. She might hold off two if she was lucky, but the others would get to Snow the moment Rose began fighting.

"Rose..." Snow's voice was weak.

"It'll be alright." She said, hoping that her own fear didn't show in her voice.

One wolf paused its pacing, crouching down as if ready to attack. Rose tried to keep her eye on the other three, but she'd seen that crouch before. The direwolf was about to strike. It gave a low growl, its eyes glistening with evil intent.

Then the wolf yipped and leapt back, the shaft of an arrow protruding from its shoulder.

An angry shout echoed from her right. Rose turned to see a figure running into the clearing and yelling at the wolves while his hands swiftly notched another arrow in his bow.

It was the ranger! Her ranger had appeared again to save them!

Rose saw two of the wolves flee with arrows tugging at their fur, but she noticed the last had turned and was circling to get behind the ranger. Acting on instinct, she threw the ax at it. It was a glancing blow, but the wolf turned towards her and growled. The ranger heard the growl and spun around, letting loose another arrow at the direwolf. The distance was too close for him to miss, and the beast fell dead with the arrow through its heart.

The ranger looked around to make sure that the other three wolves had indeed fled, then he turned and met Rose's eyes. "Are you both alright?" he asked.

Rose breathed a sigh of relief, then smiled at him. "We are now. Those wolves were about to tear us apart before you arrived."

He exhaled, his face showing relief that they had escaped harm. The ranger then walked over to the last wolf and retrieved his arrow. "This wolf's one of the biggest I've ever killed. You did well to hold them off as long as you did."

Rose didn't know how to respond to the compliment. The terror was still gripping her, as were Snow's fingers. Snow's breath was also rapid.

Then Rose heard a slight sigh from Snow, and her fingers lost their hold on Rose's dress. Rose got her eyes around in time to see that Snow had fainted and was falling away from her. She reached out but missed Snow's arm.

Fortunately, the ranger had seen her fainting and was already moving. His arm slid under her before her head hit the ground. "Easy, easy," he said, gently shaking Snow to wake her. When that failed, he took out his flask with his free hand and held it up to Rose. "Apply some water to her face. Lightly."

Rose did so, using the hem of her dress. However, Snow stayed motionless, as though she had fallen into a deep sleep. After a few more attempts, the ranger waved her off. "Her pulse is fine. She's just in shock." He looked up at Rose. "I don't know if there are other packs nearby. We should get you both back to your cottage."

Rose nodded, deciding it was best not to argue. Who knew if the wolves wouldn't turn around and attack them again, perhaps in greater numbers? "I'll lead you to our home."

He put his hands under Snow and took a breath, then he lifted her with ease. After ensuring that he had a firm hold on Snow, the ranger looked at Rose. "I realize we haven't actually introduced ourselves to one another." He said with a grin. "I'm Roland."

Rose smiled and offered her hand daintily. "I'm Rose Red."

Roland stared at her hand for a second, then opened his fingers to show Rose that he couldn't accept the gesture with Snow securely in his arms. She smiled and tucked her chin in embarrassment.

Roland chuckled softly. "You have a beautiful name. It suits you." Rose looked back to see that Roland was himself embarrassed by his comment, but he was being sincere. "So, why are you out here this time? Were you looking for Snow again?"

"No," she replied, "we were gathering aedelis cuttings for my mother to make dyes with and came upon a dwarf stuck in that log over there."

"A dwarf, here?" He furrowed his brow; yet whatever question lay there remained quiet. "I haven't heard of a dwarf venturing this far from their mountains."

"This one said he was chopping the log to get chips for his fire, but when we freed him by cutting the end of his beard, he yelled at us. Then, when the wolves appeared, he disappeared with a sack full of golden coins that he pulled from beneath the tree."

Roland looked at her quizzically, as though he knew she wasn't lying, yet he wasn't sure he could believe the story. After a moment, he shook his head. "You'll have to tell me all about it while we walk." Checking his hold on a still-sleeping Snow, he then motioned for Rose to lead the way home.

"What's wrong with them?" Snow asked fearfully. Snow had noticed what Rose already knew. Their magical bond had no effect on the wolves, just like the wolf from autumn. They were at the beasts' mercy.

Rose tried to keep her voice calm, but she heard the fear quiver in her words. "I... don't know,"

The dwarf cried out again, but his voice was fainter. "Eat them, you fiends! Eat them!" Rose realized with horror that the dwarf had abandoned them to the wolves.

Instinct told her to run like The Hunter had warned her to do, but she would easily outrun Snow. If that happened, the rabid beasts would catch her sister and kill her. Rose couldn't allow that to happen.

Her eyes caught a glint near her feet. She glanced down and saw the dwarf's small ax laying where Snow had set it down. She picked it up and faced the direwolves, ax in one hand, the knife in the other. "Snow, stay behind me."

The wolves started fanning out to encircle them. Rose could hear Snow trying to stifle her terrified sobs behind her, but she didn't dare to look behind to give a reassuring look to her sister. Rose's arms were already tired from the hours of collecting aedelis and trying to help the dwarf, and her voice had a raspiness to it as she yelled at the wolves to stay back.

In her heart, she knew she couldn't stop the four of them. She might hold off two if she was lucky, but the others would get to Snow the moment Rose began fighting.

"Rose..." Snow's voice was weak.

"It'll be alright." She said, hoping that her own fear didn't show in her voice.

my poor beard. You two are almost as much of a pain in my side as that demon bear is."

"Demon bear?" Rose and Snow asked in unison, though their tones couldn't have been more different. It was clear from her voice that Snow wanted to hear more; Rose wanted nothing more than to run home. In all their father's stories, Rose had never heard of such a thing. She felt her heart beat faster at what such a thing could be.

"Yes. That blasted demon keeps trying to steal my treasure." He then hopped over to the side of the log and dug beneath where he had been chopping. "Should have done this first," he muttered to himself.

Soon the dwarf had pulled out a small bag, but he pulled with such force that some of its contents spilled on the ground. Brilliant golden coins shone in the late sunlight.

Rose glanced at Snow, who asked the dwarf, "Where did those coins -"

"It matters not, you hussies! They're mine now and that's that. Your help doesn't warrant payment, if that's what you're thinking. I've never met worse people in all my years."

There was a small sound behind the girls. Rose saw the dwarf's eyes look that way and go wide with fright. "AH! Direwolves! An even worse turn of events!"

Rose and Snow turned to see a pack of four blue-gray wolves had crept up on them. Upon realizing that they no longer held the element of surprise, the four stood at full height and bared their yellow fangs.

The memory from last autumn rushed back as Rose saw their blue-gray pelts and red eyes. Rose took Snow and pulled her sister behind her protectively.

Chapter 31

It had been yet another long day of searching for the dwarf, though today had been the most successful since Werner had left the cottage. Twice he'd picked up the scent of the villain, but both times he could not follow it for long.

The first time, the dwarf had taken care to go through a stream and walk down it a ways before emerging on the other side. It had taken Werner far too long to pick up the trail again. After he had, the dwarf appeared to have slipped on a loose stone and tumbled head over heels into a mud bog that overpowered any scent that Werner could hope to pick up. He'd found no trace since then.

If there was one thing about the dwarf that Werner was certain of since their last encounter in the snow, it was that the little creature somehow possessed both incredible clumsiness in his movements and incredible skill in covering his trail.

Werner felt his stomach rumble. He shook his head at the overpowering hunger. Try as he might, there was only so far he could go before his bear body required a large catch of food.

Werner gazed at the sky. It was the middle of the afternoon now, and he was a fair distance from either the river or the lake. Those were his best sources of food in the forest. He thought for a moment to go for the lake, but the river was the easier of the two to fish from.

The prince had only taken a few steps when an unfamiliar scent reached his nostrils. It was an odd mix of animal and mineral, as well as blood. In all his time in the forest, he'd never come across anything quite like it. The winds carrying the scents came from the north. Curious, he turned toward it.

What greeted him when the origin of the scent trotted into view were three wolves, the likes of which he had never seen. The smallest was more than half the size of him, and he was massive to begin with. Their blue-gray coats looked like no wolf's pelt he had ever come across, and their red eyes were best described as hateful.

The three wolves growled at him, and on instinct Werner roared back. For a moment, his sudden aggression surprised Werner. He'd left the other pack of wolves alone during winter; why were these evoking such primal feelings? As he stared at them, though, there was something about these beasts that felt wrong. He felt in his very core that they were something unnatural, that they needed to be destroyed.

A year ago, the mere sight of these beasts would have terrified him. But he was a bear now. While he had no sword or bow, he had immense strength behind his claws and teeth. And besides, there was no chance that the wolves were more elusive than the dwarf, and Werner had nearly caught the dwarf when he'd surprised him during the winter.

The three wanted a fight, and his primal urges were ready for a fight as well. If nothing else, it was a chance to expend an entire winter of frustrations on beasts that he knew didn't belong in his forest. He issued another challenge at them and stamped his paws into the ground.

With a howl, the smaller two pounced. Werner chose one and rushed it, but the wolf leapt away as the other attacked. The yellow fangs dug into Werner's shoulder, and he roared in pain.

Werner snapped his head towards the wolf, but it had chosen its bite well. The beast was barely beyond the reach of his teeth. Out of the corner of his eye, Werner saw the third wolf jump at his now exposed throat. He swiped his paw and backhanded the wolf across its jaw, sending it sprawling.

Turning his attention back to the wolf still clinging to his shoulder, Werner picked his front paws up and slammed that shoulder towards the ground. The wolf released its grip before Werner crushed it, but he knocked it back with a swipe of his other paw.

The other small wolf again nipped at him, this time catching his heel. Roland spun to face it, but the wolf had hopped away. It glared at him evilly, with an unsettling sort of grin on its muzzle.

Werner took a step towards it and roared. It hopped back again, but Werner saw its eyes flick to the right. The prince turned that way and barely prevented the large wolf from clamping its jaws around his throat. The wolf's jaws instead bit into his foreleg, and the wolf let go and retreated before Werner could retaliate.

For a moment, the fighting paused. Werner was already feeling sluggish compared to his foes, but he was still free of their jaws.

Free, and capable of thinking clearly.

The wolves circled him as they looked for a new opening. Werner noticed that the large wolf was favoring its left foreleg, though Werner couldn't see why as the wolf was presenting its right side to him as it circled. The one wolf he had backhanded had blood coming from its snout, while the third was yet unscathed.

However, the prince realized that both of the small wolves were only acting as distractions. Despite its injury, the large wolf was the one that would go for the kill. If Werner could take that one out, the other two may decide to run away.

At least, that's what he hoped.

Though Werner had only taken a few bites from the wolves, all had the intent of slowly disabling him. The prince had to finish this fight quickly. While he was far stronger than the wolves, Werner was completely inexperienced in fighting with his bear form, and they were taking advantage of that.

Werner formed a quick plan and acted. He first feigned a charge toward the large wolf, then he turned on one of the small wolves, the one with the bloody snout. The wolf didn't quite escape the swipe of his paw and Werner barely caught his flank, sending the wolf spinning.

Werner took a step as though he intended to press his attack against the wolf. The other small one leapt to take advantage, this time clamping into his right leg. Werner spun, taking a momentary look at the large wolf.

The wolf was coiling for its attack. Werner continued around, letting himself look like he was vulnerable again.

The large wolf made its fatal mistake and lunged towards Werner's throat. Ready for the attack, Werner swung his paw in an uppercut and his claws tore through the wolf's neck. It yelped, but Werner wasn't able to finish the wolf off immediately. The smaller wolves had tried to attack as well.

One paw smacked a wolf onto its side, while the other wolf nipped at his heels to turn him. Werner spun the other way, knowing the trick from his days in court, and caught the wolf, pinning it to the ground. With one well-placed bite, the wolf fell still under him.

Werner turned to the last wolf. The bloodied wolf looked at him with its ears flat, then fled into the forest.

The battle was over.

Taking a few breaths, Werner spat out the blood in his mouth. Even the taste of their blood seemed tainted. Now he needed the river not only for food but also to clean the foul liquid from his tongue. Now that the fighting was over, though, curiosity set in about these invaders.

The largest of the blue-gray wolves lay spread out on the forest floor. He could see that it was dead from his slash across its throat. Cautiously, Werner approached it and found the broken shaft of an arrow protruding from the shoulder that had been facing away from him. Some hunters had already attacked the pack, but the wolf had shrugged it off. Still, the arrow had likely hindered the wolf enough for Werner to gain the upper hand.

Though, what if the hunter that had loosed the arrow is still nearby?

He sniffed the air, and his heart leapt in delight. *The dwarf's scent!* He looked back down and saw that the tracks of the wolves fell in the same direction as where the vile scent came from. Throwing caution to the winds, Werner hurried down the wolves' trail.

Two more scents soon reached his nose, then a third. While he couldn't place the last one, he knew the two. It was Snow White and Rose Red! And they were with the dwarf!

He doubled his charge, hoping that he could reach them before the dwarf caused the two any harm.

The scene that greeted him was bare and disappointing, save for another dead wolf. No one remained who gave off any of the four scents.

He followed his nose to where the dwarf's scent was strongest and found a small clump of white hair stuck in the cleft of a log. The powerful scent of the pine told him that the cuts in the tree had happened that day, but the soil around its base had weathered. The log must have fallen during the winter, and the dwarf was trying to clear it away.

Werner sniffed at the clump of hair. He then exhaled forcefully at the unmistakable stench. It was indeed the dwarf's, and Snow and Rose had walked right up to him. By the scent of the dwarf, he had bolted away from where the direwolves had approached. Werner felt his heart grow cold at the thought of the dwarf abandoning the girls to a violent end.

He tried to look for any tracks, knowing that the dwarf had so far left none. There had been four of the blue-gray wolves. Judging by the still damp pool of blood, it must have died on the spot and not too long ago. It was likely that whoever the fourth scent belonged to had found the girls and saved them in the nick of time.

Yet that last scent also confused him. It was at once familiar and unknown to Werner. At first, he thought it was the scent of The Hunter. The prince knew that the old man had driven off the wolves and saved the girls. Werner knew from the girls that The Hunter had left to hunt the North Beasts, but it had always sounded like the man had battled his way back to his frozen frontier.

He took in the air again. *No, the scent isn't right for what I remember? Is it another hunter, then?*

But if that's the case, why do I recognize the scent?

Werner followed the other wolf tracks and found an arrow lodged in the ground. It was a normal cedar arrow, as far as he could tell. That meant it couldn't be The Hunter then. The old man carried either his red mahogany arrows or those strange black arrows for the great bow.

Could it be the same scent from Rose's scarf? Werner thought about it. The idea could explain the familiarity, and the girls would go with the man if it was the ranger, but Werner couldn't be sure. *Guess I didn't know that scent as well as I think I did.*

Deciding there was nothing else to be gleaned, he followed the human prints a little further. One girl had fallen, then her tracks vanished while the two remaining sets of tracks went towards the girls' cottage. Werner thought that the girls' protector must be carrying one of them. He sniffed the ground and felt a pang of jealousy as he realized that Snow White was the one being carried.

The pieces of the encounter fell into place. The fourth scent had to belong to Rose's ranger. It was the only explanation he had as to why the girls' tracks showed no sign of worry when he approached them.

But then, why is he carrying Snow and not Rose? The feeling of jealousy grew stronger. Was Werner about to lose Snow to some wandering hero?

He could follow the tracks. If the man and Rose were talking, then he might be able to catch up and learn if his growing jealousy was for nought. Meanwhile, the dwarf had fled towards the lake, and Werner still needed to feed himself.

If the dwarf was still by the lake and Werner dealt him the killing blow, he could still make it to the cottage tonight and cut off any potential rivalry.

In the end, there was only one choice to be made. Werner continued on towards the lake. One thought occupied his mind. *Kill the dwarf. Then I can return to Snow as myself and win her heart.*

Chapter 32

"She's a deep sleeper, huh?"

Rose looked over at Roland, then lowered her eyes to her sister. Snow was still asleep, despite how long they had already been walking and the little conversation that had passed between them. "Snow tends to be."

She watched Roland carry her sister for a few seconds. Snow had tucked her cheek against Roland's chest and had her lips slightly parted, like she always slept. The ranger, for his part, had done a good job of walking as smoothly as possible to not wake her.

Rose felt jealous of her sister and wished that perhaps they could have traded places. This brought a thought to her mind. "I don't mean to pry, but you seem like you're quite familiar with carrying ladies who have fainted."

Roland flashed a guilty smile. "Never for this long, but I have been called on to do it before."

Rose feigned disappointment as best she could. "I suppose I shouldn't be surprised. The ladies of the court probably fight over your attention quite a bit."

He gave her a look of surprise. "How did you know I was part of the royal court?"

Pride welled up in Rose's chest. "I've never seen a ranger with your sigil, or that goes around wearing chain mail."

"Good deduction." The ranger gave a playful laugh and relaxed. "You're not wrong. There are more than a few who frankly love fainting in order for me and Werner to catch them. We always do, as well we should, but honestly, it is refreshing to carry someone who isn't trying to play at my heart for once."

"Oh, I see." Now Rose felt guilty for the jealous feelings earlier. Rose sighed and looked back towards Snow. "It was quite the experience for her. She's never had animals attack her before; she usually stays home with Mother while I went out with Father."

"Ah." Roland stopped for a second and slowly shifted his hold on Snow to support her better. "You seem to be ready to fend off the attack. Have you fought with wolves before?"

The memory of autumn returned, but this time it wasn't as terrifying as before. "One of those wolves tried to attack me right before the roc's storm. The Hunter saved me."

"So, you're related to The Hunter?"

Rose tilted her head. "How did you guess?"

"Your cloak. It is the same color as my scarf that I lent you when we first met."

"Yes, our father was from his tribe." Rose blushed as she remembered the scarf currently wrapped around the corner post of her bed frame. She also recalled that the dwarf had called the four direwolves, just as Snow had suspected. "That's part of why the direwolves scare me so much. My sister and I can form a bond with animals that we inherited from our father. They usually yield to the bond, unless they're in distress or have a maddening disease. The direwolves, being North Beasts, didn't flinch when we tried to use the bond."

Roland raised an eyebrow. "So those four were direwolves, you say?"

Rose nodded. "That's what we thought that the one that attacked me was, and that's what the dwarf called those four today."

Roland was silent for a few moments as he considered this. "Those direwolves must have followed the roc south. We've seen a lot of North Beasts that came into the kingdom after the roc."

"Oh." Rose was concerned by the confirmation of Snow's guess, and because The Hunter hadn't told her the true nature of the autumn wolf. Her heart sank lower. The long winter wasn't over for her yet. She and Snow had to be alert in the woods as long as the North Beasts were still around them. "At first I had thought that maybe the wolf was rabid or something, like that lynx a few years ago?"

"A lynx? In this forest?" Rose could hear in his voice that the news surprised Roland. "You've seen lynx here?"

"Yes." She pointed across to the northern range. "There's a few that like to hide in the vale up against the mountains. Mother had a favorite spot for us to gather aedelis from over there before..." she paused for a moment, "before our father died."

Roland was silent. When Rose glanced at him, she saw he was waiting to see if she had more to say. She dropped her eyes, and Roland said, "I'm sorry to hear that. I'm sure he'd be proud of the way you tried to protect your sister today."

"Thank you." They walked a few more steps in silence. Rose wasn't sure what to say next and eventually asked about Roland's family. "Are your parents alive?"

Roland nodded. "Both of them are still alive, and they're as worried about Werner as I am."

"Can they not come and help? It must be difficult searching alone."

Roland bit his lip, seemingly at a loss for what to say. That alone puzzled Rose. Roland had given her no signs he had to be secretive about who he was, though this was only their second meeting. *Why would he be worried about who his parents are? Are they bandits? Is he actually a bandit?*

The ranger let out a sigh. "My father is the king, and he can't simply abandon his throne to help me search for Werner."

Rose felt her jaw drop. When she spoke, it was almost subconsciously, "The king?! Then you're..."

He smiled and gave as much of a bow as he could while trying not to wake Snow. "Crown Prince Roland of Thistledown. At your service." He stood to his full height, and for the first time Rose saw a glint of mischief in his eyes, a glint that reminded her of The Hunter and her father. "I hope that doesn't disappoint you."

"No, no," she replied with a smile, trying to hide how flustered she'd become. "I just didn't expect I would run into the crown prince alone in the woods."

"That was quite the unexpected encounter for both of us."

"Oh?" She tilted her head, curious as to his remark. "Why is that?"

The prince laughed softly. "Have you forgotten that I first saw you in the forest in the middle of a snow flurry? That's not the usual place for maidens to be. And now I find you fending off a pack of direwolves with a knife and hatchet while protecting your sister. You leave quite the impression, Lady Rose Red."

The burning blush on Rose's cheeks surpassed any that had ever occurred before. Roland grinned at her reaction, but he held back the laughter in his eyes. His restraint helped soothe the feelings the last part of his words had conjured. The compliment hadn't been purely flattery, though the improper title came as a welcome embellishment.

She gave a slight bow. "Thank you, Prince Roland."

Roland tucked his head, his hold on Snow keeping him from bowing back and possibly waking her. "You can just call me Roland."

Rose smiled. "And you can just call me Rose."

He smiled back. "Very well, Rose. May we continue on?"

She nodded, and the conversation became lively as the woods took on more of its evening hues. The conversation bounced between Roland telling her about courtly life and Rose describing what she knew of the North Hunters. Through it all, despite their voices no longer being restrained, Snow remained still in Roland's arms.

Soon they came to where Rose could see the clearing for their cottage up ahead. "Before we get too close to the cottage, I have a request." Rose said in a low voice as she stepped in front of Roland. The two stood facing each other.

"Go ahead."

"Don't tell my sister or my mother that you are the prince. My mother wants us to marry now that our father has died, and my sister dreams of finding a prince from a fairy tale."

Roland grinned, that mischievous glint in his eyes again. "I see the intrigues of courtly life are hardly different from the intrigues of the rest of the world." He gave her a nod. "I'll keep my lineage a secret for now, so long as I can visit you again."

Rose felt her heart flutter at what Roland's request implied. "I would like that."

"Then we're agreed." Roland then stepped to the side, and the two continued walking.

They reached the clearing around the cottage, and Rose saw her mother looking out for any sign of her daughters. Her eyes found them, and she reacted first with surprise at Roland's presence and then with worry upon seeing Snow being carried. She hurried over to them. "Snow. Is she...?"

"Snow is alright." Roland said. "She's just tired."

Their mother sighed thankfully, then looked down at Snow. Her face twisted a little, then in a stern voice she said, "Snow White..."

Snow's head immediately turned to look at all of them, embarrassment clear on her face.

"SNOW!" Rose exclaimed. "How long have you been awake?"

"It's been a while now," she replied meekly.

Rose felt her face go red from both anger and the realization that her sister had been listening in on what she'd said to Roland. "You had him carry you this whole time?! You could have walked with us."

Snow tucked her chin sheepishly. "I didn't want to interrupt your conversation."

Rose looked at Roland. He gave her a smile of amusement, and for the third time, she saw a mischievous glint in his eyes. She gave him a smile before setting her gaze back on Snow. "Well, thank you for that."

There was a moment of silence after the exchange before their mother turned to Roland again. "Thank you for bringing them home, ..." Their mother hesitated for a moment. "I'm sorry, but I don't think I asked for your name."

Roland smiled as he set Snow back on her feet. "I am Roland, from Thistledown."

"Thistledown? That's a long way from here."

"He's a ranger." Rose replied calmly. The next sentence she immediately regretted. "And we're glad he found us."

"Oh?" Her mother looked at Roland. "Why is that?"

Rose turned to Roland, hoping that he wouldn't mention the direwolves that had attacked them. But the prince chose not to hide the attack from their mother. Roland gave a slight bow, then replied, "Direwolves were about to attack your daughters. I drove them off with Rose's help."

Their mother gasped and put her hands over her heart. "Direwolves, here?"

"Yes. The roc brought many North Beasts in its wake when it flew south. From what I've been told, you may have had one of them staying with you."

"You mean Goldie?" their mother asked quizzically. "He's a North Beast?"

Roland nodded. "I believe he is one of the spirit bears from the north, and it is possible that he may have a connection with my brother's disappearance."

"You think he killed him?" The accusation was unfounded, but Rose was still surprised that her mother would so readily defend Goldie. "I assure you, that bear has no malice in its heart."

"On the contrary. I think Goldie may have carried Werner to safety before wandering over to find you." Roland said with a mild chuckle. "Spirit bears don't appear often and we understand very little about them, but I've heard from your people that they are one of the few mystical creatures that will help humans rather than harm us. There're even laws against hunting them along the marchlands because of that."

"I am glad to hear you say that," their mother replied, "but The Hunter didn't believe that Goldie was a spirit bear when we informed him."

Rose saw disappointment cross Roland's face. She quickly added, "But he told us that Goldie acted like a spirit bear, so he may be a half-breed."

The prince smiled at her. "Perhaps he is." He lifted his eyes towards the sun for a moment, then turned to their mother. "It is getting late, and I must return before it gets too dark. May I return another day?"

"Of course!" The reply was a little too enthusiastic. "I mean, I would like the chance to repay you for saving my daughters."

"Think nothing of it. I would gladly protect Rose again. And Snow."

The three women laughed, then Roland said his goodbyes and walked back into the woods.

Rose watched him the longest, holding her gaze until well after he had vanished into the shadows. When she looked away, she saw that her mother had already gone back inside, and her sister was staring at her with a slight grin on her lips.

"You like him, don't you?" Snow asked. Rose blushed and instinctively thought to deny the claim, yet she couldn't bring herself to. Snow laughed softly. "Don't worry. I'll let you tell Mother about your ranger's secret when you're ready."

"Thanks." Rose said sarcastically, then she chuckled to herself. When she spoke again, it was genuinely from the heart. "And also thank you for letting us believe we were alone. It was a pleasant talk."

"You're welcome." Snow smiled warmly. "I knew you'd find your prince someday."

Rose laughed. "You did. I just didn't expect him to be an actual prince." They laughed together, then took their aedelis gatherings inside to await their mother's appraisal.

Chapter 33

Roland had maintained his dignified stride only until he was sure he was out of sight. He then turned from the direction of Fernglen and made his way back to where he had saved Rose Red and Snow White, moving at a pace that he thought would make a horse envious.

Part of his energy came from the excitement of claiming the direwolf he'd killed, but he couldn't deny the greater power came from Rose and the mystery she presented. He'd met many young women for a second time owing to his station as the crown prince. Each was unique; some brought joy when he saw them again, some dread, and many brought with them no potent feelings whatsoever.

Rose's encounters surpassed them all. Of that, Roland held no doubts. His body felt light as the evening breeze and his mind was racing with thoughts of what he might do when he got the chance to meet her again.

I guess this is what Werner meant by falling for a lady.

Once he returned to the site of the skirmish, he started investigating everything he could find in the evening light.

His feet carried him first to the direwolf. He had never seen one during his hunts in the north, but he had seen their hides. Looking at the wolf he'd killed, there was no doubt that it was one of the North Beasts.

On closer examination, he was right when he had told the girls that this was one of the largest wolves he'd ever faced. It was the largest he'd killed by a wide margin, and unless his memory was becoming flawed by the feelings of love, this was not the largest of the four wolves. The sisters were beyond lucky to be alive.

Roland lifted his prize over his shoulder, noting that it was at least threefold heavier than Snow. By all accounts, he would have plenty to tell of today's search back in Fernglen.

But he couldn't leave just yet; Rose's passing mention of the dwarf was still firmly in mind. The description had fit the small frost dwarves from the north, whom Roland had been told were the most secretive of all dwarves. The Hunter didn't hold a high opinion of them, nor did the mountain dwarves Roland was more familiar with. Roland had never followed up the revelation of the dwarf being here, letting the conversation with Rose flow as naturally as he could manage, but now he was free to look for any clues the creature may have left.

He set the direwolf down and paced around the clearing. The fallen log was there, and a small tuft of white hair was still stuck exactly where Rose had described it.

Roland looked around the tuft for the tracks of the dwarf but found none. He also found the tracks of a massive bear that had wandered onto their battlefield soon after they had left. Aside from that, and the hatchet that Rose had left behind, nothing else gave a witness to the dwarf being there at all.

This troubled him greatly. From Rose's description of the dwarf, there should have been some tracks around the size of a rabbit's hind paws. Yet aside from the undeniable tuft of beard, there wasn't a trace that the dwarf even existed.

"It's like he's a ghost," Roland said quietly to himself. There was something profoundly unsettling that there was a creature like the dwarf that he couldn't track. That didn't bode well, given what he knew the creatures were capable of.

He then chuckled to himself to ease the tension. "First a mysterious bear, and now a stuck-up dwarf," he whispered to himself, as though worried his words might somehow carry on the wind to Rose's ear. "What wonder will you have for me the next time we meet? Maybe a roc?"

Roland laughed loudly at the thought. Leaving that question unanswered, he cast his gaze to the bear tracks. Nothing about them caused him concern, save for perhaps their size. Their owner had to be the largest bear he'd come across. Even the spirit bear tracks he'd crossed in the north paled in comparison.

The tracks wandered up onto the site in a hurry; then once in sight of the place, it investigated both the dead direwolf and the tuft of the dwarf's beard before it seemed to follow his and Rose's tracks. Curious, Roland followed the trail but found that it only lasted for a few steps before the bear had wandered off towards the lakes.

Roland glanced towards the sun. Given the time of day, it was probable that the bear had been on its way to catch a fish from the mountain streams when it found this small battlefield and had merely taken a glance at what had happened.

There was more than one thought in Roland's mind that the bear could be Goldie, the spirit bear. He wanted to follow the tracks, but Roland could tell that they were already several hours old. The bear had come upon the place not long after he and the girls had left, and night would fall before he had a reasonable chance to find the bear near the lake.

Roland made a note of the spot and of the bear's possible domain, then retrieved his direwolf prize. Seeing that the direwolf tracks headed towards Fernglen, he had the wolf over his right shoulder while he firmly held his bow in his left hand. If the rest of the pack was nearby, he would be ready for them.

It wasn't long before he tossed the direwolf aside and readied his bow. Two other blue-gray shapes were laying down up ahead.

Roland slowly approached them. They were indeed direwolves, and one of them still had Roland's arrow lodged in its shoulder. Yet as he got closer, it was clear his arrow wasn't the injury that killed it.

He took a slow breath. Three sets of direwolf tracks converged on those of the bear. Who had attacked first was unclear, but it had left these two dead and the third fleeing with a bloody trail in its wake. The bear tracks had only a few marks of blood for the first few steps, then the dirt had either covered its source or the direwolf blood had dried.

Roland thought back to where the bear started following his and Rose's tracks. If such a beast had attacked while he was holding Snow, Roland was certain that it would not have ended well. Mentally, he berated himself for being so cavalier. Even with two daughters of a North Hunter, the forest was still not a place to lower his guard.

More alert than he had been since his reunion with Rose, Roland again picked up his direwolf kill and set his course for the manor.

The twilight had fully set in when he returned to the manor. He greeted Lord Arrenton's servants at the gate, who, after overcoming the surprise of the direwolf, informed him that the lord and his wife were washing up before dinner.

"That's fine. I should clean up as well after my hunt today."

"Did you find any sign of Prince Werner?" one asked.

Roland held his tongue as an idea formed. Once he was certain of it, he replied, "I found no sign of Werner. But I do have a request for one of you."

"Your majesty?" The servants looked at one another for a moment.

"Do you know someone who is good at gathering aedelis plants?"

"Jacob would," one of them said.

Jacob gave the man a look, then replied, "Yes, I know a few people in the town and on the other side of the forest who gather aedelis and menulia."

"Tell them I want the best cuttings they can provide by tomorrow evening."

The servant gave him a confused look. "May I ask why, your majesty?"

Roland could not withhold a grin as he created a story. "I have taken a sudden interest in them, but don't know the proper method to gather them. I would like the best I can find so that I may study the plant."

"Prince Roland, if you want the best cuttings of aedelis, they come from a widow on the north side of the valley. She lives somewhere in the forest and only ever brings the finished dye to market, but I assure you her plants would be the best you're looking for. Her dyes are without equal within a week's ride."

How much should I wager that he's speaking of Rose and Snow's mother? "Do you know where she lives in the forest?"

Jacob glanced away. "No, I don't. Forgive me for bringing it up."

"It's alright, Jacob. Gather what you deem best from the local cutters. Fill my satchel full of cuttings and that will suit my purposes. I will view them tomorrow evening after I return."

The servant bowed, and Roland continued on to his room. "Tell Lord Arrenton to not hurry himself and that I will be down to dine with him after a while."

Roland closed the door and smiled. *To study the plant indeed. Only, not the aedelis plant.*

Chapter 34

Snow was outside with her sister, getting ready for another long day of gathering. It had been three days since their encounter with the direwolves, and to alleviate their mother's fears, the girls had gone to another patch on the other side of the woods yesterday.

It was proving to be a productive place to gather. This spring's cuttings from that patch of menulia were some of the best that their mother had ever worked with.

Their mother's mood had markedly improved since that first trip. Some of that was because she was working the craft that had defined much of her life, but Snow was more than aware that it was also the sudden presence of Roland, and Rose's admirable but futile attempts to hide her affection.

Snow felt convinced that part of the reason her mother had allowed them to continue going into the woods was so that Rose might run into the prince again, despite sending them away from where the direwolves had attacked.

Snow hoped for it, too. Her plan to help Rose by becoming a student of the forest was working, but it had nearly got them both killed by the direwolves. The prince had been the only thing that had saved them, and now Snow hoped they would keep crossing paths to fully break Rose of her terrors.

It took great effort for Snow to remember not to tell their mother about Roland's royal bloodline. She knew that their mother would be stunned by the news, but it was Rose's secret to tell when she believed the time was right. Snow's will could wait, even if her tongue didn't want to.

At any rate, it was an amusing irony to see how her sister, who had begun looking down on Snow's love of fairy tales as they grew older, was now living one out before her eyes. A mischievous smirk broke onto Snow's face as she dreamed of how their third meeting would go. Fairy tales had a habit of using threes for significant events.

"Hello, the house!"

Snow saw Rose's head spin. Smiling, she turned to see the prince walking up to their cottage. He still had his bow and sword, but this time, he had a large satchel over his shoulder. Snow was certain that it contained a gift for Rose, and she hoped she would get to see what was inside when Rose opened it.

"Roland!" Rose barely held back her delight at saying his name. Snow turned her gaze to their mother, who had a knowing grin.

Roland wore a smile that was both happy and nervous. Snow didn't believe that the prince had any penchant for nerves from the talk he'd had with Rose while Snow had pretended to be asleep. Snow tried to hide a grin. The prince must be stepping out of his routine with whatever was on his mind. *A good sign.*

"How are you doing today?" Roland asked, directing the question at her mother.

She smiled at him. "The day has started well, Roland. It's gotten a little better with your presence, though." He turned a little red at the compliment.

He's definitely the solitary type of prince. Snow thought.

"You flatter me." Roland remarked with a slight bow, then he held up the satchel to her. "This is for you."

Snow couldn't hide her surprise that the gift was for her mother, then felt her jaw drop as the prince pulled out bundles of aedelis from the satchel. "I've heard you are a master dyer, so I thought I would bring some aedelis when I came this morning."

Her mother was at a loss for words. Snow was no better, still stunned at what the gift was. It therefore fell to Rose to answer the prince. "Thank you very much, Roland. Snow and I were just about to go out and gather some menulia plants ourselves." She looked at the cuttings, then eyed Roland. "You obviously need some practice, though. Most of these were not quite mature enough to be gathered."

"Forgive my inexperience." Roland replied, his eyes showing no disappointment at the appraisal. "Perhaps you could teach me?"

All three of them gasped, though Snow thought their mother may have been the loudest. A smile creep across Snow's face at the exchange. Roland was making the most of the opportunity Rose's words had given him. He may even have planned for that exact reaction.

Her sister's delightful smile told Snow that the proposal was what Rose wanted. As if they had spoken as much in their minds, both Roland and Rose turned to her mother, who hadn't yet recovered.

A moment passed, then her mother sighed with a smile. "I suppose this would be enough for Rose to cover for your 'training' expedition."

"I'm grateful." Roland then turned to Rose. "When would you like to go with me?"

Rose glanced at their mother, who nodded. Rose smiled at Roland. "I can leave right now if that's fine with you."

"Your terms are acceptable." Roland said with a grin.

Rose beamed at the answer, then she hurried inside. The act confused Snow. All their gathering supplies were already sitting outside.

"I trust you will look after her," her mother said.

Roland put a hand over his chest and bowed slightly. "I will guard her with my life. No harm will come to her."

"I'm glad to hear it." She then lowered her voice. "Rose is quite taken with you."

He grinned. "The feeling is mutual."

"Good."

Rose reappeared from the cottage. In her hand was Roland's scarf. "I forgot to return this to you when you were here the other day."

The prince took the scarf from her hand and deftly tied it around his neck. "Thank you. There were a few evenings where I was missing its warmth. Hopefully, it served you well."

"It did," she replied, then before Snow or her mother could ask any more about the scarf, Rose picked up her satchel and took a few steps towards the tree line. "May we begin?"

Roland chuckled. "I'll follow your lead."

Snow watched the two go. Roland had his even strides, while Rose gave the impression that she was walking on air beside him. Snow's heart fluttered. This was the third meeting. *Surely* -

"Snow." her mother whispered.

"Yes, Mother?" she whispered back.

"I want you to follow them. Make sure your sister doesn't end up doing anything foolish."

"But what about the cuttings?"

Her mother chuckled and lifted a bundle from the satchel. "Roland brought more than enough for the two of you to carry in a week, and from the look of it, Rose was overly harsh in her assessment. You two could probably stay here for a few weeks for what I could make out of this bushel."

It was indeed an impressive number of cuttings. Snow glanced towards where Rose and Roland had disappeared. "But what if I get caught? That may ruin their time together."

"Just stay at a distance and don't get lost, like when you followed Goldie."

"Okay, Mother. I'll keep my eyes on them."

"And Snow?" her mother's voice had dropped to a more serious tone.

"Yes?"

"Keep an eye out for Goldie as well. He may take exception to Rose being around a strange man and try to run Roland off."

"Or Roland will fight..." Snow caught her breath before she could finish the joking remark. Roland had shown no fear when he jumped into the fray against the direwolves. Even though Roland had said he knew of the laws against hunting spirit bears and that he thought Goldie might be one, would the prince allow an unknown bear to get anywhere near Rose?

Roland might even kill Goldie by accident, since Goldie didn't look like a spirit bear.

She nodded, understanding what her mother meant. "I'll do my best." She then took her headscarf off and handed it to her mother. "So that they'll have a harder time spotting me."

Her mother laughed softly. "Good luck."

Snow gave her a smile, then followed her sister and the prince.

Chapter 35

"So, what are your actual intentions for this expedition?" Rose asked after the two were out of sight.

Roland looked at her and smiled. "Well, my intentions are twofold. The first is that I want to get to know you more."

Rose felt her cheeks burn a little at his words. "And the other reason?"

"The second is to see if perhaps you can lead me to Goldie."

That took her by surprise. "What do you want Goldie for?" she asked slowly, intrigued by what his answer would be.

"He may be able to lead to Werner, or at least to where he left Werner."

She tilted her head a little. "Do you still believe that Werner is alive? Hasn't it been weeks since he disappeared?"

Roland nodded. "If a spirit bear is involved, yes."

"And what makes you so sure Goldie is the one who found him?" She knew The Hunter believed that Goldie wasn't a spirit bear, yet she didn't want to crush Roland's hopes either.

The prince took a few moments before he replied. "Spirit bears are solitary creatures. I've heard that you only see two adults together during mating season up north. I believe two of them coming south would be unusual, even in the wake of a roc's storm."

Rose nodded. *Father said as much in a few of his stories.* "If that's the case, I can help you look for him now. He shouldn't be too hard to see in the woods. That coat of his will stand out."

For a moment, Roland raised an eyebrow at her. "I'm curious about something."

"What?"

"You call it the woods; I know it as a forest. How do you distinguish between the two?"

Rose couldn't hold back a soft laugh. Of all the questions that Roland could have asked, she never would have thought of that. "My father always referred to it as the woods. He said that while it may seem big, this forest wasn't anywhere near the size of the northern forests. So, he always called it the woods." She then shrugged and said, "I guess it just became a habit for us to call it the woods as well."

Roland nodded his head. "That's reasonable. I've heard the same from The Hunter."

Rose held her tongue. Questions of Roland's connection to The Hunter played out in her mind, but she didn't know which one to ask first. It felt foolish to ask how he knew The Hunter, given that the high chieftain visited the royal court often enough when he came south.

Rose wanted to ask about how Roland got the scarf, but what if it was simply a gift of friendship like her mother had suggested? Roland was clearly a capable hunter in his own right, but would that be enough for an outsider to gain such a token?

Or, she thought as she remembered what Snow had said that night, *is he the one who underwent the hunts? The one the king and The Hunter spoke for?* It would certainly make sense for a prince to be given such an opportunity.

"Do you have any idea where Goldie would go during the winter?" Roland asked, breaking the long silence.

Rose glanced over at him and shrugged. "His tracks toward the end of winter always headed towards the lake. Maybe he's in the hills behind it."

"Is there any aedelis on the way there?"

"Yes. Why?"

"I think it would seem bad if we returned to your mother with nothing to show for our 'expedition'."

Rose laughed, then pointed to a hillside some distance away. "There's usually a good patch on that hill. We can search over here and then stop up there around lunch."

"Sounds like a good plan to me." The two then spent the rest of the morning searching for any sign of either Werner or Goldie's tracks. They had no luck in the endeavor, but Rose could see that Roland was enjoying himself. Even as the sun climbed towards midday and they reached the aedelis patch, the prince never lost the grin on his face.

After they ate their food, Rose and Roland turned their attention to appeasing her mother. The prince was a quick hand once he knew what to look for, and within an hour, they had a sufficient pile of cuttings for Rose to carry in her satchel. "I think that should be good."

"Need any help packing the cuttings?" Roland asked as he stowed his dagger.

Rose shook her head. "I can manage this part on my own. I don't want them crushed too badly before we get back."

"Alright." Roland stood up and grabbed his bow. His eyes settled on a target tree, and he calmly loosed his arrows at it. Once five struck in and around the prominent knot, he walked over and retrieved the arrows, then repeated the process. Rose tried to concentrate on storing the cuttings properly, but soon she was simply watching the display of marksmanship.

"May I try?" she asked after the sixth volley was being walked back.

"Sure." Roland replied, then he motioned for her to meet him halfway. "The bow is pretty heavy, though."

Like Father's? She took the bow from Roland's hand, and he handed her an arrow. To prove she knew what to do, she quickly nocked it and adjusted her grip. Roland stood behind her back shoulder, letting her attempt the shot without offering his assistance while being positioned to offer critique.

Rose went to draw back the bow. At first, she struggled against the power in its limbs, but slowly the arrow found its way back to her cheek. The slow draw compared to Roland's hurt Rose's pride. It made her feel weak.

Once she believed she'd compensated for the bow's strength, Rose loosed the arrow. The force of the bow threw her aim wildly as it sprang back into form. Her arrow landed far beyond and to the left of the tree.

Roland chuckled. "Not bad, but I think you need a lighter bow."

"I know," Rose said as she handed the bow back. "At least I could draw yours. It's lighter than my father's bow, and I couldn't even string his." Then, worried that Roland may take offence, Rose added. "Yours feels good in my hand, though. It's very well made."

"You have a good feel for a bow's quality." Roland motioned to his bow. "This one comes from your people as well."

"Really?" Once again, she wondered at the strange relationship the prince had with her people. Rose decided now was the chance to press the issue. "How are you so familiar with my father's people? I can believe that you would know The Hunter simply because he and your father are friends, but from the way you talk and the gifts you've received, there must be more than that."

"That's an old story." Roland chuckled and motioned to sit down. "It was when I was a young boy, maybe ten or eleven, and I thought I could hunt in the forest just as well as any of my father's rangers. I'd practiced enough with a bow that I knew I could hit a buck at a good range, so one day I slipped out of the castle in Evesham before dawn and happened upon a small herd.

"There was a magnificent buck among the herd, but there was also a smaller one who would strike the does when the large buck wasn't looking. I decided I would kill that one, and so I drew back and loosed my arrow at him. I hit him right in the side and the entire herd fled when they heard my bow."

"I was feeling pretty good about myself when I heard a yowl behind me. I spun around to see a big mountain lion crashing down next to me. At first, I panicked and lost all my arrows when I upset my quiver, so I reached for my knife. A moment later, I realized the lion wasn't moving. Then I saw the red arrow shaft.

"When I looked towards where I thought the arrow might have come from, The Hunter was standing right there, silent as death itself. He looked down at me, and I wasn't sure what to make of the look he gave me. It was at once angry and curious. The Hunter then asked me my name. I told him who I was, and that I had gone out to prove I could hunt as well as a ranger. He then asked why I had taken the smaller buck, and I answered I had chosen that one because it seemed like it was harming the others.

"Then The Hunter smiled and said, 'Well done, hunter. Remember this though; always be aware of your surroundings. You are not the only hunter in the forest.' He then threw that lion over his shoulder like it was a rabbit and we followed the trail of my buck until we found where it had died. He then carried it too, and we returned to the castle."

The prince laughed as he pictured the scene of his return. "My father and mother were terrified when they learned what had nearly happened to me, but The Hunter said he would take me under his wing whenever he came south until I was old enough to go out on my own."

He exhaled and looked out at the trees. "I've been in love with the forests ever since. Its beauty and its danger. I feel better among the trees than anywhere else." Roland ran his thumb along the hem of the red scarf reverently. His eyes met hers, a grin spreading across his face. "Not a fitting passion for the heir to the throne, but true nonetheless."

Rose smiled softly. "Maybe, but it suits you." She couldn't help but marvel at the story. It would fit right alongside the ones her father had told her and was also strikingly similar to how The Hunter had saved her from the direwolf, but it was what Roland said about how he viewed the forest after nearly being killed that stood out to her. Her magic and heritage protected her while she was growing up in the woods, yet the direwolves had shaken her to her very core. Roland had neither gifts, yet he had responded by falling in love with the potential danger.

"I still can't believe you're really a prince." She said idly.

The comment struck Roland, for he drew back into his thoughts to mull the statement over. Rose wasn't sure what part of her words had caused it, nor what his feeling about those words may be.

Perhaps it was that he thought she believed him to be lying about his tales, but she was certain that he was telling the truth. She'd been watching his eyes, and like he had said when they'd first met in the snow, she believed his eyes weren't lying to her.

"... did I say something wrong?" she finally asked.

Roland turned his eyes towards her. They cleared with unspoken laughter. "No, no. It was simply a stray thought." He smiled and stood. "Let's keep looking. We don't have long before I should get you back home."

Rose glanced at the sun. It was about halfway down the afternoon sky already. "I guess so. Let's head to the other side of the lake. You may find a fresher track over there."

Roland nodded. He went to lead her down the hill, but paused for a moment. The prince smirked. "Don't turn around too quickly, but so you're aware, someone's been behind us this whole time." His eyes then glanced over her shoulder before he took the lead in going around the lake.

She tilted her head at the remark, then noticed that he chose a path that let her look back in the direction his eyes had lingered. Rose cast a quick glance that way, and she immediately knew whose cloak was attempting to hide in the brush.

How long have you known she was following us? She left the question unasked, feeling safer by knowing that Roland was taking The Hunter's advice to heart.

They continued their search along the side of the lake and into the low hills beside it, though they moved at a slower pace than before so that Roland could keep Snow in view. Yet, as the sun hung low in the sky, the two found themselves on a low rise overlooking the lake, with no signs of Goldie having come this way.

Roland decided it would be of little use for them to go on any further. "Even if we find a track now, there's hardly a chance I could find him before nightfall, and I'd rather approach him during the day."

"That's probably a good idea. I'm sorry we couldn't find Goldie today. I'm sure you'd like him," Rose said as they looked across the waters. It was looking like it would be a beautiful evening. A few fluffy clouds dotted the sky, and there wasn't a hint of a breeze. The air still had some early spring chill to it, but Rose found it pleasant. She turned to the prince. "Though now I wish I had let you follow me back when we first met. It may have saved you a lot of searching."

Roland breathed a laugh. "True, but I hadn't fully decided if he was a spirit bear yet or not, and even then, I would have worried my father even more if I hadn't returned that night."

"Oh? Why's that?"

"He arrived in Fernglen that afternoon. Partially, it was to inquire about how my search was going, but he also intended for me to return to court. If I had stayed out, the royal court would have wondered if I was now lost as well. As it was, meeting you and learning about Goldie has bought me more time to search for my brother."

Rose smiled. "I'm glad he let you keep searching. If you hadn't, those direwolves would have killed us."

"I'm glad, too. I wanted to meet you again." Roland then laughed softly. "Though I will say that meeting you has proven to be quite the experience."

Rose tilted her head, eyeing him curiously. "How so?"

"Well, it's not every day a prince meets a maiden in the snowy forests whose sister is riding a bear. And then the next time we meet, I'm saving you and your sister from direwolves. I can safely say that none of the ladies of court have provided such interest."

Rose felt her cheeks burn at hearing Roland comparing her favorably to the nobility. She had never considered herself alongside them since her life was so different from theirs.

Though, she supposed, *that may be why Roland enjoyed our meetings so much.* "I guess that's true. I will admit that I'm glad today hasn't been quite so..." she almost said 'exciting', but didn't want Roland to think that he was boring her, "... so dangerous."

He chuckled at her choice. "I can't argue with that. It has been nice to just be with you."

She stepped beside him. "I agree." They stared into each other's eyes, slowly drawing closer together. The breeze gently tugged at them, but otherwise, the moment seemed perfect.

"No, no, no!" a shrill voice cried out in the distance before it dropped too low to make out what it was saying. They both turned towards it and saw a tiny figure hopping about in the reeds along the shore.

"Is that...?" Roland's voice trailed off.

"Yes, that's the dwarf." Rose said, then she spied another figure hurrying to the dwarf's aid, her blue cloak flowing behind her.

Rose ran after Snow.

Roland was right beside her.

Chapter 36

Snow exhaled loudly. Everything felt like it hurt. Her feet, her legs, her lungs. The beating of her heart made it sound as though it could burst through her chest. There had been no sign of Goldie that Snow could tell, but whatever Rose and Roland were doing was not simply going to cut aedelis. Snow didn't believe that the two had seen her yet, but she was also barely able to keep up.

The early morning had passed without too many complaints. The pair talked as they maintained a slow pace towards the aedelis patch. Snow simply needed to stay out of sight and daydream about Roland carrying Rose off to his castle.

All that changed when they made some unheard agreement, drifting apart and moving quicker now that they weren't in constant speech. It took Snow a while to realize that they were on parallel paths looking for any signs of Goldie. She had to try even harder to stay out of two separate lines of sight.

Rose was leading Roland all over the woods, and Snow was struggling to keep up. There had been several times Snow had lost sight of Rose and Roland and had run to get them back in her sights, only to have to scramble for cover as the two had stopped just over the rise or around the bend. By the time they'd actually reached an aedelis patch and stopped to gather and eat, Snow felt like she was ready to sleep for an entire week.

It was by luck that she hadn't fallen asleep when the two began their search again. Snow felt her body strongly argue to rest a while longer, but she forced herself up. It was a small mercy that the pair decided they would search along the side of the lake where the land was gentler. There was also less brush for her to hide behind, so she had to follow from a greater distance.

A few hours later, when the two finally stopped and were gazing over the lake, Snow sank to the ground in exhaustion. She didn't want to think about having to still walk home that evening. Yet, as she watched them, with the sky in the first stages of the sunset hues and the lake barely stirring down below, Snow could feel their attraction slowly pulling them closer together.

Maybe this is where they kiss for the first time! Snow smiled at the thought, then tried to sneak even closer to get a better view.

A movement near the shore caught her eye. When she turned, Snow could barely withhold a laugh at the sight of the dwarf hopping along the shore with his beard pointed comically towards the water. She watched him hop about, then grab onto a protruding rock. His beard kept pulling him towards the water, and Snow soon realized that the poor dwarf had gotten a fishing line tangled in his beard. Forgetting to watch for Rose's kiss, she hurried over to the dwarf just as he lost grip on the rock.

"AH!" the dwarf exclaimed, grasping for anything to hold on to.

Snow reached out and caught his hand. "I've got you."

"Ow! My beard! Pull that fish in and save my beard."

Snow tried to pull against the fish, but the muddy shore was causing her to slide and nearly fall. The dwarf kept yelling in pain as the fish tried to go deeper into the lake.

Rose and Roland soon ran up to them. "What happened?" Rose asked.

"What kind of fool are you!?" the dwarf exclaimed. "Can't you see that blasted fish is trying to drown me?"

"Help me hold him." Snow said. Rose hurried to help Snow while Roland grabbed the line and pulled against the mighty fish. Yet despite his strength, Roland couldn't seem to gain his footing on the muddy shores and all four were being pulled towards the water.

"Rose, cut the line!" he shouted.

"NO!" the dwarf cried. "You'll lose me my dinner if you do."

Roland kept fighting the fish, but his eyes turned to the dwarf. They were stern, with a determined fire behind them. "Do you want me to let go and let the fish eat you?" he said in a threateningly calm voice.

"Of course not!" the dwarf replied, "But -"

"Rose, cut the line."

Rose already had her knife out and looked at Snow. Understanding the look, Snow nodded and took a firm hold on the dwarf. A moment later, Rose cut the line free.

"NOO!"

Snow expected that Roland would drop the line, but instead he wrapped it around his wrist in a fluid motion and dashed along the shoreline to the rock that the dwarf had grabbed at earlier. Setting his foot against it, he slowly reeled the fish in by wrapping the line between his forearms. Snow wondered if it hurt to have the line cutting into his skin, but then she remembered the chain mail under his jerkin. Roland would be fine.

"Well, at least someone has a brain among you three." The dwarf huffed and looked to his feet. "Ah, my shoes are ruined! Just my luck running into you two."

Rose turned on the dwarf. "If it wasn't for Snow, you'd have already been dragged into the water."

"Pish-posh," the dwarf said with a wave of his hand, then he tried to untangle the fishing line from his beard. "Oh, my poor beautiful beard. How these fools have fouled you so."

Us? Snow thought. *Why does he blame us?* Snow looked at her sister and could see the incredulous look on her sister's face at the remark, but Snow motioned for her to be quiet before she made a reply. Instead, they split their gaze between Roland's struggle with the fish and the dwarf's futile attempts at freeing the fishing line from his beard.

"How did you tangle your line like this?" Roland jested as he nearly had the fish on the shore. "There are knots all along it."

"Never you mind that! Just finish catching that stupid fish. Oh, my poor beard and shoes..." The dwarf continued his futile attempts to pull the line out of his beard.

Snow tried to help the dwarf, but the little man shouted and complained at each slight tug. "OW! Who taught you manners? That hurts."

"I'm sorry, but -"

"BAH! You and your sister are no help to anyone. Oh, my poor beard."

At this, Snow saw her sister's face sour, and Rose replied mockingly, "You could always cut it off and start over."

"AND DEFACE MYSELF?!" the dwarf exclaimed. "Have you no shame!?" The little man reached for a nearby stick and went to swing it at Rose.

Rose put her hand up to protect herself, but Roland stepped in the way and caught the stick. "Enough!" he said forcefully as he ripped it out of the dwarf's grasp.

"Oh, you're in league with these hussies, are you?" The dwarf shook his fist at Roland. "I should get you as well."

"Is that a threat?" The prince's voice went dark, and the fire in his eyes shifted to cold fury.

The dwarf lowered his hand as the eyes locked onto him, though he still spat venom when he spoke. "Who do you think you are, you buffoon?"

Roland touched his dagger. "I am Crown Prince Roland of Thistledown, and I think you will take your fish and leave now."

For once, the dwarf was at a loss for words. "Well... I uh..." He muttered to himself as he walked over to where the fish was now lying on the shore. The dwarf took out his small dagger and cut the fish open. "Wretched interlopers. Ruined my beard and my shoes."

Snow watched as he cut towards the fish's stomach and reached inside. When the hand returned, it was holding a bag. "What's in there?" she asked.

"Never you mind, you..." the dwarf didn't finish the threat as he caught Roland's eyes again. He then stamped his feet impetuously and said. "My staff would've dealt with you." He then turned and fled south along the reedy shore, though he missed that two small orbs fell out of the bag as he did so.

They waited until he disappeared, then the three of them moved towards the two orbs. Snow gasped. They were pearls, the likes of which she had only seen being sold by merchants from the east.

"Where did he get those?" Roland and Snow asked in unison.

"I don't know," Rose answered, "but that's the second treasure he's taken with him."

Snow perked up. "That's right. He had those rubies and coins under the tree when we saw him the first time."

Roland didn't reply, instead walking over to where the fish was laying.

"What do you think the treasure means?" Snow asked. "Clearly it's what he was after instead of the fish itself."

"It's the same as when he lied about cutting wood for his fire." Rose looked at her sister. "Snow, I'm getting a bad feeling about the dwarf."

"So am I." Roland replied. The girls looked to see that he was kneeling, with one hand pointing to the ground. "I think I know why he kept mentioning his shoes."

Snow and Rose walked over to see a trail of little footprints in the soft ground. Snow tilted her head in confusion. "What of it? He's just leaving tracks."

"I went back to where Rose said the dwarf was when the wolves attacked you," he explained. "I found the tuft of his beard right where she said it would be, but there were no prints. Seeing this," he motioned to the tiny footprints, "I think the shoes were enchanted to leave no trail behind."

He stood and looked sternly at Snow. "I don't know much about magic, but I would suggest avoiding the dwarf from now on. Magic can do many things, and a creature as ungrateful as him may cause you great harm."

"But he hasn't yet," Snow replied.

"Because he doesn't have his staff." Rose answered slowly.

Snow was about to ask why that would be important, but she recalled the stories in her mother's books. Dwarves were beings whose cultures revolved around magic, not unlike the North Hunters, but dwarven magic was of an entirely different nature, more similar to that of fairies and trolls. From her mother's tales, the magic could even change the shape of things, or people. "But why would he use his magic on us? All we've ever done is try to help him."

"Not the way he sees it." Roland's voice had a menace in it, and when Snow turned, she saw a look in his eyes. The intensity with which Roland was looking down at the dwarf's trail reminded her of the direwolves. She inadvertently took a step back at the sight.

Snow turned to Rose. Her sister was also looking at the eyes, and the intensity didn't seem to bother Rose. In fact, the initial worry her sister had shown was turning into a thin smile the longer she watched them.

Roland exhaled, and the eyes returned to their normal state. He wrapped his arms around the great fish and lifted it over his shoulder. "Now then, if you two don't mind, I think we should get moving and surprise your mother with a late dinner offering."

The girls laughed, but as they took the first steps towards the cottage, Snow felt her legs tighten up. She fell clumsily to the ground and laughed at herself.

"What's wrong, Snow?" Rose asked worriedly.

She looked up and smiled to calm her sister's concerns. "My legs aren't used to chasing you all over creation."

They all laughed again, and Roland handed the fish to Rose. "I can carry you back, then."

Rose struggled with the weight of the fish for a while, but once she mimicked Roland and tossed it over her shoulder, she looked to be handling it alright. The prince then asked that Snow ride on his back so that he could keep his bow ready should the dwarf reappear.

Once she'd secured herself, the three began their walk back towards the cottage.

Chapter 37

Where are you going?

The question had plagued Werner ever since he had noticed the pattern the dwarf was following. His foe would wander around seemingly without intent, then when the dwarf found what he was looking for, he would make a straight path into the forest.

Whenever Werner followed the scent, he found himself in a hidden meadow. The dwarf had walked over practically every blade of grass in the meadow from the smell of it, so Werner couldn't determine what the dwarf was doing, but once he was finished with that mysterious work, the dwarf then wandered off again. At the end of the winding new trail, the dwarf would turn back to the meadow again.

The prince first noticed it the day after Snow and Rose had crossed paths with the dwarf. He'd followed the dwarf's scent towards the lake, then he tracked his foe into the night until Werner had stumbled on the meadow.

Not finding the dwarf, he rested nearby until morning and set out again. It had now been the fifth time he had followed the scent trail here in the last two days.

There was something about this meadow. Werner could sense a presence to it that was unsettling. It was the same as the direwolves he'd fought, that there was something unnatural afoot. The dwarf didn't carry that presence, so Werner decided it was something that the dwarf was doing in the meadow. Maybe it was something magical. Maybe it wasn't.

Whatever it was, Werner needed to figure out what the dwarf was up to, and quickly. The answer to that question could mean the end to his months-long hunt.

But do I stay here or keep hunting?

The straightforward answer, that Werner should stay and wait for the dwarf to return, carried a dangerous risk. If the dwarf realized Werner was now stalking the meadow, he would likely move his treasure trove to another place like he had with the winter meeting ground. That would put Werner right back where he was now.

Actually, it would put Werner in a worse position, for if the dwarf had discovered him and acted in that manner, Werner may not know that the dwarf was doing it. Werner might stalk the meadow for days while the dwarf was off to some other place.

I can't risk that. I'll follow the freshest trail and see where it goes. If I find nothing, I'll return here and see what I can learn.

The new trail took him towards the northern hills. There the dwarf had run into his blackbeard friend from winter again, but given the strength of the scents, their meeting had been brief. All that said, the trail couldn't be more than a few hours old.

Werner felt his heart leap at the thought of catching the dwarf today. Even if it had been a constant thought as of late, he clung to that hope without cynicism.

Werner repeated his new mantra. *I will get you. If not today, then tomorrow.*

He took in the dwarf's scent. Once their meeting had concluded, the little man had then gone down the hillside, but instead of going back to the meadow immediately like he had been, the dwarf had gone over towards the lake.

Smiling to himself that he had made the right choice to not trust the meadow, Werner wandered down to where the dwarf had stepped into the water.

Suddenly, the dwarf's scent changed. The prince looked down and saw the imprint in the mud of something large lunging from the waters. Werner checked the scent again and chuckled. *He's startled.*

The dwarf's scent moved on from here, so whatever had attacked hadn't eaten the dwarf. Werner breathed a sigh of relief. He wasn't sure if the curse would lift if something else killed the dwarf, and he didn't want to risk that outcome not working.

He sniffed the air again. The dwarf had taken off toward the meadow but had returned sometime later. Werner moved to where the dwarf had come back to the lake and found a chaotic trail of broken reeds that extended towards the south of the lake. Some reeds looked like something had smashed through them, but as he looked at the reeds closer to the lake from those that were smashed, many of those reeds appeared cut or stripped by something else entirely.

The scene puzzled Werner. If the smashing resulted from whatever had lunged at the dwarf, then what could cause the cutting marks? Maybe the dwarf's dagger, but there were simply too many reeds that were damaged for that to be the answer. There had to be something else going on.

About a hundred yards down from where the damage to the reeds began, Werner found another clue. A fishing rod lay in the mud, with its spool entirely empty. He looked at the reeds and saw that the damage still continued on.

The prince glanced from the rod to the reeds a few times, then laughed. He continued following the damaged reeds, knowing that at the end he may find the dwarf struggling against whatever he had hooked in the lake.

The jovial thoughts of his upcoming triumph changed when he caught five scents emanating from the southwestern shore. One was a fish, two were of the girls, one was that strangely familiar scent...

And the last was the scent of the dwarf.

All were right next to each other.

Werner hurried along the shore. There he found what remained of the dwarf's fishing line, but everyone had already left. The prince looked to the ground. His fears were alleviated when he saw human tracks walking away, though once again Snow's tracks disappeared next to the man the girls were with. The mysterious stranger stoked his jealousy, but Werner forced it from his mind. Courtly games could wait for now. Werner could instead be thankful that the girls had again faced the dwarf and had again walked away unscathed.

Hopefully, they don't cross him again.

He then turned to sniff out where the dwarf might have fled to, but it was only a moment before his hopes soared. *Tracks! He's leaving tracks!* And not only tracks, but two small pearls were barely visible in the mud beside one of the prints. It had to be some of the dwarf's treasure. *Could it be...?*

Werner rumbled through the landscape as he tried to follow the trail before the sun fully set. The dwarf had rounded the lake to the south, then cut east. Right as the light faded, Werner found himself back at the meadow.

Instead of charging into the grass, though, Werner stopped. The dwarf may still be there, but the prince no longer enough light to see him. Werner resolved to keep his decision from earlier in place. So long as the dwarf didn't know that Werner knew of this place, the prince could continue plotting to set an ambush.

But now the ambush would have a new component. If those pearls truly belonged to the dwarf, then it was possible that the dwarf was moving all of his treasure into the meadow. The various trails into the forest must be from the little man gathering his caches that he had hidden for some unknown reason.

Werner recalled the conversation with the second dwarf. The treasure must be part of the deal that the black beard had referred to. If Werner could find that treasure and move it while the dwarf was gone, the dwarf would come looking for it. After all, he had cursed Werner over the mere potential that the prince might be a thief. What would he do if the entire trove were to be taken?

I'll return in the morning. Werner turned and quietly left to find a place to sleep. *Tomorrow will be the day. I can feel it.*

Chapter 38

Roland had kept his eyes alert to any movement in the evening light as they walked back to the cottage, yet nothing appeared. He was thankful for that. Keeping watch for danger had let him idly listen to the sisters. Some of their talk centered on the dwarf and Roland responded with what he knew of frost dwarves, but mainly the sisters were discussing Snow's thoughts on the day's events.

Their discussion allowed him to think about other things. The dwarf's threats drew his ire, but Roland could only dwell on them for a moment before he was again thinking of Rose. The encounter with the dwarf had interrupted the moment above the lake, and Roland found he wanted to create that moment again.

In fact, I want her to meet my mother and father. He thought as they reached the clearing around the cottage.

As they walked up to the cottage, the girl's mother greeted them. "I see Snow needed to be carried again."

"My legs refused to go another step." She replied with a laugh.

Their mother simply shook her head, then regarded the fish that Rose had slung over her shoulder. "And how did you catch this monster?"

Rose set the fish down. "We ran across the dwarf again. He was caught in the line, and we freed him from it, but he threatened us afterwards."

"He did?" She looked at Roland with worry.

The prince nodded. "He mentioned that if he had his staff, he'd do something to us. I think it would be wise to avoid him in the future."

"I agree." Their mother said while picking up the fish with some difficulty. "I dare say this is the largest fish I've seen since their father caught one like it four summers ago."

"It is quite the fish." Roland replied. Then a thought came to mind, and he asked somberly, "How did your husband die?"

Snow and their mother turned slowly to Rose. Her eyes dropped for a moment. "He died two summers ago, when the North Hunters attacked a roc eyrie."

"I'm sorry to hear that." Roland said softly. "I was told about that battle. I didn't realize your father was one of the hunters who fell fighting them."

"He died slaying the largest one." Snow replied with a little forced cheer to her voice.

The prince felt his heart quiver, though he kept the knowledge from showing on his face. He knew the man at once, though he had never learned the man's name. The

Hunter's grandson. That fact alone was enough to strike Roland.

They are The Hunter's great-granddaughters! That means if I were to ask for Rose's hand, -

"What of your family, Roland?" their mother asked. "Do your parents still live in Thistledown?"

Roland put the thoughts away for now as a grin spread over his face. "I suppose they didn't tell you yet?"

She eyed her daughters. "Tell me what?" Roland couldn't quite see Snow's reaction, but he fully saw the smile breaking through Rose's defenses. Rose looked at him and nodded to tell him to reveal his heritage.

He breathed a laugh. "Well, I was born in Thistledown, but my full title would be Crown Prince Roland of Thistledown."

It took every fiber of his being to stop from joining the girls' laughter at their mother's reaction. Her jaw was agape, and the fish fell to the ground with a thud. She hurriedly tried to pick it up. "Forgive me, I -"

Roland held up his hand. "There's no need to apologize. Rose had asked that I keep it a secret from you, and I am quite content with being viewed as a ranger."

Their mother bowed her head in appreciation, though she shot a glance at Rose that landed harmlessly amid Rose's joy. "Would you like to stay for dinner?"

Roland smiled as the anticipation of his answer held their attention. "I would love to stay, but it is getting late, and Lord Arrenton doesn't enjoy keeping his gate open at all hours of the night waiting for me." He bowed to their mother. "I would like to come again, if that is all right with you."

"Of course, my prince!" she said, once again sounding a little too enthusiastic. "You're welcome any time you'd like."

"Thank you." Roland laughed. "Just Roland will do."

Their mother bowed respectfully, and Roland turned to the sisters. "I'll see you two soon," he said, though he knew his gaze lasted far longer on Rose than it did Snow. He was terrible at showing impartiality in her presence.

"Don't wait too long!" Snow exclaimed.

"I'll do my best." He told her. His eyes once again reached Rose, who simply nodded with a barely suppressed smile. He nodded in reply and left for the manor.

This time, the journey passed unnoticed. Roland was in higher spirits than the first time he'd met Rose. It had been a grand day, even with no sign of the bear. The moment just before the dwarf's interruption stood out above them all. He wished to complete that moment soon.

Even so, the dwarf worried him. He knew now that it was indeed a frost dwarf. There was little he knew of the beings, save that they were strong in magic and dismissive of other races. Even the mountain dwarves disdained them, calling them 'gnomes' to distance themselves from their northern cousins.

That one of their kind is here and threatening the girls... I'll have to deal with this quickly.

Roland reached the manor, pondering how he would accomplish such a thing. He walked into the main hall and immediately saw his father and mother standing there. Roland knew in an instant that they were waiting for him.

"Mother!" He called as he went over to embrace her.

"Roland!" she said, then once they had let go of each other, she asked, "Have you found anything?"

"No, not yet." He could see the despair in her eyes and hoped she wouldn't ask anything further about the matter.

"What of your forest maiden?" his father asked.

"I have come across her again." Roland had expected the news to excite his father, but the answer was received with melancholy. "What is it?"

"The high king has called for a tournament in Delriata. We will make plans and alliances for the future while you compete before the other kings and nobles. I've received letters from several of the kings of a marriage alliance with you."

His shoulders dropped in despair. "How soon?"

"We will leave for Delriata tomorrow."

Roland looked away, attempting to contain his emotions. The fate that had once seemed destined for him had reappeared to hold sway over his life. It put him in a cruel position. His father had already received offers for his hand and the times were tense, especially after the roc's storm. With Werner gone, Roland would have to marry to ensure a continuation of their bloodline and stability in their kingdom.

His marriage to a commoner after receiving such advances had all the potential of scandal. It may even lead to a break in the existing network of treaties under the high king.

Rose...

"Give me one more day," he said after a few moments.

"Roland," his father started, but Roland held up his hand.

"You gave me leave to pursue Rose for another week yet. I will accept any decision you make if I cannot find her again tomorrow, but grant me that one day to see if she will accept me."

His father looked hard at him for several moments, then at his mother. Roland didn't take his eyes off his father.

The silence lasted until his father chuckled. "Very well. I can grant you one day, then we will leave together."

"You needn't stay on my behalf." Roland replied.

The king laughed. "Why not? I should like to meet my new daughter-in-law when you bring her back with you."

All three laughed together, and Roland hugged his parents. "I must take my leave. There are things I wish to get ready tonight."

"Go," his father said with a wave of his hand.

"Good luck, Roland," his mother added.

Roland turned and hurried to his room. He was there for only a moment before he left with a tournament bow and quiver in hand. Soon he was knocking on the door of Lord Arrenton's master armorer.

"Alright, alright! Who's beating on my door at this -" the armorer yelled as he swung the door open, then he froze at the sight of Roland. "Oh, Prince Roland. What can I do for you?"

"I need your help in wooing a woman."

The armorer scoffed. "Me? What would I know of wooing a lady fit for you?"

"For one, you can determine if this bow is too heavy for her." Roland said, as he handed the tournament bow to the armorer. The prince then took his bow from his shoulder. "I need your weights to guess at her draw."

"What would a lady want with a bow?" he asked.

"She's from the north." Roland replied.

The man understood at once and rushed to get his weights. He had Roland draw the bow back to where the prince had seen Rose starting to struggle with its power, then he took it to the proper stand and added weights on the string until they reached the draw distance at forty-five pounds. They then assessed the tournament bow.

"It's a bit heavy," the armorer said after saying the weight of fifty-two pounds, "but she'll grow into it soon enough."

"Good." Roland was pleased that he had guessed the right bow to bring. He possessed several bows for the tournaments, all much lighter than the one he carried into the forest yet still capable of dropping large game. Roland had commissioned the bows so that he could be a part of the archery competitions throughout the day rather than a mere few rounds. He'd won many tournaments, but now this bow would be used by his greatest target of all.

"Is there anything else you need from me?" the armorer asked.

"Can you examine it to ensure that there are no defects? I have grown used to my bows and don't have an unbiased eye towards them."

The armorer nodded. "I can do that quickly enough."

An idea sprung to mind. "Can you have someone replace the grip with one stamped with roses?"

The man eyed him for a moment before remembering that Roland was giving the bow away. "I know a man in town who can, though it is late already."

Roland handed him five gold coins. "Will this be enough incentive to rouse him from his bed?"

The armorer gawked. "I should say so!"

"Good." Roland handed him five more. "For your help."

Smiling from ear to ear, the man took the ten coins. "I'd say that's more than fair for the long night ahead of us. We'll finish our work before the mid-night watch ends."

"Thank you. I will return before first light."

"Why so early?"

"It's a fair distance to where she lives. I'd like to start as soon as possible."

The man chuckled. "Very well. Good luck, my prince."

"Thank you." Roland turned and left the armorer to his work. As he headed to his room, he asked a servant to ensure that someone woke him when the mid-night watch ended. Once he reached his room, the prince lay down on his bed and thought of his plans for tomorrow.

There was yet one area near the maidens that he could look for Werner; in the northern hills overlooking the forest, past Rose's cottage. If there was no sign of his brother there, then Roland would have to give up the search for good. There was little else that could be done. Still, Roland had to make that last effort.

Then there was also the matter of Rose Red.

Roland laughed as he felt the anxious energy building within him. He'd be up all night if he dwelled on her. He knew she would appreciate the bow, even if she chose not to follow him back. It would allow her to protect their woods as her father had.

Still, he hoped she would follow him.

Roland could picture how his brother would react to his plan. "Of course, you would give a hunting bow to a lady you fell for," Werner would say as he rolled his eyes, then he would start giving Roland advice on how to woo her into accepting the proposal. Roland would then have rejected all of that advice as romantic nonsense.

I hope you can meet her, Werner.

Tomorrow was the day. Roland would go out early and find a place in those hills to hide the bow, then go for Rose.

Either he would find his brother, or no one would.

Either he would return with Rose having accepted his proposal to be his wife and queen, or he would return alone.

One last chance, Roland. Loose the arrows and see if they strike true.

Chapter 39

The sun had been up for a few hours, and Rose was outside tending to the blooms around her mother's garden with a smile on her face. Snow had yet to roll out of bed. Her mother said that Snow was refusing to get up because her legs felt like lead, and Rose couldn't help but chuckle at the thought.

That's what you get for spying on us.

The thought wasn't malicious. Her mother had told Rose that she'd been the one to have Snow follow them, in case Goldie appeared. "Snow's connection to Goldie is stronger than yours." Her mother had said. "If he decided to attack Roland to protect you, your sister stood the best chance of calming him down."

"Do you honestly think he would have attacked Roland?"

"I don't know. In the end, it didn't matter."

It didn't matter.

Rose hadn't answered her mother, her thoughts immediately pointing to Snow going after the dwarf and all that had occurred afterwards. Therefore, Snow had interrupted the moment with Roland.

But as the morning had progressed and her sister had still not appeared from their room, those thoughts faded as she revisited the prior evening. Both Roland and Rose knew Snow was nearby, yet that hadn't stopped them by the lake. It had been the frantic cries of the dwarf. All Snow had done was try to help the dwarf, which had caused Rose to go after her sister.

And could Rose even blame the dwarf for the distraction? While he was the cause of the interruption, it was with the frantic cries of someone desperately in trouble. The little man may be an ungrateful liar, but that was no reason to let him be pulled into the lake and drowned.

Rose shook her head and laughed softly. *Even if we didn't kiss, Roland did catch quite the dinner for us. Maybe next time...*

She smiled, then turned her focus back to tending the plants while her mother did Snow's chores.

The sun was well into mid-morning before Snow finally emerged from the cottage. Rose could see the slight limp in her sister's steps from the soreness, but Snow's face was as cheery as ever.

"How do your legs feel?" Rose asked.

"They're sore, but the more I walk, the better they feel."

Rose laughed. "It's funny how that works."

"Yeah, but Mother has a sense of humor about it. She asked if I would take the dye she's already bottled to

Middleton and pick up more materials. Sounds like it will be a good year for her."

"Oh?" Rose had heard nothing from their mother about going into town. "Do you want me to go with you?"

Snow smiled mischievously. "I think we both were hoping you had other plans for today."

"I don't even know if Roland will show up today." Rose replied, knowing what they were hoping for. "He's never appeared two days in a row."

Her sister shrugged. "Maybe today he will."

"Maybe," Rose replied with a smile.

Snow then turned her gaze to the north. "I was thinking of something this morning. The Hunter was going to take us north now that it is spring. When do you think he'll come back?"

Rose inhaled and held onto the thought. That had been the plan for them ever since their father had died. Back in the autumn, it hadn't concerned her beyond the knowledge that she might leave and never return to the woods. She would be among hunters and could finish her training. Then she would have a choice to make of remaining in the north or not.

Now though...

"You hesitated." Her sister remarked with a wide grin. "You really do like him, don't you?"

Rose couldn't hold back a smile, but this time there was no embarrassment behind it.

"Hello, the house!"

Roland! The two hurried towards the voice. Snow beat Rose to the oak tree, but Rose slipped past her to reach Roland first. "You returned so soon?"

"I did," he said as he opened his arms. Without thinking, Rose stepped into him, and they embraced. "I was hoping that you would go out with me again to look for Goldie."

"Of course! Let me get my things together." Rose ran back to the cottage, slipping past her mother, who stood in the doorway. She put some bread, cheese, and dried meat into a knapsack, then ran to get her cloak from her room.

She only paused when she caught a momentary glimpse of her father's bow in her mother's room. Rose considered if she could take it or her old training bow with them, to prove that she was capable of hunting like Roland and her father were.

The thought was fleeting. Roland wasn't a North Hunter who might place far more stock in such a thing. Not to mention that it was just yesterday that Rose had said she didn't have the strength to use her father's bow. It was an unnecessary gesture.

When she emerged from the cottage, Rose could see Snow staring in wide-eyed glee towards Roland, and though her mother had her back to Rose, her mother clearly had both hands up to her mouth.

"What is it?" she asked.

All three turned to her. Roland, who had seen her when she had reappeared, replied, "Just news from the court. I'll tell you after we're done searching."

"Okay." Rose didn't fully believe that it was some courtly news given her family's reaction, but she didn't question it. "Should we get going?"

Roland nodded, and the two turned towards the woods. "What do you think of the hills to the north? It's about the only place I haven't searched yet that's nearby."

She gave him a wide smile. "Alright."

Chapter 40

Snow and her mother watched as Rose and the prince walked away with barely contained glee. Roland had told them he had to return to court, and what his intentions were for this outing. Her mother had approved of the plan only a few seconds before Rose had reappeared, and it had taken everything in both of them to not give away any signs of the plan to Rose.

Snow waited until long after they had disappeared before she looked at her mother. "How soon do you think they'll be back?"

Her mother laughed softly enough that her voice didn't have any chance to carry on the wind. "I would expect it will be sometime this evening."

"Why not sooner?"

"He has something else on his mind. I think he will spend as much time as he can to make one last attempt to find his brother, then he will ask Rose at the last moment."

"Oh." Snow replied sadly. She had forgotten about Werner when Roland had mentioned that he had to return to court and wanted Rose to go with him. She dropped her eyes to the ground. "Do you... think Werner made it?"

There was no reply. Snow didn't need one.

After a few moments, her mother sighed and turned to another matter. "Well, are you still up to go to town while I prepare a proper dinner for the occasion?"

Snow nodded. "Yes. I'll have to leave now to make sure Rose isn't home before I get back."

"Good. I have a basket ready with what I've already prepared. Get some food and don't linger too long in Middleton."

She nodded, and the two went inside. Her mother reminded her of the order in which to visit the merchants in Middleton, and what her arrangements with each were. Snow recited the list back twice, then hugged her mother and was on her way.

The sun was reaching the middle of the morning, and Snow was making good time towards town. She had already crossed the dividing river and was walking along its banks with a spring in her step. Roland was planning to ask Rose to marry him, and she didn't want to miss the moment her sister came home. Snow knew that Rose would accept the proposal.

In her mind, she kept track of how long she had left before Rose might be home. Of course, she couldn't know the exact time, but if Roland proposed near evening as her mother expected, then Snow would be home an hour or two before Rose did.

Even so, she was walking as fast as her sore legs would allow. The thought of Rose and Roland together numbed the pain she felt. Her sister was getting the fairy tale story Snow had always hoped for the both of them.

Now that Rose has her prince, maybe I will find mine in the north.

A shadow passed overhead. Snow looked up to see a falcon circling above her. It was a majestic bird, and as she looked closer, she noticed it had blazing orange feathers over its eyes, as though flames were erupting from them, and its tail was more like a swallow's with long outer feathers that grew shorter towards the middle.

A sun-browed falcon? She'd only seen such a bird once, the day her father had gone north the last time. *Is that hunter in the woods?*

The falcon passed over her again, appearing to study her. Snow quickly tried to reach out to it with her bond, thinking of how impressed Rose would be to see the bird again, not to mention Roland.

But the falcon didn't heed her.

It wasn't like with Goldie, where his mind was a mystery too strong for her magic, nor was it like the direwolves, whose very being had resisted being swayed. In trying to sway the falcon, she could feel that it had fixated so strongly on something that a quick attempt at the bond couldn't reach it.

At first she thought to make a stronger attempt, but then she recalled the tales of the falcon's vengeful ways. Snow looked at its legs and saw a tattered cord still dangling from one foot. It was a trained falcon, but it had been a long time since it had seen its master.

It continued on its flight, and Snow stopped to watch. She didn't know when she would see another falcon like it again, and she had some time that she could admire the bird.

The falcon went only a short distance before it flapped its wings and dove to the ground behind a bush.

Snow heard the shrill voice of the dwarf call out from where she saw the falcon dive. Instinctively, she knew the bird was attacking him. Setting the basket down, Snow hurried over to help.

As she rounded the bush, Snow found the falcon had taken hold of the dwarf's staff and was trying to fly away with it. The dwarf had one hand firmly clamped on his staff and the other grasping a root from a stump in the ground. His voice was calling out, "Get away! Get away! Eat someone else, you fool bird!" Snow could also see the end of the staff flickering, as if the dwarf were trying to conjure magic through it, but the struggle was breaking the dwarf's concentration.

Just as she reached the two, the dwarf's grasp on the root failed. The falcon began to carry him off, but Snow reached up and grabbed the dwarf's ankles. The falcon was not strong enough to lift her as well, but it was determined to not let go of the staff. They pulled against one another, with the dwarf crying, "OW! Let go, you hussy! You're hurting me!"

"Let go of the staff." She said.

"You fool girl! Like I would do something so stupid. Let me go! Or else -" His hand slipped from the staff, sending him and Snow tumbling back while the falcon winged away, satisfied that the staff no longer had the dwarf attached to it. The falcon carried the staff over the trees, not letting go while it remained in Snow's sight.

The dwarf was livid. "Now you've done it, girl! My jacket is ruined, and you've lost my staff!"

"I saved your life." Snow tried to reply gently, but her voice carried an edge of frustration.

"As if that matters!" The dwarf scurried over to the stump and pulled out a sack that was hidden within it. A few small rubies fell from a hole in the side, which were hurriedly retrieved by the dwarf. "Even my satchel is torn because of you. And this is the last one I needed." He turned and shook his fist at Snow. "Now my day is properly ruined. If I still had my staff, I'd deal with you right here!"

"But -"

"Not another word from you! You've been a pain in my side since the moment I first saw you and that stupid sister of yours. Be gone and leave me alone!" And with that, the dwarf rushed into the woods, leaving a bewildered and frustrated Snow in his tracks.

The nerve of him! And all I've done is to try and help him.

Snow stared towards where the dwarf disappeared for a while, then she returned to her basket. She tried to put the incident out of her mind. She had saved the dwarf, and she would make it to town and back without further incident.

Today will be a great day, no matter what that dwarf thinks.

Chapter 41

Frustration with the meadow had hit a boiling point hours ago, but Werner was sure that the dwarf had hidden his treasure somewhere nearby. The stench and tiny footprints were all concentrated in this part of the woods. If he could find the treasure trove, then Werner could begin his planned ambush to kill the dwarf and end the curse the prince was under.

His nose worked over the grass and rocks as best it could, his eyes alert for anything that could be a giveaway as to the trove's location. In the back of his mind, he worried that the treasure was being handed off to another dwarf whose prints Werner would never find, but his nose reassured him that no other dwarvish scents were here. *Where is it?*

Time moved on, and Werner was keenly aware that the dwarf could return at any moment. If that happened and Werner didn't find the treasure, the dwarf might spirit the whole trove away the first chance he got. Then

Werner would be back to where he was, without a clue where the dwarf could be hiding.

And Werner wasn't sure what he would do should that-

There!

Werner could see a faint corner in the grass, as though cut by a tiny shovel. The prince chuckled. Though Werner hated the dwarf, he couldn't deny that the little fellow was clever. The square cut of sod was so neatly placed that Werner was sure only the most experienced hunter could have found it, and then only if they were looking for the dwarf's treasure.

He dug his claws into the sod's edge and lifted it, surprised that it was nearly six feet wide. Even more surprising was what lay beneath it; a trove of treasure the likes of which would have made Finley and Mauvelin turn green in envy. Fine cut rubies that captured and enhanced the rays of sunlight, and gold coins so meticulously polished that they reflected every enhanced ray the gems gave off. There were pearls too, though not in nearly the quantity as the former two.

While he stared in awe for a few seconds, Werner's thoughts wandered to what he would do now that he knew where the dwarf's treasure was. Simply piling up the treasure in the meadow wouldn't work. The place was so covered in tall grass and brush that the dwarf could easily sneak in without him knowing, and if Werner were to attack the dwarf, the little creature wouldn't have far to go to find a hiding place.

And Werner had already spent months trying and failing to run him down. There needed to be a better way to catch the dwarf.

Werner huffed. *If I were still human, I would set a trap like we set for the bandits.*

His mind raced, but then an idea formed. Werner smiled as best as his muzzle could, then he put the sod back over the treasure. Turning towards Snow and Rose's cottage, he ran like he rarely had before. There was little time, and the longer he took, the sooner the dwarf might return from whatever foray he was on.

It was days like today where he was glad to be a bear. No man could run half as fast, nor for as long as Werner did to reach the cottage. A true blessing from the curse.

When the cottage came into view, he sniffed the air. The only prevailing scent was of their mother; both Snow and Rose were away, and that familiar fourth scent had gone in Rose's direction.

Despite wanting to see the girls again and perhaps learn who that scent belonged to, the two not being home was probably for the best. *I don't want them following me and having the dwarf curse them as well.*

He rumbled up to the cottage. Werner reached the white rose tree right as the girls' mother came out of the door. "Well, hello, Goldie!" their mother called out to him. "How have you been? The girls haven't seen you in weeks."

Werner shook his head to acknowledge her, then turned his nose towards the cottage.

"Do you want to go inside?"

He nodded, and she stepped aside. Werner lumbered into the cottage, barely listening to what their mother was saying to him. He went to the stack of blankets and took hold of the large quilt that Snow always laid out for him during the winter.

"Why do you want that?" she asked.

Unable to think of how to express his plan, he gently lifted the quilt in his mouth and looked up at her with pleading eyes.

Their mother crossed her arm in a mockingly stern pose. "Will you bring it back?"

He nodded emphatically.

"Will it be in the same condition?"

Werner turned his eyes. *I doubt it...*

Their mother laughed. "I suppose you can take it with you. Just make sure you bring it back when the girls are here. They'd love to see you again." She then straightened up as an idea struck her. "Could you be here tonight?"

Werner shrugged quickly, not wanting to delay his plan any further than he had to. *I hope I can, though it wouldn't be as a bear if I have any say in it.* He then went out the door and was about to run for the hidden meadow.

"Goldie, have you come across a dwarf in the woods?"

Werner turned sharply. He knew the girls had come across the dwarf at least twice, but it was possible that their mother knew more about the dwarf than they did. He nodded and listened for what she had to say.

"What do you know of him?"

So much for that hope. Werner shrugged. It wasn't as though he could tell her all that he had learned about his foe, and even that wasn't much to work with. *Just tell the girls to avoid him until I'm done with him.*

"Well, he keeps saying that if he had his staff, he would harm the girls. Are his threats -"

HE SAID WHAT?! Werner stood up on his hind legs and growled loudly, letting the quilt fall to the ground.

Any qualms that Werner had harbored about killing the dwarf vanished. Though Werner had worried that the girls might face the same fate if they crossed the dwarf, the fact the little man had promised to do so made him a mortal enemy that must be slain.

"Easy, easy," the girls' mother said as she reached up to stroke his cheek calmingly. She sighed. "I guess that's all I need to know. I pray they never come across him again. Can you protect them from him?"

With my life! Werner nodded his head emphatically. He then took the quilt firmly in his mouth and hurried towards the dwarf's treasure. The end of his curse was at hand. *Mark my words, that dwarf will not live to see the suns-*

"Oh, before you go," their mother called to him, "there's a young man with Rose who's been looking for you. He thought that if you are a spirit bear that you may be able to help him find his brother."

Werner eyed her in confusion. *Why would anyone think I could help him find their brother out here? I've been a bear for months now.*

Their mother smiled. "And if you see them, don't try to scare him away. His name is Prince Roland, and ..."

Werner didn't catch what she said after that. His jaw fell open in surprise, letting the quilt thud onto the ground again.

ROLAND!?!? Roland is here?

In a moment, he understood the familiarity of the ranger's scent. Just like with The Hunter and the dwarf, it was his brother's that he knew from before he'd been cursed. His brother had been the one that had been gallivanting all over the forest since before the snow had melted. And if what she said was true, Roland was still looking for Werner. *But why? Surely, he doesn't think I could have survived that storm.*

He then thought about what she had first said, about him being a spirit bear. If that was what his brother believed, then had Roland braved the storm to come back for him, only to find the trail that led to that cursed encounter? Had that sent him into a winter of vain searching only to cross paths with Rose?

The sound of laughter brought his wandering mind back from his thoughts. He wondered why the girls' mother was laughing, then he realized what a sight it must have been for her to see a bear stunned by the mention of a prince. After picturing it in his mind, Werner was sure he would have been laughing through tears as well.

Sheepishly, he snatched up the quilt again and looked at her. She was only now recovering from his reaction and getting back to her feet. "Ha! Oh, I wish the girls had seen that! But then, you know of Prince Roland?"

Werner nodded.

"And do you know his brother?"

He nodded again, thinking about how she would react if she only knew who she was asking that question to.

She straightened up. "Is he alive?"

Repetitively, Werner again bobbed his head. *Not that anyone would recognize me, but yes, I'm alive.*

"Can you lead us to him?"

Werner shook his head, knowing that the only way that they would see him in his real body again was for him to kill the dwarf. And he was wasting precious time to set his ambush. He turned, and despite some pleading from the girls' mother, he hurried back to the treasure trove.

An hour later, Werner looked at his work with pride. Despite the problem of scooping jewels and coins with his bear paws, he had gotten about half of the dwarf's treasure into the thick quilt. He tugged at it a few times, and while it was a foregone certainty that the blanket would be returned with dirt and grass stains, it would hold the weight while he dragged the treasure away.

Now, he simply had to place the treasure where the dwarf would see it, and it needed to be near enough that Werner could reasonably make it back and get the rest before the dwarf returned. He scanned the hills, looking for such a sight.

His eyes finally settled on a suitable outcropping at the very eastern end of the lake. It lay to the northeast of where the dwarf's treasure was, and if the setting sun were to hit it in a few hours...

Werner could see the plan fall into place. With the sun going down, the treasure would be like a beacon to anyone west of it. While he left the treasure exposed on the outcropping, Werner would hide and wait for whoever the gleam of the treasure attracted. Some passersby could stumble upon it, but Werner could run them off and return to waiting until the dwarf arrived.

I will wait as long as I need to, and even if I have to run you off again and again, you'll never abandon your treasure. You will have to kill me before I kill you.

And I will be coming to kill you.

For the girls' sake.

Chapter 42

The rest of the journey to town was uneventful. A few people waved at Snow when she entered, and after sharing some quick greetings, she went to the first man on her list. The money from selling the dye to the tailor would pay for everything else Snow had to get.

"Snow White!" Jack the tailor said cheerily as he caught sight of her. "I'm glad to see you survived the winter."

Snow smiled at him. "We did. It was quite the experience."

"That it was." He said as he hobbled over to her. "I nearly died when that roc flew in."

"Oh no!" she exclaimed. "Were you caught outside as well?"

"I was. Had gone to Fernglen to deliver a dress for Lady Arrenton and decided to help the lord and the princes clear out a bandit camp. Had to wait for The

Hunter to join us so we were still deep in the woods when the storm hit. Then, as we were making our way back to Fernglen, a tree snapped in half and fell on me."

Snow gasped, causing Jack to pause his story for a moment. Her own memories of the storm swept in, and she was thankful that no trees had fallen on them. "How did you get out?"

"Prince Roland and the others dug me out, as well as a few others. One of the bandits died under that tree; we had taken them all prisoner before the storm struck." Jack exhaled heavily. "I'm grateful to be alive, but I wish Prince Werner hadn't died. It's been rough on the nobles, not to mention the royal family."

"Do you think he's dead?" Snow asked quickly.

"How can he not be?" Jack said sadly. "He wasn't prepared to survive in such conditions, and though I hear Prince Roland is still searching for any sign of him, it's been all winter. All he's likely to find are Werner's bones."

Snow cast her gaze downward at the thought. She didn't want to see Roland discover such a sight, not after all he had done for them. And especially not today, with what Roland had in mind.

"Sorry," Jack said in a somber tone, "I suppose you hadn't heard about that with how deep the winter was."

"I had heard that Prince Werner was missing, but I must have forgotten that it was during the roc's storm." For a moment, she questioned why Roland had never mentioned that, but neither she nor her sister had ever bothered to ask. Snow thought to mention Roland's theory about a spirit bear, but simply shook her head.

Even I can't hold much hope in that outcome.

"That storm was a rough thing for a lot of us," Jack continued. "Made a few folks wonder if we'd even make it through to spring. I swear I've never heard of such a long winter. Good thing your father's folks kept most of those beasts confined to the north. How are they doing?"

Snow shook her head. "I don't know. The Hunter hasn't come south since the roc's storm. There must have been a lot of North Beasts to deal with."

"I've heard as much." He then shifted to his cheery tone again. "But it's spring now. Good things are on the horizon. Now, does that basket contain what I think it does?"

"It does." Snow set the basket on one of the tables and pulled out a few of the bottles. The tailor took one of them and put the dye through a couple of tests. Snow watched, but even after all these years, she still didn't quite know what the man was looking for.

After a while, Jack turned to her with a wide grin. "This may be your mother's best batch yet! I'll add another tenth to our normal arrangement."

Snow accepted the trade heartily and exchanged the dyes for the coins and empty bottles. She then went to the other merchants her mother knew in Middleton. At each, while the owners greeted her with wide smiles and cheerful voices, she heard similar stories of hardship over the winter. A few, such as the miller's wife and the apothecary, had died during the roc's storm, while others had succumbed over the long cold.

The news hurt Snow's heart, and she wondered if Fernglen had suffered just as badly. "I suppose we were more than lucky that day." She said to herself after leaving the last stall.

Outside of the town, Snow fixed her gaze westward. There was still plenty of time to get home. She exhaled and put the sorrowful news to the back of her mind as she remembered what awaited her.

The moment she was back in the woods, she let her joy take hold and skipped along the riverbank with a basket full of empty bottles, cheeses, nuts, two flasks of cider, a large jar of flour, and a pouch of medicinal herbs. There was also a small money purse with the leftover coins the tailor had given her. All told, it was a successful and swift trip. She could now enjoy the journey home.

Perhaps it will be the last time I take this way.

She looked upon the scene with wide eyes, appreciating her father's woods once again. The leaves were rustling in the spring breeze, and the cold waters of the river churned over smooth stones. It was beautiful in spring.

A few birds darted past her. Snow stopped and focused on them. She felt the bond forming with the bluejay, then she looked to the pair of sparrows chasing it off. Snow exhaled, and the bond formed. All three flew to her and landed on her shoulders.

Snow laughed at them as they sang to her, and she offered them a few of the nuts she'd bought before releasing the bond. They flew away, happy with the exchange.

Three! I swayed three! Snow skipped even higher as she continued towards the cottage. *I can't wait to tell Mother and Rose that I swayed three!*

The path carried her back to the place where the falcon attacked the dwarf. As she recognized it, a lingering question slowed her steps. *Why did the falcon attack? Did the dwarf's staff have something to do with its master's death?*

Roland's concerns about the dwarf echoed in her mind. A pit formed in her stomach as she wondered, *Should I have just let the falcon complete its vengeance?*

She sighed and looked towards the bush, then above it to the hills beyond. The falcon had flown that way...

There was a glittering light in the atop one of them. *What new wonder is this?*

She strained to see it. It looked like some golden beast was sitting on the hillside, but she couldn't make out anything about it besides that color.

Something struck her on the back of the head. Snow was unconscious before she hit the ground.

Chapter 43

It had been a beautiful morning going through the woods with Roland. The two had spoken of many things as they wandered through the northern hills, but as midday approached, Rose became increasingly aware that Roland's thoughts were elsewhere. His pace had become too quick to keep up any length of conversation, and his gaze constantly went to their surroundings. The few times she had drawn his attention, he would simply answer her question and get moving again.

Rose found it worrying, yet she made the choice to observe rather than ask a question. Roland was leading her well into the northern hills. It was about the farthest from Fernglen he could go. The prince only had until the early afternoon if he was to return before dark.

She studied Roland a while longer. *It's like he's running out of time. But time for what?*

Their pace continued until shortly after midday, having made something of a circle among the hills. Roland took a glance towards the sun, then turned to her and pointed to a knoll to the south. "How about we stop there to eat?"

Rose audibly gasped.

"What is it?" Roland asked in a concerned tone.

Collecting herself, Rose pointed to the cairn. "That's where my father is buried."

The prince stood silent for a few moments. "I'm sorry, I didn't realize that was his cairn."

"No, it's alright." She said gently. Then she breathed a laugh and added, "I would have liked to introduce you to him."

"I would have been honored to let you." Roland replied, apparently relieved that she had taken the suggestion so well.

The pace to the knoll was much slower, and the prince was more talkative. "What was your father like?"

"Like The Hunter, but younger." Rose smiled. "The Hunter is my great-grandfather, and Father was his favorite among his grandchildren. The two hunted everything together. Few in the north could match them. Father even became the chief of our tribe. Everyone expected that Father would become the next Hunter after The Hunter died. But then, things changed."

"What happened?"

"He met my mother." She said with a laugh. "Father volunteered one year for the winter hunts, and he met Mother as she was searching for better aedelis patches. They said it was love at first sight. Father found her again over the summer, then when he returned north, he asked all the chiefs to allow him to renounce his place and live in the lowlands."

"He did that for her?" the prince asked.

"Yes. And from what The Hunter said, all the other chiefs rejected the idea until The Hunter gave his blessing."

Roland nodded knowingly. "He, of all people, would know what it is to accept a lonely position. So, your father stayed south in our kingdom and made these his woods, so your mother and the two of you could be safe."

She nodded. "And for everyone else in this part of the kingdom as well."

"Did you go out with him much?"

"Yes. You could say I was his daughter, and Snow was Mother's daughter. He took me all throughout the woods, but not so much into these hills."

"Why is that?"

"The wildlife in the hills is larger and more crafty, and my father preferred to hunt them alone. Besides, it was closer to the north, and any North Beasts that made it south would first have to cross them. The hills were the wall of his fortress, so to speak, and he didn't like me being near them."

"Did Goldie go this way at all?" Roland immediately exhaled and glanced away. "Sorry, I should have held my tongue."

Rose laughed softly. "No, it's alright. I know how much finding him means to you. His track went north originally, but he had ventured in all directions by the end of winter."

The prince gave her an inquisitive look. "What do you think he was looking for?"

Rose shook her head. "I don't know. We gave him food and shelter, and I'm pretty sure he was the only bear not hibernating, so I can't imagine what he was doing out there. Snow tried to find out the day I met you, but Goldie chose to go in a circle and take her home."

"And even The Hunter didn't know what Goldie is?"

"Not when he left to go north again."

Roland sighed as they stepped into the clearing of the knoll. "That the bear is a mystery even to The Hunter..."

She chuckled. "I know. I believed he knew every creature in the world as well." Rose then looked at her father's cairn and left Roland to go stand beside it.

Rose could feel her thoughts fade as she gazed at the cairn. Rose could see the withered gifts from the prior autumn and felt a pang of guilt that she had yet to bring a gift because of the roc's storm. Yet the tender memories of her father also overwhelmed her. Times that she would cherish the rest of her life.

There was also a new gift on the shelf, evident by the bright hue of the wood compared to its weathered counterparts. It was a single arrow. A mark of respect from one hunter to another.

Rose stared at it for a few seconds, unsure who would have left the arrow there since none of her people had come south this winter, at least that she was aware of.

A hand rested on her shoulder. Rose stepped back and leaned against Roland, and the two stood in respectful silence for a while.

Rose exhaled and turned to Roland. "Thank you for bringing me here."

"You're welcome," Roland said as he led her to a rock in the middle of the meadow. "But I wish I had realized that the cairn was for your father."

Rose looked at him curiously. "Why?"

"Because of what I planned to give you here." He walked to a nearby bush and pulled up a bow and quiver, which he then held to Rose. "I wanted to give you these so that you can protect yourself and your family. I saw the cairn of a hunter and thought it was one who had died here, instead of thinking that your father had been brought back to you."

She stared at the gifts. "I don't know what to say," was all she could manage. She glanced up into Roland's eyes. He looked pleased with her reaction.

"Let's eat first," he said, "then you can try the bow."

Rose nodded in agreement, yet in her excitement, the meal disappeared quickly. She was eager to assess the bow. Roland seemed amused by this and also finished his meal in short order.

Their hunger satisfied, Rose led Roland to the line of stones her father used. The prince then handed Rose the bow and quiver. Rose tied the quiver's belt around her waist while Roland drew his bow and loosed an arrow at a nearby tree. It settled near the center of a scar where a large branch had broken off from the main truck during the long winter. "Aim for that."

Rose set an arrow against the side of the bow and drew the string back. Slowly and shakily, her hand reached her chin, then she took aim at Roland's arrow.

She took a breath and held it as her father had once told her she should. Her arm was quivering from the power waiting to be released from the bow, but this time, the bow wasn't too much for her. Rose focused on Roland's arrow, waited a second, then slowly exhaled and loosed the arrow.

The bow jumped in her hand, and the arrow jumped as well, barely catching the top edge of the scar.

"Not bad." Roland said. "You hit the target on your first try."

Rose looked at him with a wide grin. "Thanks."

"Try again, but this time don't think so hard. The longer you hold the draw, the more tired you'll become. Only draw when you're ready."

Rose nodded and focused on his arrow. She then drew while aiming, and loosed her arrow far quicker than the first attempt. It struck closer to Roland's arrow than the first.

Seven of the remaining nine arrows made their flight towards the scar in the tree. A few flew wildly, causing both her and Roland to laugh, but three found a home near his arrow.

Satisfied, she went over to collect the arrows from the target.

"You still have two arrows in your quiver." Roland noted. It wasn't an accusation; rather, his eyes betrayed a knowing curiosity about her habit.

She met his gaze and grinned. "My father told me that I should always keep a few ready, in case something unexpected happened."

He smiled back. "He was a wise man."

Three more times, Rose let nine arrows fly towards the target. Each time, the arrows settled closer together. A triumphant smile became fixed on her face. *I'm no longer powerless.*

"You're a natural with a bow," Roland said as she returned from the tree with a full quiver. "Just like your father was."

"You knew him?" she asked.

Roland nodded. "He was one of the hunters who oversaw my hunts. I never learned his name, but he was a good man."

Rose heard the paws before she could reply. Fear caught her in an instant as she spun to the left and saw the direwolf slinking through the brush, trying to surprise them. The red eyes settled on her, and gleamed.

Her heart stopped, and she said weakly, "Roland!"

Roland already had an arrow nocked. "I see it."

"Then kill it!"

"Nock your arrow," he said.

"What?"

"Nock your arrow."

Rose nearly asked again, but then she realized what he was telling her to do. She breathed slowly to steady her heart as she nocked an arrow and prepared to draw her bow.

The direwolf bared its fangs at them and slinked between the bushes, trying to get out of sight before making another attempt to attack them.

Beside her, Roland remained as calm as ever. "Don't worry. I'll take it down if I need to."

She waited until the direwolf made a misstep and exposed its side to her. She drew back and loosed the arrow. The bow bucked again in her hands, and the arrow cut the top of the direwolf's shoulder before disappearing into the underbrush.

The beast ducked down, but it didn't run away. Its red eyes stared at her hatefully.

And for the first time, she stared back at those eyes without fear.

Swiftly, she nocked a second arrow and waited for her next opportunity. When it came, she adjusted for her earlier miss and let the arrow fly.

The arrow dove deep into the direwolf's side, piercing through its heart. The beast gave a last wail, then it fell dead.

"Well done, huntress."

It took a moment to realize that she had actually heard the words, that it wasn't her imagining her father's voice speaking to her. Rose turned to see that Roland was smiling at her as he returned his arrow to his quiver.

Rose felt the smile crossing her face as the rush of hearing those words being said to her settled in. "I had a good teacher."

Roland breathed a laugh. He then walked towards the direwolf, and she followed. "You need more practice for strength and stamina, but you should have no problems protecting your mother and Snow with that aim."

She nodded, feeling as though a weight had lifted from her shoulders. Ever since that first direwolf had attacked her, the woods had no longer felt as innocently safe as it had her entire life. Now, though, she could face the danger herself and win. The woods may never again be the same carefree refuge it once was, but Rose could go unafraid into her kingdom again.

Aside from that dwarf, of course. He was no simple beast, and Rose couldn't shake her worries about him after his threats by the lake. She hoped that encounter would be the last time they crossed paths.

She pushed the thought of the dwarf to the side as Roland had her retrieve her arrow from the direwolf, then they searched for where the first arrow fell. After Roland found it hiding in a small bush, he handed it to her. "Let's continue our search for Werner."

Rose smiled. "Okay, but first I want to do something."

He looked at her curiously. "What is it?"

"I want to leave a gift for my father." She took the bloodied arrow that had killed the direwolf and walked over to the cairn, setting it right beside the others.

I killed my first one, Father. Right beside you. I hope you could see it from up there.

After a few moments beside the cairn, she rejoined Roland. "Let's get looking for your brother."

The search continued for several hours more, and Rose noticed that Roland's temperament was changing again. Though he still tried to speak cheerfully, his face hinted at an anxiety building deep within. She thought about asking what the matter was, even though she knew it had to be about Werner, but she remained quiet. If Roland wanted to tell her what was on his mind, he would do so.

For now, she kept her eyes alert for any sign of Goldie or of Werner.

Despite their best efforts, the sun reached the point where they would need to stop the search in order to return before dark. Rose got Roland's attention and said as gently as possible, "It's getting late. We probably should turn back now so we can meet Snow on the trail."

"Is there anywhere else that a cave could be on this side of the forest?" Roland asked.

Rose shook her head. "Not that I am aware of." She saw the grief in the prince's eyes. "What is it?"

He hesitated to collect his thoughts, then exhaled slowly. "I have to leave the forest. The high king has called for a tournament in Delriata, and my father wants me back in court because of problems both within and beyond our borders. It is a duty I have to uphold as the heir to the throne."

She inhaled sharply. *So that's the news that he told Snow and Mother.* "But your brother..."

He dropped his eyes. "I still haven't found any sign of him."

Guilt stole into Rose's heart. "I'm sorry. I shouldn't have distracted you from searching for him."

"Don't be." The prince said, then paused before speaking again. "If I haven't found him now, then he didn't make it through the winter."

There was a moment of dead air as Roland prepared to speak again. Rose studied his face, and couldn't understand why he was fighting to withhold a smile after telling her that he had to abandon the search for his brother.

What could be on his -

"Rose, I..." Roland laughed, then said, "I want you to come with me back to court."

Rose knew what he meant in an instant, but couldn't bring herself to believe her ears. "Come with you?"

"Yes." He nodded, the corners of his lips still struggling not to bend into a boyish grin.

Rose glanced away for a moment. She felt her cheeks start to burn. In her heart, she wanted to say yes, but she was overrun with questions. Would her mother and Snow be allowed to come to court as well? Would she never go into the woods again, mere moments after she'd conquered the direwolf? Could she give up her woods just like that?

Yet when she met his eyes again, the questions faded away. Roland was here in the woods of his own choice, and he was the crown prince. There was no way he would deny her this part of her life when it was so integral to his own. And Roland had also shown fondness to both her mother and Snow. Why would she think he wouldn't bring them along as well?

Snow's question from that morning came to mind. *You really do like him, don't you?*

Rose smiled, knowing the answer. "Roland, I..."

Her eyes caught something in the distance. It shone brighter than any flame she'd ever seen, like it was some pure source of light resting on the side of a hill. Her curiosity took hold. "What's that?"

Roland turned and studied the light for a few seconds. "I... don't know." He looked back at her. His eyes were glinting in mischief, and a wide grin had formed. "How about we take a closer look while you decide?"

Rose chuckled, knowing that she was already certain about her decision. "Alright."

Chapter 44

Werner stepped away and looked at the pile of treasure with what passed for a clever smile along his snout. After all these months, everything was finally falling into place.

The treasure sat on the open hilltop with no holes or brush for the dwarf to hide in. On one side, the trees were several hundred feet away, and the ground was a gentle slope that wouldn't do much to slow Werner when he charged uphill. Away from the trees, the hill gave way to a cliff that fell some fifty feet towards a shallow lake. He had walked along the cliff's edge several times and there was no path along it to be found.

In other words, it was the perfect place to stage an ambush.

The prince could see it all now. The dwarf would come storming into the clearing and right up to his treasure, paying no mind to his surroundings. Werner would hide in the trees nearby. Once the dwarf reached the treasure and started cursing at how to even move all of it, Werner would try to sneak up on the little man.

Whenever the dwarf saw him, Werner would charge and keep the dwarf against the cliff's edge until he'd either killed the dwarf with his own paws or sent the little man flying to his doom.

Then I'll be free.

He felt his spirit rise at the thought. The prince would be himself again, and then he would go back to Snow. He hadn't given much thought as to how he would approach her yet; maybe once he'd returned to Fernglen alive, he would ask for Roland to lead him into the forest, and he could "happen" upon their cottage.

Or I could just ask to have Roland introduce me to Rose. Apparently, they're close now.

He laughed at the thought. To think that both princes had fallen for the two sisters. It reminded Werner of several of the tales in the girls' mother's storybook. The only damper on the feeling was that Rose knew what Roland looked like. Werner would likely have an uphill battle with Snow, considering she only knew him as a bear.

Werner had mulled over how she would react to that knowledge, and how to prove it. As much as Snow liked fairy tales, there would be no simple way to show that he was the bear that had stayed with them once he was human again.

Well, except for the stories and certain things she had said to him, yet while such stories would easily prove his story, they would also be fairly uncomfortable to bring up. He knew he would have a minor crisis if the animal he'd taken in and treated as an intelligent pet turned out to be a cursed princess. How would Snow react?

That was a fear for later. First, he needed to get the rest of the treasure. If there was any of the trove remaining in the meadow, Werner feared that the dwarf might have a moment of clarity and hide what remained of his trove before looking for the lost portion. Who knew how long that would take? It could be days or even a week before the dwarf found a suitable spot and got that portion hidden.

After a few attempts at failing to fold the quilt again, Werner took the quilt in his mouth and flung it over his shoulder. He would look strange to anyone who saw him, but likely less strange than he'd been while dragging the treasure up the hill.

Again, he charged through the forest, in a race against the dwarf's strange cycle. There was always the chance that the dwarf would be in the meadow when Werner arrived. Inconvenient, but at this point it was a welcome possibility.

Maybe I can kill him now rather than later.

Hearing that the dwarf had threatened Snow and Rose removed any caution that Werner had been acting with. The dwarf would not get another chance to hurt the two. Not while Werner was still alive.

When Werner reached the meadow, he could smell that the dwarf had not visited during his absence. Werner chuckled as he tore off the sod and began awkwardly shoveling the treasure onto the quilt. He worked at a frantic pace while trying to make sure not a speck of the trove remained.

Twice Werner thought he caught the dwarf's scent, but it was a fleeting moment on the wind. The third time it approached far quicker than the dwarf had ever moved. Werner tried to smell where it was coming from and eventually his nose told him to look up. He spied a falcon gliding overhead, with a small stick in its talons. The scent disappeared shortly after.

I must be getting paranoid that he'll sneak up on me. The prince shook the thoughts from his head and finished loading the treasure onto the quilt. After a brief search to make sure there was nothing left to find except his tracks and the grooves of the loaded quilt, Werner set out for the hillside again.

As he dragged the remaining half of the treasure past a small stand of trees, the wind changed direction. He caught the stench of the dwarf and immediately dropped the quilt. The scent came from the hidden meadow.

Werner glanced around for a hiding place. There was a small hollow in the trees that would suffice. If the dwarf came running down Werner's trail, there was no cover that could protect him. The prince grinned and slipped into the hollow. *Maybe it will end now.*

He waited, but the dwarf's scent didn't get stronger. Instead, the scent weakened as though the dwarf were going in a different direction entirely.

Werner left the treasure behind and followed the scent, hoping that he might discern more about how the dwarf was reacting. He had thought that surely the dwarf would see his prints if nothing else.

Yet, the scent never got closer to him.

After deciding that the dwarf was running around in some sort of mania, he went back to the treasure and began dragging it towards the hill.

The dwarf's scent still hung on the breeze while Werner got closer and closer to his destination. The prince glanced towards the sun and knew that it had reached the right position for the pile to become a beacon.

Not much longer.

Then he caught Snow's scent intermingling with the dwarf's. Werner dropped the quilt and took a step towards the scents. *Is he -*

Then Werner smelled blood.

NO!

Werner took off at once, leaving the remaining treasure behind.

Snow was in trouble, and he was perhaps the only one who could save her.

Chapter 45

"Wake up, you stupid girl! I didn't hit you that hard."

Snow groaned as she slowly woke up from the sudden blackout. She tried to rub the back of her head, but her wrists were stuck together. When she opened her eyes, Snow saw that there was a rope around them.

She bolted upright, a motion which made her nearly fall over again from dizziness. Snow touched the back of her head. Her headscarf felt damp. When she brought her hands back in front of her, she found her fingers stained red.

Is that -

"What have you done with my treasure?!"

She looked at the dwarf. The little man was holding his dagger directly at her heart. Scared, she replied, "Treasure? I don't know of any treasure-"

"Don't lie to me! You and your stupid sister and that archer friend of yours are the only ones combing through this part of the forest. You must know something!"

"Please, I -"

"Oh, are you merely the fool in their plot? The quiet, ignorant fool who they leave behind so that they can run off with everything?"

Snow opened her mouth to reply when the glistening light caught her eye again. She stared at it, drawn to the question of what caused it. As she stared, the dwarf's accusation made her realize what the light had to be.

"What the devil are you -" the dwarf spat as he followed her gaze, then he leapt into the air. "That's it! It has to be!" He then sheathed his dagger and pulled on the rope around Snow's wrists. "Come on! I'll deal with all of you at once!"

"But -"

"Would you rather I deal with you now?" The dwarf asked as he touched the dagger at his side. She shook her head. "I didn't think so. Now get moving!"

Snow was forced to keep up with the dwarf's maniacal pace or risk falling and being dragged by the little man. It was nearly an hour before they entered the clearing that the trove sat glistening in. The sheer amount of wealth that sat before her stunned Snow. *How long has he been gathering this treasure?*

"By Jove, that's only the half of it!" the dwarf exclaimed when they were a dozen yards from the pile. He yanked on the rope and Snow nearly fell to the ground. "What have you done with the rest of it?"

"I swear, I don't know," she replied.

"Don't you be lying to me."

"Let her go!" a voice commanded.

Snow turned to see Rose and Roland hurrying up towards them from the bottom of the hill. Both had an arrow ready on their bows. For a moment Snow smiled, but then the dwarf pulled her down onto her knees. He then hopped behind her and drew his dagger.

"Where's the rest of it?" the dwarf yelled.

"The rest of what?" Roland's voice was stern, and his eyes were in their cold fury compared to the fiery panic Snow saw in Rose's eyes.

"Don't act so innocent to me! My treasure. Where is the rest of it?"

"We don't know," Rose replied.

"Don't lie to me. You had this hussy distract me while you made off with it, and now you've come to hide the rest of what you stole?"

"Why would we place it here?" Rose was incredulous, but Snow kept glancing at Roland. The prince was waiting for an opening. *If I can push the dwarf away...*

"Why should I know? It's your plan." Snow felt the dwarf's dagger cut against her arm. She gave a cry of pain, then looked to see blood staining her sleeve. "You'll tell me where the rest is," the dwarf said darkly, "or I will kill her."

Rose nearly dropped her arrow in shock, while Roland's arms were shaking in impotent fury. Snow could think of nothing to help them. She knew that her sister and Roland hadn't moved the treasure, but the dwarf was beyond reason.

The little man spat onto the ground. "So be it, prince. You want me out of your forest, but what if there's no forest to leave?"

The dwarf began chanting, and Snow saw confusion cross Roland's face, as well as terror on Rose's. She looked towards where they were looking and saw that the treasure was faintly glowing with a reddish light.

Is it getting brighter?

A roar cut through the tension. Snow turned to see Goldie charging out of the trees straight towards them. In his eyes was a wrath she had never seen before. Even when facing the direwolves, Snow had never felt such terror as looking into those eyes.

Roland stepped in front of Rose and drew back his bow. In an instant, Snow remembered the prince had still never met the bear. Rose put a hand on him, but Snow couldn't hear what she said over the dwarf's cries behind her.

"AH! The demon bear! Kill it! KILL IT!" The dwarf pressed himself behind Snow as if seeking her protection.

Instead, Roland lowered his bow and pulled Rose out of the way.

The dwarf's voice cracked. "What are you doing, you fool?! KILL IT! That bear has been after me all winter."

"What a coincidence. That bear's been staying with the girls all winter." Roland responded as he drew his dagger.

The dwarf stammered incoherently, then he threw Snow into the bear's path before his little feet fled towards the cliff. "Eat her! Eat her and not me!"

Goldie didn't stop or go around Snow. He instead leapt over her and continued to pursue the dwarf.

Snow watched as the dwarf moved swifter than any man could dream, but the ground-shaking charge of Goldie was swifter still. He nearly caught the dwarf several times, but the dwarf was the more agile of the two and at the last moment, he kept leaping aside to safety. Goldie tripped and rolled twice, but soon he was no longer losing his footing.

Snow caught the look in Goldie's eyes. That desire to destroy the dwarf burned furiously in them, perhaps now even more so than when he had first charged up the hill.

Then the dwarf found some measure of courage, and at the next dodge, he slashed Goldie's leg, leaving a trail of blood flowing down the bear's leg. Yet Goldie appeared to not even acknowledge the attack, nearly crushing the dwarf under one mighty paw.

"Are you alright?"

Snow turned to see that Rose and Roland had reached her, and Roland had unsheathed his dagger. She held up her hands, and the prince cut the rope.

"I'm fine." She replied as she rubbed her sore wrists. She then turned to Roland. "You have to help Goldie."

Roland nodded and took his bow in hand, hurrying after the two combatants, with Rose and Snow following as quickly as they could. Goldie had hardly let up on his furious attack, and even armed with the dagger, the dwarf was retreating up towards the cliff side.

The dwarf was trying to get to the trees, but Goldie was blocking his path, forcing the little man closer and closer to the cliff's edge. Goldie made another charge, but the dwarf leapt past the swiping paw and cut at Goldie's leg as he rolled away.

This only enraged Goldie more. Twice more, he charged; twice more the dwarf dodged and slashed. Snow could see the dwarf's eyes change from fear to determined hatred.

One of the pair was going to die.

"Can you hit the dwarf?" she yelled to Roland.

"Goldie's not giving me a good opening," came the reply.

Snow turned her attention back to the battle taking place. Goldie had pinned the dwarf against the cliff and looked like he was readying for another charge. With a grin on his face, the dwarf backed up right to the edge.

She saw what the dwarf had in mind just as Goldie took reached the dwarf. Despite knowing she was too late, she cried out, "Goldie, no!"

A moment later, the dwarf leapt to the side, hoping that Goldie would tumble over the edge. But the bear was ready for the ruse, and his mighty paw lanced out. Snow saw the moment when the dwarf's face turned from triumph to terror, then the mighty paw struck him. There was a crunching sound, and the dwarf's body flew over the cliff and down towards the lake.

Snow didn't hear when the dwarf hit the water, but she knew he was dead before he ever got that far.

She continued onward, reaching Goldie as he looked down from the edge. Seven cuts were reddening his black coat, which seemed to be more golden with each passing moment. Her heart sank. If he was a spirit bear, as Roland believed, was Goldie now dying in some peculiar fashion? Snow didn't know if spirit bears died like everything else, or if they were truly more spirit than mortal.

No. I won't allow it. She reached out and touched his shoulder. The bear spun in surprise, but then calmed once he saw it was her and rubbed his head against her hand.

"You're hurt." Snow tore the cut sleeve of her dress to staunch the wounds. Behind her, she could hear Rose and Roland looking on. Their voices were hushed, as though they were stunned by all that had happened.

I'll get you patched up. Don't die on me, Goldie. Don't -

"Snow, look." Rose whispered.

When she lifted her eyes, Snow froze. Goldie was now golden from head to paw and seemed to be changing shape. She stared in amazement as he looked more and more human, until at last the light faded and she was face to face with a golden-haired man barely older than herself, dressed in fine clothes beneath a leather jerkin.

He looked down at his hands, a smile forming on his lips. Then their eyes met. These, at least, had not changed. It was still Goldie sitting in front of her. Just, he was no longer a bear.

For a while, no one spoke. What could Snow say in the face of such a sight? The golden-haired man also appeared at a loss for words.

The first voice to speak was Roland's. It was a loud, joyous voice. "Werner?"

The golden-haired man turned, and his smile grew even wider. "It's me, Roland." He called as he got to his feet.

Roland let his bow fall from his hand as he ran towards them and embraced Werner. "You were the spirit bear the whole time?! What happened? How did you end up like that?"

"I... I can't breathe."

Roland looked at him for a moment, then smiled and let Werner out of the crushing embrace. Werner took a couple of breaths, then relayed his story. "That dwarf cursed me with a magic staff after I lost track of you in the roc's storm. I'd stumbled upon one of his treasure troves, and the next thing I knew, I was a bear. After that, I wandered the forests until I found Snow and Rose's cottage. They and their mother took me in while I hunted for the dwarf." The prince made a mischievous face. "Speaking of which, how do you know these two? Don't tell me you'd been hiding them all these years, and that's why you love being in the forest so much?"

Roland laughed. "No. I met them while I was looking for you."

Werner looked at his brother with a knowing smile. "So I've heard. Their mother told me about how you were still looking for me when I stopped at the cottage to get a quilt to drag all that treasure up here."

"You stole the dwarf's treasure?" Rose asked.

Werner nodded. "I just had to ask how I thought Roland would bait a trap for a dwarf, and the pieces fell into place." He then looked back at his brother. "Still, you never stopped looking for me? I would have given up on myself after the first day."

"Of course I never stopped looking for you! I couldn't find any signs that you were dead!" Roland gave Werner a playful punch in the shoulder. "I never gave up hope of finding you. Neither did Mother."

"What about Father?"

Roland shrugged with a grin. "It has been a few cold months, though he only lost hope for a moment. Most considered you dead the day after the storm."

Werner laughed. "And I may have been, if I hadn't found the girls." He then turned to Snow and hesitated a moment before answering. "I've wanted to thank you both for sheltering me during the winter. I don't know what I would have done if you two had left the door shut or turned me away after seeing me at your door."

Snow still could not find the right words to speak. Goldie was a prince this whole time!? Rose finding Roland was one thing, but to think Goldie had been Roland's missing brother!

Fortunately, Rose still had her wits about her. "You're welcome, my Prince. And I should thank you as well."

"Oh? And why is that?"

Rose moved to stand beside Roland. "If you hadn't been going out all winter, Snow wouldn't have followed you that one day. If that hadn't happened, I would have never met Roland."

"I suppose you're right." Werner's eyes danced between the two, then he grinned. "You take too much after The Hunter, Roland. You had the girls puzzling over your name every evening until I left."

Snow felt her cheeks burn, though not nearly as much as Rose's did. Roland merely shrugged. "I didn't mean to do that. We just never bothered to tell each other our names." He then looked at the pile of treasure. "What do you think he was attempting with that chant?"

Werner shook his head. "He could have been trying to use his magic to change it like he did to me, but the magic he used on me looked bluish-green, not red." The prince turned to Snow. "Do you have any ideas?"

Neither Snow nor her sister knew what the magic could have been for. Snow then realized she was still the only one not standing, and the torn sleeve of her dress was still in her hand. Her eyes then darted to where the wounds had been. Whatever else the magic had done, the wounds were no longer there. She looked back into Werner's eyes. "Your wounds have healed."

He checked himself to confirm what she said, then smiled at her. "It would appear so. You're still bleeding, though." He then took the torn sleeve from her hand and gently wrapped it around her arm. "I'm sorry I couldn't stop him before he attacked you."

Snow smiled back. "Was the dwarf the danger you were pursuing every day over the winter?"

Werner nodded. "I ran into The Hunter that first morning when I went out. He said that the only certain way for me to break the curse was to kill the dwarf. That's why I didn't want you following me, and why I haven't been back since the snow melted. Though I had planned to return to thank you once I was myself again."

"Thank me?"

"For taking me in during the winter. I don't think I would have survived if you hadn't."

Snow chuckled as she remembered that night. Then her cheeks turned red as she remembered the rest of the winter.

"What is it?" Werner said with concern.

"I don't know. It's... I was just thinking about you by the fire during the winter." She chuckled softly as Werner also looked uncomfortable at the memories.

Werner gave her a sheepish smile. "I didn't know how to explain that I wasn't always a bear when I couldn't even speak."

"I understand," Snow said slowly, "I just... I don't know what to do now."

Werner sighed. "I... don't know either."

Snow glanced towards her sister. Rose looked around the circle, then settled her eyes on Roland. Snow saw a thought spring to her sister's mind. Snow knew that look. It was a mischievous thought that her mother would have thought of and would adamantly approve of.

With a confident grin, Rose said, "Well, I know what I'm going to do." And as Roland turned to her, she lifted her heels and kissed him.

Snow and Werner could only look between themselves and their siblings, Werner in shock and Snow in muted glee.

After a few seconds, Roland pulled back and smiled at her. "Is that a yes?"

Rose was beaming as she answered, "Yes."

Epilogue

One year later...

The nobility lined the cathedral as the bride walked slowly down the aisle alongside The Hunter, her pure white dress embroidered with menulia-dyed snowflakes. At the end of the aisle stood the prince, his surcoat emblazoned by the sigil of a bear. Snow smiled at Werner, then glanced to her left. Roland and Rose stood next to her mother, and in Rose's arms was their newborn son.

Her mother could see Snow barely withheld a chuckle, and there was no question about what was going through her daughter's mind. Roland and Rose had been married within the week of returning to Fernglen and were already growing their family; now it was Snow and Werner's turn to do the same.

The ceremony had concluded, and the court was doing its favorite traditions as the celebration moved to the main hall of the castle. It would continue like that until sunset, then once Snow and Werner had left, the nobles would carry on until long into the following day. That had been the festivities had gone the previous year with Roland and Rose, and their mother was sure it would play out the same this time.

At first, she had served the function of the bride's mother as expected. For those who had been at the prior wedding, the conversation was cordial. Yet there were many from the other lowland kingdoms and more than a few foreign dignitaries who hadn't heard her firsthand account, and she found herself surrounded by this company soon enough.

"What did you think when Werner told you he was that bear?" was the common question on everyone's lips.

She would then tell them of having the four return to the cottage and tell her of the battle with the dwarf, then that Werner had been Goldie. "Somehow, the surprise was less so than when Roland told me he was a prince. I suppose I was still in high spirits from Roland saying he would ask Rose to marry him." Then, she told about how after they all ate the meal she had prepared, they left for Fernglen.

There, the questions would turn. What did she think of living in castles now? How was her relationship with the king and queen? She'd repeated the process countless times now, and while the tale hadn't lost its luster, those questions had long lost their charm.

Finally, she excused herself and made her way toward the balcony overlooking the gardens. Here was the place where she could still find peace in the hustle of courtly life.

At the far end of the gardens, facing towards their old cottage, were the two rose trees. Under her supervision, the king had ordered them moved to the castle he'd bestowed upon her after Roland and Rose's marriage. They had their own gardener assigned to them, but more often than not, she had continued to care for the two so that they remained as beautiful as ever.

Perhaps even more so than before. The attention had gone down to even where the two stood in the garden. Snow's bush was in the shade of a mighty silver maple, while Rose's sat in the shadow of nothing the whole day through.

She gazed down at the two and thought back to that time not so long ago. To the joys, the trials, and to her husband. "If only you could see the girls now, my love. They've grown so much. You'd be so proud of them."

"I know he would be."

She turned to see The Hunter, his face beaming with pride of his own. She smiled back at him. If there was anyone else who knew how her husband would think of today, he would.

The Hunter bowed his head. "You raised them well. I could not be more proud of who they have become."

"Thank you." She said as she wiped the tears from her eyes. "Has anyone found out what that dwarf was trying to do?"

The Hunter shook his head. "The frost dwarves remain silent about the incident. I fear we will have to learn his intentions on our own."

He excused himself, and she returned to gazing at the roses for a while longer before rejoining her daughters.

She couldn't hold back a smile at the finery that clothed the two girls, and at how even now they were still the girls from the woods despite all that now surrounded them. Roland was much the same as she had known him, having always been the forest rogue, while Werner had supposedly mellowed dramatically following his adventures as a bear.

Last of all, her eyes fell on the newest member of the family, and she wondered what the child would see in the years ahead.

She smiled. Only time will tell.

Afterword

Thank you again for reading my adaptation of *Snow White & Rose Red.* I had a lot of fun writing it, and I hope that even with the changes I made that it still holds true to the classic fairy tale.

I would like to thank Alia and Eliana for alpha-reading the book and providing feedback, as well as my mother. I greatly appreciate the help you all gave.

I'd also like to thank Luisa Galstyan for the beautiful cover she created. It was a pleasure working with you and I'm grateful for how you were able to bring the story elements into the artwork.

If you, the reader, have any feedback, I would love to hear your thoughts as I continue in my own writing endeavors. My website and social media information is on the copyright page if you'd like to reach out.

Until next time, take care, and may God bless you in the days ahead.

www.ingramcontent.com/pod-product-compliance
Lightning Source LLC
Chambersburg PA
CBHW021956130726
47903CB00014B/1468